SIN AND DECEPTION

SIN AND LIES

BOOK TWO

SIENNA SNOW

Cover Design: Artscandare Book Cover Design

Editor: Silla Webb

www.siennasnow.com

ISBN - eBook - 979-8-88535-021-1

ISBN - Print - 979-8-88535-022-8

AI Disclosure

No generative artificial intelligence (AI) was used in the writing of this work. The author expressly prohibits any entity from using this publication for purposes of training AI technologies to generate text, including, without limitation, technologies that are capable of generating works in the same style or genre as this publication.

TROPES LIST

- Dark Mafia
- Antihero
- Alpha Hero
- Bodyguard
- Boss's wife
- Second chance
- Enemies to lovers
- MM
- MMF
- Why choose
- Revenge
- Forbidden Romance
- menage romance
- Suspense
- Off-limits romance
- Hurt you to save you
- Protector

- Spicy Romance
- Forced Marriage
- Forced Proximity
- Billionaire
- Found family
- Girl squad
- Kink/BDSM
- Touch her, and you die
- Hate to love you
- Strong heroine
- First Love

Author's Note
Content Warning

This book is a dark romance with subject matter that may trigger some readers.

- Forced Marriage
- Domestic Assault
- Sexual Assault (light on page, discussion of past in graphic detail)
- Physical Assault
- Violence and graphic death
- Body mutilation (not on page)

ONE

N ERINE

"You've been a very naughty girl, Angel." Theo's stern words pierced the air like a sharp blade, making me tremble with fear.

On my other side, Xander's large, rough hand gripped my chin tightly, his expression unforgiving and filled with anger.

"Are you ready for your punishment?" he asked in a low, rumbling voice that sent chills down my spine.

It was a dangerous blend of desire and fury that I couldn't resist.

Fear tightened around my heart as I desperately fought against the restraints keeping me in place. My eyes flicked between the two men, their familiar darkness flashing with rage and sending a wave of panic through me, replacing my usual submission. I struggled to understand their anger, trying to push through the fear and confusion clouding my mind.

How had everything spiraled out of control? Doubt crept in, gnawing at my resolve. Did I truly deserve this punishment? What if they were right?

The thought paralyzed me as my heart waged war between guilt and defiance. "Please," I whimpered, my voice trembling. "Please, let me explain."

But their eyes only grew darker, shadows looming over me and filling me with dread.

"Just listen to me," I pleaded, my voice diminishing as their anger intensified.

"Enough!" Theo shouted, making me jump at the sound.

His imposing figure loomed over me, his anger palpable and capable of shaking me to my core. The thought that they could be this angry with me left me reeling.

His steely gray eyes bore into mine, unyielding and unforgiving. "We know all we need to know."

A violent shudder wracked my body as I tried once more to escape the leather straps binding my wrists. The harsh material dug into my skin, leaving painful red marks that I knew would last for days.

"But you don't," I pleaded, desperate to make them understand.

"Stop talking!" Xander's voice was sharp and commanding, with the threat of punishment hanging in the air without him needing to say another word. They stood on either side of the bed, their stormy eyes shooting bolts of furious lightning over my naked body.

Helpless and at their mercy, I weighed my options. They had stripped me as soon as we entered the luxury penthouse suite. I had thought they meant to devour me with love and pleasure, finally releasing me from the torture I had endured for the past two years without them.

Leaving them was one of the hardest things I had ever done, and enduring those two years without their love, touch, and guidance was even harder.

The three of us formed a team, united against every challenge and obstacle that came our way. Yet, there was one thing that had driven us apart.

Me.

And now, that love wasn't coming back.

I had ruined everything, and they would make me pay dearly for it. Xander's fingers glided along my cheek and down to my neck, gripping it tightly. I looked up at him with pleading eyes, shaking my head slowly.

"Xander, please don't," I whispered.

"You betrayed us, Angel." His words were like a knife twisting in my stomach, an accusation I couldn't deny. I had truly betrayed the two men I loved most in this world. But I had my reasons.

"I can explain," I begged again, my words barely audible through my tears.

But they had no interest in hearing my explanations. It was torture, knowing deep down that if they just listened to me, they might spare me from whatever punishment they planned.

Agony coursed through my body as I lay bound on the bed. My heart shattered into a million pieces. Theo and Xander stood over me, their expressions cold and unfeeling.

But their words only reinforced my despair.

"We don't want to hear it," Theo said, his hand reaching down to pinch and twist my nipple, sending shockwaves of pain and pleasure through me. His grip was like a vice, squeezing harder and harder until I cried out in agony, the sound echoing through the room. Xander, standing behind me, tightened his hold around my neck, choking off any escape attempts.

I glanced back and forth between them, fear coursing through my veins as I awaited their next move. Theo licked his lips hungrily while his gaze roamed over my trembling body before he turned to Xander with a taunting smirk.

"Revenge."

The word echoed in my mind, filling me with terror. I struggled against the leather straps holding me in place, desperate to break free. I had seen firsthand what these two were capable of when fueled by anger and vengeance, and the thought of being on the receiving end of their wrath made my blood run cold.

It was then that I realized just how much danger I was in. How could they do this to me? We were supposed to love each other and face anything together. Even after I left and disappeared for two years, I always believed we would find our way back to each other.

But not like this.

Never like this.

"Please," I whimpered again, my body going limp in defeat.

The bindings held firm, refusing to give even an inch. They were too skilled at restraining their victims. A fact that was painfully clear at that moment.

"Do you remember what it felt like, Angel?" Theo asked, his fingers releasing my nipple and trailing down to cup my breast. His palm slid further down, stopping just above my hip as his thumb pressed into the tender flesh there.

I cried out at the sensation, a mix of desire and fear coursing through me.

"Theo," I pleaded.

"Answer the question. Do you remember?" he demanded, pressing his thumb harder into my skin.

Desire washed over me in a wave, but the overwhelming fear of my situation quickly overcame it. The two emotions battled fiercely within me, tearing at my troubled soul.

"What?" I finally managed to gasp out in exasperation.

"To be with us? To have us love you? To have us"—his fingers trailed teasingly close to my center, circling just inches away from where I ached for him to touch me. He relished this torture, taking pleasure in watching me squirm and writhe beneath him. He had always enjoyed it, apparently even now in this twisted scenario we found ourselves in. "Fuck you?"

"Yes," I breathed out, my voice shaky with emotion. "I could never forget."

"And do you remember," Xander asked, lifting a brow, "what we did for you?"

"Of course," I replied. "I would never forget. Never."

Xander removed his hand from my throat and walked to the end of the bed. My feet were tied to the posts of the bed, leaving my thighs wide open. He gazed between my legs, his eyes landing on my pussy. The heat of his stare seared me, leaving me quivering and squirming. One look from either of them could leave me crashing over the edge, but the look in his eyes told me he wanted much more than merely to gaze upon me.

"I loved tasting you, Angel," he told me, as if reliving a memory.

My mind spun, and my body was on fire from their nearness and words.

A desperate urge to unveil everything consumed me. I yearned to explain why I had left, where I had gone, and what I had done during my time away. However, their gazes left me unable to discern whether their intentions were malicious or not. The fear of further provoking their anger paralyzed me.

Theo's hand let go of my hip, and he moved to join Xander at the end of the bed. Standing shoulder to shoulder, they gazed down at me as if I were a precious artifact in a museum, something to be admired and revered.

All I craved was for them to love me again.

To touch me.

To kiss me.

To fuck me.

"Remember how it felt when I pushed my cock inside

you, Angel? Remember when I fucked you so hard that you couldn't walk the next day?"

Of course, I remembered. Those memories lingered in my mind every day. Their absence in my life left an emptiness that tainted my very existence.

Without them, I was a woman without a heart.

I yearned for their touch and their gaze upon me once more.

Every single day.

But this?

This torture they were inflicting upon me?

I had no yearning for this. Not once.

"What are you going to do to me?" My irritation bubbled over as I questioned them.

Xander shook his head slowly while Theo once again wore that infuriating smirk on his face—a trait that always annoyed me. At times, Theo reveled in his snarky attitude and condescending tone. Unfortunately, even that could not diminish my intense desire to be claimed by him—rough and unapologetically.

Enough was enough.

I needed to feel him inside me again. To feel Xander's presence alongside him. But with each passing moment, it became clear that they weren't here to fulfill any of my desires.

They were here for revenge. And they would do whatever it took to exact their vengeance. The determination in their eyes sent shivers down my spine.

"We're going to show you what you missed, Angel," Xander growled.

"Do you think I don't already know?" I scoffed, no longer attempting to conceal my irritation. What was the point? It would only give them further satisfaction.

Their hands trailed up my legs, starting at the ankle and moving slowly upward. They kneaded my thighs with gentle pressure, igniting a fire within me that caused me to gasp for breath.

"What's wrong, Nerine? Are you feeling excited, beautiful?"

I remained silent, staring down at them as I attempted to control the intense arousal that surged through my body from their touch. No one had touched me like this since I had left.

I wanted more.

I craved everything I knew they could give me.

But I couldn't trust them. Their teasing actions would not lead to fulfilling my desires. The cold glint of cruelty in their eyes told a different story than their hands.

As Xander's thumb brushed against my vulva, a cry escaped my lips at the overwhelming sensation. Theo gripped my hip and lifted my body from the bed, peering between my spread thighs with an intensity that made me tremble with anticipation.

My gaze flickered to his lips, remembering the intense pleasure he had given me with his mouth. I could still feel the lingering tingle of his skilled and intuitive touch, knowing exactly how to make my body writhe with ecstasy. His mouth was like a part of me, sharing every sensation and amplifying them to new heights.

Neither had ever left me wanting, and Theo's mouth was always my favorite source of bliss. The way he would tease and taunt me built up the anticipation until I was begging for release.

"Your pussy is as exquisite as I remember it being, Angel," Theo growled hungrily.

His words sparked hope within me. Maybe he would finally touch me the way I needed him to, giving me the release I so desperately craved. Perhaps he would press that god-like mouth against my most sensitive places and take me to paradise with him.

"Theo, please," I hissed, wiggling my hips suggestively and giving in to my primal desires.

"I think she wants you to fuck her with your tongue, Theo," Xander chimed in with a chuckle. "Remember how much she loves that?"

"I think she wants both of us to fuck her," Theo grinned, reaching out a finger to brush against my entrance and reveling in the sight of how wet and ready I was.

"Please!" I cried out, not caring anymore about pride or explanations. All I wanted was for them to ravish me, to claim me as their own once again. We could deal with everything else later, but I needed them now more than anything.

But first? I needed to be fucked ferociously by the two men I loved most.

"Isn't she adorable?" Xander mocked.

"Adorable?" My anger flared at his words, and I opened

my mouth to defend myself when they both silenced me with a simple phrase.

"Shut up."

With those two words, my heart sank.

Theo released my legs with his words, walking further away from the bed. To my dismay, Xander followed suit until they stood too far away to give me what I desired.

I wanted to plead with them to return. I tried to assure them I would do anything and everything they desired. They knew how to pleasure me perfectly, but I also learned how to make their bodies sing. We were like three perfectly matched souls, intricately aware of each other's intimate desires and fantasies.

"Guys, please," I pleaded desperately, feeling like I was losing them all over again. "You know that I—"

"You don't deserve anything from us, Angel. You know that."

Theo's words lingered in the air. When Xander joined in, I realized there was no turning back from the pain I had inflicted.

"You broke our fucking hearts, Nerine. You left us standing with our dicks out, looking like a couple of fools. You have no idea what kind of damage you've done."

"So why should we let you explain yourself?" Theo asked."

"You destroyed everything we had," Xander added, his voice heavy with disappointment and betrayal. "And now you want us to forgive you?"

"There's no forgiveness, Angel," he said, shaking his head

firmly. "None. How could you do this, Nerine? How could you leave us without an explanation and expect everything to be okay?"

My heart shattered at his words, crushing the tiny shred of hope I had clung to.

"So what now?" I asked, knowing there was no turning back from the hurt I had caused. "Are you going to kill me?"

Throughout all these years together, I never imagined I would face this end at the hands of the two men I loved most in the world.

"Oh, no," Theo chuckled darkly, sending chills down my spine. "We just want you to understand how it feels to be left behind."

My eyes widened in shock and desire as I watched him turn to Xander, his strong hands cradling his face before pulling him into a passionate kiss. The intensity of their love was palpable, filling the room with an electric energy that left me both elated and envious.

Their kiss was deep and intimate, their bodies pressed close together as they explored each other's mouths with fervent abandon. It was evident that their connection had only grown stronger since my departure. While I was happy for them, I couldn't help but feel a pang of jealousy at being left out of this moment.

I watched as they trailed their hands over each other's bodies, eagerly groping at each other through their jeans. Their lustful kisses grew rougher with each passing second, reflecting the primal need they felt for each other.

Finally, Theo pulled away, and Xander sank to his knees

before him. With deft fingers, he unfastened Theo's jeans and pulled out his impressive cock. My eyes widened in awe as I took in its size and thickness, my body trembling with memories of the pleasure it brought me when Theo expertly used it to make me scream in ecstasy.

Xander leaned forward, parting his lips as Theo's throbbing member disappeared into his mouth. I gasped at the sight, my body aching with arousal as I watched them together.

Theo's head fell back in bliss, his hand entwined in Xander's hair as he thrust his hips forward, driving his cock deeper into the warm depths of Xander's mouth.

"Fuck ... yes..." Theo growled, lost in the pleasure coursing through him. Xander kept his eyes closed as he continued working Theo's shaft with his talented tongue, moaning at the sensation of having Theo inside him again. He reached up to cup Theo's balls and elicited another guttural cry from him.

Theo couldn't take it any longer. He pulled away from Xander, his cock glistening with saliva as he reached down to grab Xander's arms. With a predatory grin, Theo quickly unfastened Xander's jeans and shoved them down his legs, revealing a rock-hard cock that was begging to be touched. Roughly, he pushed Xander down over the edge of the bed, leaving Xander with his hands braced against the mattress and his pert ass raised in the air. Our eyes met as I stared between my open thighs, shamelessly watching them.

"Do you see what you're missing, Angel?" Theo taunted

me as he poured lube onto his length and began stroking himself slowly.

My mouth went dry at seeing him, and the ache inside me intensified with every passing second.

Then, without warning, Theo lined himself up and thrust forward, burying himself deep inside Xander's tight heat. Torn between turning away and watching intently as they moved together in perfect synchrony, I screamed out my frustration.

"Don't do this to me!"

Their lips curved as they kept their focus solely on me. They never broke eye contact as Theo pounded into Xander with increasing urgency. My gaze flicked back and forth between them, watching as their faces flushed with pleasure and hearing their moans fill the room.

Watching them together had always been arousing for me when I actively participated in their love play. But now, being forced to watch from a distance felt agonizingly wrong.

"Please ... untie me," I begged, desperation creeping into my voice. "I want you both so badly... I need you..."

Instead of showing mercy or acknowledging my pleas, they continued with vengeful satisfaction evident on their faces. This entire situation was a cruel game to them, and they were relishing my pain.

"Please," I begged again, my shame forgotten in the face of overwhelming desire.

In response, Theo thrust harder and faster, their bodies slick with sweat as they moved together in perfect harmony.

With a roar of release, Theo came hard inside Xander, shaking with the force of his orgasm.

He never broke our intense stare as he reached forward to take hold of Xander's cock, working him until Xander cried out and released himself onto the bed.

They took a moment to catch their breath, and I watched, awash in the deepest pain, the most intense desire, and the excruciating loneliness that consumed me.

Theo pulled out of Xander's trembling body, and he stood up, their gazes filled with disdain as they looked down at me. My skin was slick with sweat from arousal, and my heart felt like it was cracking wide open as they shook their heads.

"We don't want you anymore, Nerine. You'll never be our Angel again," Theo said coldly.

My entire being cried out in protest, tears streaming down my cheeks as I struggled against the restraints once more. But it was pointless. They were finished with me.

"No!" A loud cry tore from my throat in protest, tears streaming hotly down my cheeks as I struggled against the restraints once more. But it was all futile.

The movement jolted me awake, gasping for air.

As I opened my eyes, the darkness of my bedroom surrounded me, and I could still sense the lingering pain from the dream.

Or was it a nightmare?

No matter either way, I was still living in the midst of my personal hell.

My tiny apartment felt as empty as ever, mirroring the

void in my heart and the loneliness that had consumed me for two long years. Running a hand down my body, I longed for the touch of the two men still holding my heart captive. Dreams like this had become all too familiar, and yet each time I woke up, the torment lingered, reminding me of what I had lost.

I rose from the bed and walked into my tiny bathroom, stopping to stare at my reflection in the mirror above the vanity. Standing naked and trembling, I couldn't help but trace a gentle finger over the obscene scar carved into my lower abdomen by my violent dead husband, Andraius.

Whore.

Years ago, I had killed Andraius in self-defense, but the consequences still haunt me, even now.

I shook my head, setting those memories aside, and instantly, my mind shifted back to Theo and Xander.

I angled my body and glanced over my shoulder to study the tattoo etched down my spine. It was two dragons with their tails wrapping around the waist of an angelic figure. It symbolized our connection, our bond, and the love we shared.

I sighed, knowing this wasn't where my thoughts should linger, but my body craved their touch, making me too restless to fall back asleep. Perhaps these dreams were an omen of the darkness looming on the horizon, warning me to prepare again.

Two

N ERINE

The rows and columns of the spreadsheet blurred into one large, illegible mess. I squinted, attempting to make sense of it all and concentrate.

I sighed with frustration and did my best to ignore the chaos swirling around me in the office of SinCity Distillery. Its Firewater whiskey had become a cult favorite after a popular Hollywood actor used it as an ingredient in everything he served at one of his parties. The drink's Black label recently went viral after being featured in a blockbuster action movie. This resulted in a surge of new orders, creating a bottleneck for fulfillment at a small production facility.

I did my best to stay focused and input the crucial

production data as quickly as possible. However, the chaos of the office kept invading my thoughts, and I found myself having to double-check my work.

Unfortunately, my biggest distraction today was the dream I had awakened from this morning. I still couldn't shake the lingering fear it stirred up. Images of Theo and Xander haunted me even after I locked up the apartment and came to work. It felt like two figures were sitting on my shoulders, and no matter how hard I tried, I couldn't flick them off. It was maddening, and if I didn't figure out a way to cope soon, it was going to start causing serious problems.

I couldn't afford any problems. My life depended on everything running smoothly without drawing attention to myself. I could easily attract unwanted notice if I made mistakes or talked to the wrong people.

"Hi, Rina," Sarah, our admin assistant, said as she set a pile of files on my desk. "These just came in."

Stifling a groan at the sight of the large stack of invoices, I reminded myself to be grateful for this mundane job. It provided the cover I needed to protect my identity, which was the most important thing.

Work was work.

Still, I longed for the privilege of my old life.

If any of my coworkers knew my real name was Nerine Angelos, the missing Godmother of the Night and Queen of the Angelos Mafia, not one of them would have been able to keep that secret.

Luckily, I'd perfected a demeanor, making the truth an outlandish possibility.

It sounded strange to my ears, too, sometimes.

But that was all in the past. I wasn't the same woman I had been when I left, and I would never be the old Nerine again. It was best that I remained grateful and humble for that fact.

So, instead of rolling my eyes and pushing the work away, I politely smiled at Sarah and thanked her for the work.

Outside my office windows, the Las Vegas Strip stretched for miles. The daytime view contrasted sharply with the glittering neon chaos I observed from the small apartment I lived in during the evenings. I resided at the Ida Hotel and Casino, owned by my employer, Penny Lykaios's husband, Hagen. From my bedroom, I had a perfect view straight down the Strip, showcasing the dazzling neon lights and bustling streets.

Thank goodness for blackout curtains, though, or I'd never be able to catch a wink of sleep. I laughed, thinking about how different my life was now.

My friend Penny had been a lifesaver for me, not to mention an inspiration.

She was a brilliant chemist and the founder of SinCity Distillery, a successful woman in her own right. She was also married to one of Las Vegas's most prominent casino and hotel owners. With the indulgence they offered the public, they were the king and queen of the Las Vegas underworld if such a thing existed.

My dear friends, Nyx Drakos and Devani Patel-King, had recommended me to them. Nyx was Penny's cousin-in-law, and Devani was my mentor, trainer, and knowledge bearer.

Honestly, I wasn't sure what to call her. By day, she was the Indian precious gems mogul known as the Queen of Diamonds. In her other life, she was the so-called retired director of Solon North America.

Everything was so different now. It was staggering to think about the changes I'd gone through and the stark difference between my lifestyle as the Angelos Godmother and the woman I presented as now.

I drastically changed not only my demeanor but also my appearance. Gone were my cobalt blue eyes concealed behind dull brown contacts. My once-lush raven hair now sported a hue of honey-golden dark blonde, which I achieved through intensive sessions with a hair specialist.

Sometimes, when I looked in the mirror, I couldn't recognize myself because I appeared so different.

But all in all, I achieved my goal of hiding in plain sight and being remarkably uninteresting.

So far, so good, at least.

I felt confident enough in my façade to move through the office, hotel, and casino unnoticed. But rarely did I venture much farther into the city. It wasn't a risk I was willing to take.

Luckily, I never had any reason to go anywhere.

Everything I needed was in my apartment or nearby. Suppose something came up that I didn't have. In that case, I'd have it delivered. That was the point of all the new apps and services.

Unfortunately, nothing I built in Las Vegas eased the turmoil at the center of my life.

To escape, I tore my family apart and destroyed my world. The agony of being separated from the men I loved for two years was one thing, but I let them believe someone had kidnapped me, along with my mother and sisters.

It was only half-true, a story concocted to conceal the actual plan, which was to protect everyone I loved. To achieve my goal, I had no choice but to stay as far away from them as possible. The pain of being separated from my mother and sisters was another excruciating part of my reality.

My mother and Fiona hid under fake names in Arizona, and the twins, Ariana and Christina, were in school in Washington and Oregon. I felt utterly closed off from all of them.

We were all spread out across the country, and some days, it seemed as if we'd never sit in the same room together again.

I hated it.

My thoughts wandered to Devani as I gazed out the window at the MGM sign flickering in the distance. Below it, throngs of tourists poured down the elevated sidewalks, resembling an endless army of ants.

Without Devani's help, I never could have pulled this off. She was invaluable, assisting me in obtaining false identification and paperwork with new names for myself and my family. As the retired director of Solon, a spy agency that operated outside any country's legal framework, Devani had contacts and resources I could only dream of having.

Certainly, her retirement was just for show. She would never truly relinquish control of Solon. I think everyone behind the scenes understood that all too well.

The idea of going through another year like this, away from my family, was infuriating. I had contemplated our next move for months and needed Devani's insight.

I reached for the encrypted phone I had stashed away in a secret compartment of my briefcase to call her, but it started ringing just as I grabbed it. I looked down at the caller ID and recognized the number immediately.

"Fiona!" I said with apprehension, knowing that whenever my youngest sister called, it was usually for some trouble. She was brilliant but also cunning, and I could never anticipate what she would say next.

"Nerine! You won't believe what just happened!"

I could practically hear her bouncing with excitement on the other end. "I won't? Then maybe you should tell me!"

"Okay, well..." she hesitated. "Before I share the details, I need you to promise not to get mad, okay?"

I furrowed my brow. "How can I promise that without knowing what you did?"

"Just promise!" she insisted urgently.

"Fine," I relented. "Is everyone okay, Fiona?"

"Yes, everyone is fine," she reassured me. "It's good news."

"Then why would I get mad?" I asked cautiously.

"Just listen; you'll see," she hushed me. "I wrote a book."

My jaw dropped. "A book? That's incredible! You've always loved writing."

"Well, that's the thing..." she said hesitantly. "You know how I'm always reading?"

"Yeah," I replied.

Fiona was an avid reader who became obsessed with the trending genres on social media, and romance topped her list.

"It's a dark mafia romance novel. It's titled Sin and Deception."

I blinked in disbelief and shook my head, uncertain if I had heard her correctly. "What kind of book?"

She laughed nervously. "They say to write what you know, right?"

"Dark romance? Mafia?" My stomach twisted uncomfortably.

"A dark romance involves power plays and possibly some bondage or something similar," she explained casually. "You know, dominating men who enjoy getting a little rough."

"Uh, okay, whatever," I replied, feeling increasingly uneasy.

Maybe I was overreacting. It was just fiction, right? But as she kept talking, my discomfort grew.

"Going back to writing what you know, what do you know about romance?" I asked pointedly. "Especially the type of relationship you described?"

"I know romance. I've dated. Maybe I don't have much experience, but I borrowed some plot points from others," she admitted sheepishly.

"From where?" I already felt a sinking sensation in my gut.

"From you," she confessed.

My heart skipped a beat. "You did what?"

"I only borrowed a few details," she reassured me. "And I'm telling you now because I don't quite know what happened, but the book went viral. It's become an international sensation."

"Viral?" My heart raced with panic.

"Popular bloggers showcased it on the clock app or something, and sales have skyrocketed," she gushed with excitement. "It hasn't dropped out of the top 100 on popular platforms for the last two weeks, and it has thousands of reviews across all of them."

"You waited two weeks to tell me this?" My stomach churned with anxiety. "Fiona, how could you keep this from me?"

This couldn't be happening.

"Don't worry, Nerine! It's all going to be fine," she reassured me frantically. "I promise nobody will trace this back to us. I swear, I changed the details."

How could she be so naive? My mind raced as my heart pounded in my chest.

Okay, first things first. I needed to read this book ASAP and devise a plan for damage control. Who knows what kind of consequences could come from this sudden fame?

"Send me this book, Fiona. Right now."

Excitedly, she exclaimed, "I'll email you a copy when we hang up. But, Nerine, you're going to love it!" Her words resonated with pure enthusiasm as if she couldn't wait for me to dive into the book she had written.

"I based it on your life as the Godmother of the Angelos Mafia," she continued. "The heroine was forced into marriage with the new Godfather to save the family, being the eldest daughter. But in the end, she escapes, saving herself and her family. I changed all the names, details, and locations, so don't worry."

My stomach churned with unease at Fiona's description of the book. She had taken events from my life and twisted them into a fictional tale for the world to consume. How could I not worry?

"Send me the book, Fiona," I requested firmly.

But deep down, I knew this book was not just a harmless story. It held secrets and truths that could endanger my family and me. Yet, Fiona remained oblivious to it all.

"I thought you'd be happier," she pouted. "It's a big deal to make it to the top of the charts like that.

"I'm proud of your success and artistry," I sighed wearily. "But, Fiona, I have to ensure you aren't putting any of us in danger with this book."

Listening to her protests and reassurances, my heart ached for my dear sister. She had never witnessed the horrors I endured at the hands of Andraius after our forced marriage. Mama had made sure to keep her sheltered from it all.

But now, with this book published and gaining popularity, all our efforts to protect Fiona seemed pointless.

"We're not in danger!" she insisted once more. "I wouldn't do that to us."

I couldn't stay mad at her for long. She was innocent in all of this, unaware of the consequences her actions might bring.

"I know, sweetheart. You wouldn't intentionally put us in harm's way," I assured her. "Send me the book. I'm looking forward to reading it."

"Thanks, sis," she said, a hint of relief in her voice. "I love you. Please don't be mad at me."

"Let me read the book, then I'll decide how mad to be," I replied sternly. "And, Fiona, if I tell you to unpublish this thing, you need to listen to me, okay?"

"Okay," she agreed reluctantly. "But millions of readers already bought it. You can't put that cat back in the bag."

"I'll call you back later, okay?" I managed to say before hanging up.

As I waited for Fiona's email, my mind raced with thoughts and fears. All the sacrifices and pain we had endured over the past two years—were they all for nothing?

Oh, Fiona, what have you done?

Three

T HEO

Seated behind the intricately carved oak desk, I gazed out the window at the vast Angelos estate. Beyond the tall trees encircling the property, the city of Boston thrived with life, its sounds muted by the thick walls of my office.

I couldn't shake the twinge of guilt as I looked at all this luxury I hadn't earned. I was the acting Godfather of the Night for the Angelos Syndicate, with Xander's assistance... if he ever bothered to show up.

My fingers tapped impatiently on the desk, recalling how Nerine loved this spot. Xander and I had brought her right here once, years ago, when she first assumed the title of

Godmother of the Night. A small smile tugged at my lips at the fond memory.

But my mind quickly returned to the present, filled with tough choices and memories of past events that brought me to where I am today. None of it was easy. Xander and I faced numerous challenges and sacrifices to get to this point.

Our main priority now was defending our territory and protecting the Angelos family from enemy syndicates, particularly the Stratos from Chicago, who had been breathing down our necks for far too long. Today, an important strategy session awaited us if only Xander would bother to show up on time. He would never have dared to be late if it had been Nerine waiting for him.

I compelled myself to set aside these thoughts and concentrate on our successes. Together, we had successfully thwarted every attack against us and solidified our reputation as a force to be reckoned with. After Andraius's death left us vulnerable, we ensured to form strong alliances. We made it clear that anyone who dared to cross us or our territories in Boston and across New England would face dire consequences.

However, despite our achievements, I felt uneasy in this position as acting Godfather during Nerine's absence. I had only stepped into these shoes because there was no other option. Xander had refused to take on the role himself, and I couldn't blame him. His true strength lay in being an enforcer and second-in-command, his very presence striking fear into those who dared to challenge us.

But no matter how much we justified our decisions. I

couldn't shake the disappointment and frustration of not being able to see Nerine fulfill her destiny. This title was always meant to be hers. We fought tooth and nail for her to reclaim her birthright. And yet, she was nowhere to be found.

I sighed, watching the trees swaying gracefully outside my window as a gentle breeze blew. Their fluid movements reminded me of Nerine and how effortlessly she carried herself. She was a mesmerizing sight, possessing a sharp wit and a tongue that could make even the toughest men weep.

The thought of never seeing her again was unimaginable. We had explored every lead in our search for her after her kidnapping, but each one came up empty.

It seemed that whoever had taken Nerine, along with her sisters and mother, did so intending to protect her from their enemies. But who? And how? Those questions, frustratingly elusive, haunted me day and night.

The Angelos family had countless enemies, and narrowing down who could have orchestrated such a plot was impossible. We investigated every organization, big or small, but none seemed powerful or organized enough to pull off such a feat.

I exhaled deeply and continued to gaze at the tranquil scenery. The burden of responsibility and worry weighed heavily on my shoulders, along with the fate of the Angelos family. Still, I only wanted Nerine to return safely and reclaim her rightful place as my queen, the Godmother of the Night for the Angelos Syndicate.

When Nerine vanished, we were desperate for answers.

We first contacted Solon, an underground spy agency that had previously protected her. The mere mention of their name sent chills down my spine, aware of their capacity for dangerous secrets and covert operations. We hoped they could illuminate her disappearance, but instead, they refused to assist us, citing jurisdiction issues or some other convenient excuse. My suspicions about them grew as months passed without any updates on Nerine's whereabouts.

We then reached out to Nyx Drakos, who had introduced Nerine to Solon in the first place. But even she seemed genuinely devastated by Nerine's absence. Maybe she had no idea what had happened to our beloved. But I couldn't shake the feeling that someone at Solon held valuable information about Nerine's fate.

Despite our frustration and exhaustion, we refused to give up on finding her. Nerine had counted on us to protect her and her sisters from harm, and we had let her down. The weight of that failure sat heavily on my shoulders. It was personal to me. How could I face Nerine if we ever found her? Would she ever be able to trust me again after this colossal failure? I couldn't even bear the thought of marrying her now. She deserved someone better than me—someone stronger, smarter, and more capable of protecting her.

But who was protecting her now? The thought both terrified and enraged me. Had Nerine let someone else into her life? Someone who wasn't me or Xander? Was she safe? Was she even alive?

I often found myself lost in thoughts about what I would do if I discovered she had died. The mere possibility sent shivers down my spine and brought tears to my eyes. I could never move on if that became a reality.

Instead, I pretended she was still alive and well, living her life somewhere, untouched by the chaos and danger we faced. It was the only way to get through each day without falling apart.

But those dark thoughts still lingered like an unending nightmare that threatened to engulf me. That's why I immersed myself in work, attempting to keep my mind occupied and distant from the darkness that constantly hovered over me.

I glanced at the door again, hoping Xander would walk through any moment, so my mind shifted to some other priorities. And just as if he had heard me, the door burst open.

Xander strode in, looking like he owned the room. His serious expression added to his natural aura of confidence and made him more appealing.

Nerine liked to call it his god of lust and sex pose, and I couldn't disagree.

At that moment, he reminded me that I wasn't alone in this mess.

My earlier annoyance with his lateness dissipated immediately.

"About time," I grumbled, reverting to my usual snarky demeanor.

Xander waved a book before slamming it down on my desk. I squinted at the novel with its innocent-looking cover and butterfly design. Across the top was 'Sin and Deception,' written in bold letters, hinting at a darker story within.

Then he dropped a piece of paper beside it—an article from a newspaper he had printed. I frowned as I read the headline: "Author of Sin and Deception Reveals the Inspiration Behind Her Sexy New Sensational Best Seller!"

I glanced up at Xander, who, on closer inspection, seemed beyond agitated.

"Are you suddenly into dark romance now that Nerine's not here?" I joked, trying to lighten the tense atmosphere. "I always pegged you for a mystery or sci-fi guy."

Xander dropped heavily onto the chair across from me, his energy filling the room and making it feel almost volatile. He looked like he was about to explode with frustration.

"What's all this about?" I asked, gesturing toward the book and the article. And why did he look like he was about to burst?

"Someone wrote a dark mafia romance novel," he started, leaning forward and pointing at the article. "And it has striking similarities to Nerine's life."

I raised an eyebrow. "It's just a romance novel. What's the big deal?"

"Don't you understand?" Xander exclaimed, his voice growing louder. "The author claims that she drew details from real life for this book, and although she never refers to Nerine by name, it's far too similar to be just coincidence."

"You think Nerine wrote this book?" I snorted, knowing that Nerine preferred to keep her life private.

"I don't know what to think," Xander admitted, his

hands on my desk as he leaned closer to me. I tried not to stare at his lips for too long. "But I have a feeling it could lead us to her. We have to check it out."

"Seems like a stretch, Xander," I said, trying to inject some reason into the situation.

"No, it's not!" he insisted, standing and towering over me. I reached out and placed a calming hand on his, hoping to soothe him.

"I know you miss her," I said gently. "But we have to be realistic. This seems far-fetched."

"At first, yeah," he admitted with a nod. "But listen—the book is about a Mafia family and its eldest daughter. There's a violent coup that results in the murder of her father and younger brother. Then she is forced into a marriage with the new Godfather to save the family."

"That does sound strange," I agreed, still skeptical. "But why would Nerine write a book like this? It doesn't make sense."

"That's what I can't figure out," Xander said, gripping his dark hair in frustration. "The author uses a pen name, and I can't find any clues about their true identity."

"Plenty of romance authors use pen names," I pointed out.

"I know," Xander sighed, looking distraught. "I just feel like we need to investigate this."

I shrugged helplessly. "Well, go ahead then."

"I already did some digging," he confessed. "But I couldn't find anything solid. The author is good at keeping their true identity hidden."

I could see the disappointment in Xander's eyes, and my heart went out to him. But deep down, I couldn't shake the feeling that this was just another dead-end lead that wouldn't get us any closer to finding Nerine. Where was she, anyway?

"Keep digging," I urged, my voice barely above a whisper as I tried to calm the storm inside me. The possibility of finding Nerine brought back a flood of memories and pain, making it hard to maintain my composure. "Go talk to the publisher. See if you can get more information from them."

I knew Xander needed this, whether it led anywhere or not. He had been suffering from terrible nightmares ever since Nerine went missing, constantly blaming himself for her disappearance. It broke my heart to see him like this, knowing I couldn't do anything to ease his pain. Maybe he needed to feel like he was doing something—anything—so he wouldn't drown in his dark thoughts.

Who was I to stand in the way of that?

"Keep me posted," I added, hoping to see a spark of hope ignite in Xander's eyes. It had been a long time since I had noticed that glimmer of optimism in him. In response, I also tried to let some of his positivity seep into me. We both needed it at this point. Time had turned me cynical and bitter. We climbed into bed every night without our beloved Nerine, feeling like another failure.

We were both consumed by guilt and self-blame. But we also clung to each other, desperately trying to keep one another afloat amidst the sea of agony and tragedy we lived through.

We couldn't have done it alone.

As Xander turned to leave, I stopped him. Standing from behind my desk, I closed the distance between us.

"Xander," I said softly, pulling him into a tight embrace. It was as much for me as it was for him. With a deep sigh, he returned the hug, and we stood there for what felt like an eternity, communicating everything we couldn't express in words.

I loved this man with every fiber of my being. Losing Nerine, the first time had shattered us, but somehow, this tragedy brought us even closer together.

But even as I held him close, I couldn't shake the feeling that a part of us was missing—and perhaps it would always feel that way. After a moment, Xander pulled away, and his words confirmed my fears. He looked into my eyes, his own filled with painful shadows.

"I love you, Theo," his voice trembled with emotion. "Now, let me go find our Angel so we can be whole again."

He kissed me fiercely before turning and walking out the door. I sank back into my chair behind the desk, feeling a heavy weight on my shoulders. Our precious yet maddening Nerine was at our enemies' mercy. The relentless ticking of a clock in my mind reminded me that each second that passed could bring her closer to harm and suffering. And if we never found her, the pain and torture Xander and I had endured for months would become a lifelong sentence.

We had no choice but to find her.

I grabbed the book Xander had left on the desk and started reading, attempting to distract myself from the overwhelming emotions that threatened to consume me.

Four

N ERINE

My senses heightened as I wove through the crowds of tourists checking into the luxurious Ida Hotel and Casino. The air was filled with the scent of perfume, sweat, and excitement, mingling with the constant chatter and camera clicks. My eyes scanned the area, carefully inspecting every face I passed. It felt like I now had a giant red target on my back.

I had spent the last few hours holed up in my office, curled up on the couch, poring over every detail of my sister's book instead of doing my actual job. It was a daunting task that left me sick with fear. My hands trembled, and my knees shook with every step, my mind spinning from the disaster Fiona had created.

Thanks a fucking lot, baby sis.

All I wanted was to get to my apartment, lock the door behind me, and activate my top-of-the-line security system. However, the hundreds of bodies milling about the luxurious hotel lobby made it challenging. Coping with an endless stream of oblivious tourists was one of the downsides of living in Las Vegas.

After finally making it through the expansive atrium, I paused to observe the wide-eyed vacationers as they gazed at the stunning stained glass ceiling above them. Certainly, it was a beautiful artwork that took months to install. Still, their obliviousness created traffic jams that annoyed me endlessly.

Living in a hotel was a surreal experience—both good and bad. On the one hand, I could have food brought to my room at any hour or blend in with the crowds when I wanted to escape. On the other hand, dealing with massive crowds daily became tiresome—especially when they often watched where they were going. Many of them thought that paying for the "luxury" package entitled them to VIP treatment, and they would take advantage of it by shouting at employees and disregarding those around them.

Man, I was grouchy.

I blamed it all on Fiona.

As I continued toward the apartment tower, my mind spun from the disaster Fiona had created. All because of a damn book.

Why couldn't she write about some obscure romance in a lesser-known genre instead of taking the romance industry by storm with a well-crafted saga that mirrored my scandalous life?

The parallels between the story and my reality were too much for my comfort. The more I read, the more uncomfortable I grew. What was I going to do?

The book described a betrayal by a trusted member of a Mafia family—similar to what happened to me. It even included the brutal murder of my father and youngest brother, followed by my forced marriage to the man who'd betrayed the girl's father. And if that wasn't close enough to my trauma, the main character endures horrific acts of violence, rape, and body mutilation—things I had personally experienced.

It felt like a personal betrayal. Why would Fiona write about such intimate aspects of my life? She may not have experienced it firsthand, but she knew what I had gone through and saw the scars I carried.

Only a select few outside my family knew about the word etched onto my abdomen by the monster I had married. If anyone caught wind of it, they would see the book was about me.

There were only two significant differences between our stories: the setting was in Chicago instead of Boston, and the two heroes only had a relationship with the heroine. There was no trouble situation. Even then, the mannerisms, speech patterns, and interactions between the male leads and the heroine were eerily similar to those of

Theo and Xander, the two men who held my heart to this day.

And, of course, she had to write a passage in which the younger sister complained about being left behind by her twin sisters when they visited, the older one in a "sparkling city of sin and indulgence." It didn't take a genius to figure out that she was referring to Las Vegas, or, as it's commonly known, "Sin City."

Yes, she was upset when Ariana and Christina went, but she wasn't even eighteen. Complaining about it in a book felt quite silly.

How could she not see that it would be easy for others to make the connection? As the smartest of the four sisters, I expected more from her. The book was a ticking time bomb, loaded with personal information and secrets. Hell, I was one too.

When I reached the front of the elevator leading up to my apartment, my anger and despair surged like a volcano, ready to erupt. Who knew whose hands it had already fallen into? The moment it went viral, chaos ensued, and there seemed to be no end in sight as more and more people continued to read it.

I prayed that this would all blow over, but deep down, it was wishful thinking. It was like hoping for unicorns to magically appear and whisk me away to a different realm.

My disappearance only fueled the fire, stirring up anger and revenge from Xander, Theo, and others who wanted to use me.

As I waited for the elevator doors to open, I noticed a

group of men hanging around the security desk. They wore dark suits despite the sweltering heat of Las Vegas. My instincts urged me to be cautious and alert around them.

Quickly, I reached into my shoulder bag and slipped on a pair of oversized black sunglasses before draping a scarf over my hair. Turning away from them, I hoped they hadn't seen me. With a sigh of relief, I entered the elevator as soon as the doors opened. I was finally alone again.

But even in the solitude of the elevator, I couldn't shake off the anxiety that had taken hold of me. Every passing day, I grew more and more accustomed to being alone. I missed Theo and Xander terribly. Their touches still lingered in my heart wherever I went. But with this prolonged separation, it became a little easier to accept.

That is, until now. Fiona's book shattered the peace and contentment I had worked so hard to achieve. Once again, despair consumed me. As the elevator ascended, I leaned against the wall and counted the floors until we reached my apartment on the eighteenth floor.

As soon as the doors opened, exhaustion swept over me. My safety routine kicked in as I scanned both sides of the hallway before entering my apartment. Once inside, I checked every corner of the room to ensure everything was as I'd left it. Then, feeling a sense of relief, I double-locked the door and activated the security system.

"Safe," I whispered to myself, feeling a weight lift off my shoulders as I embraced the security of my space. Sealed inside this room, no one could hurt me. But outside? In the world? That was a completely different story.

The mere thought of being recognized sent a chill down my spine. Chaos would surely follow if anyone identified me. Thankfully, my extensive training under Devani and others equipped me with the skills to protect myself and stay aware of my surroundings. But even with all my knowledge and abilities, I knew nothing was foolproof.

I walked over to a small nook in the corner of my apartment and gazed at the family portraits displayed on a set of shelves. The smiling faces of my sisters and mother offered solace and comfort amidst the chaos around me.

My heart ached as I shifted my gaze to a picture from my youth before all the horrors and tragedies struck. Papa stood tall and regal in it while little Linus beamed with his mischievous smile. The pain of losing them still felt fresh, as if their murders had occurred just yesterday.

I couldn't bear the thought of my mother and sister experiencing the same terror. I had to protect them at all costs.

"I'll do whatever it takes to keep you safe," I whispered to their photos. The guilt I felt over my inability to save my father and brother weighed heavily on me.

On some days, the logical part of me understood that there was nothing I could have done to prevent their deaths. But the girl who had lost her father, brother, and innocence could only blame herself for not seeing it coming.

I vowed to do whatever it took to lessen the damage of Fiona's book. Sighing heavily, I collapsed onto the couch and kicked off my shoes, tucking my feet beneath me.

"Oh, Fiona, what have you done?" I reached into my

purse, pulled out my eReader, and opened her book, desperate for answers.

Frustration boiled inside me as I thought of all the potential problems swirling in my mind since Fiona's phone call.

If anything were to happen to my family...

Images of two beautiful little boys flashed through my mind, and I couldn't help but envision all the tragic losses I might endure—losses I wasn't sure I could ever overcome.

I ran my trembling fingers through my hair as tears streamed down my cheeks. How could I fix this? I had to fix this. I had to do something.

But what?

An avalanche of emotions—fear, worry, anxiety, and despair—overwhelmed me, and sobs broke from my lips. I'd longed for freedom, but not like this.

FIVE

Xander

As I gazed out the window of my private jet, I couldn't help but feel disconnected from the serene scene outside. Fluffy clouds drifted lazily in the bright sunshine, creating a stark contrast to the darkness that consumed me at that moment. Restlessness enveloped me as I paced around the small cabin like a caged lion, unable to find peace.

All I could think about was Nerine. Her disappearance had taken over my life, and every lead we followed seemed to go nowhere. But I clung to a sliver of hope that this might be the clue that would lead us to her. My mind couldn't stop racing with thoughts and worries, but I refused to give in to despair. Everything had changed since Nerine disappeared, for me, Theo, and all of us. Our lives were forever altered, and there was no going back.

Instead of succumbing to sadness, I immersed myself in the quest for Nerine with unwavering determination. I scrutinized every detail, overturned every stone, and diligently chased down every rumor.

Finding Nerine became my sole purpose, even if it meant risking my life.

"Are you going to pace around the entire damn flight?" Theo's irritated voice pulled me back to reality as he looked at me with a raised brow.

"I can't sit still," I admitted, feeling guilty for putting him under more stress.

"Everything's going to be okay, Xander. You need to try to relax," he said with concern.

But relaxation was impossible.

Ever since I woke up that morning and found Nerine missing, any sense of calm had vanished from within me.

On top of all the anxiety and fear was the constant worry that Theo would pull away from me again and retreat into his shell just as we were finally getting close again after years of estrangement. He tended to shut down when things got tough, distancing himself from anything and anyone that caused him pain. I wanted to believe that the past two years of hard work had made us stronger, but there were still moments when it was clear that he hadn't fully forgiven me for my past mistakes. I wanted to move on and focus on the present and the future, but Theo always seemed to keep one foot in the past.

Perhaps my obsessive focus on finding Nerine revealed my unwillingness to move on from the past. It might be time for me to accept that nothing would change until we brought her home safely.

"We need to get our shit together before we land," I muttered, trying to distract myself from thoughts about our relationship.

"Agreed," Theo said with a sigh. "I have a contact in Las Vegas who might be able to help."

My annoyance quickly turned to outrage at his words. "Shocking. Which one is it this time? The security expert or the casino owner?"

"Must you bring that up now?" he asked, exasperated.

"What? Your countless affairs?" I couldn't help but let bitterness seep into my tone.

"Xander!" Theo's voice rose as he barked at me. "Seriously, not now! Can't you ever let that go? So what if I slept around after we broke up? What did you expect?"

"God forbid I expect you to keep your dick in your pants," I retorted, unable to stop myself.

"Not this again," he groaned, gripping his hair in frustration. "We've talked about this a million times. It's all in the past! We need to focus on finding Nerine now. For God's sake, I have resources that can help us. Why not use them?"

His plea struck a chord within me, and I knew he was right. We needed all the help we could get in this desperate search for Nerine. It was time to put the past behind us and work together, no matter how difficult it may be.

"It's hard to stay focused when you behave as if our issues don't affect anything around us. You never want to talk about us. I can't tell where I stand with you or where you stand with me, especially regarding our relationship."

My mind spun, unable to focus through the haze of anger and desire swirling between us. The tension crackled in the air, fueled by unspoken words and unresolved issues. His eyes flickered with a flash of anger at my accusation, but I refused to back down. Our relationship was a constant battle, marked by uncertainty and unexpressed emotions.

"Are you questioning my commitment to you, Xander?" he growled, his voice thick with frustration. "You're the one who ended things in the first place! Did you forget that?"

"How could I forget?" I shouted, my anger swelling like a tidal wave. "You remind me every chance you get!"

"You make me remind you every single time you complain about me sleeping with other people. You left me!" As he spoke, a note of hurt crept into his tone, bringing back the pain we both felt when our relationship fell apart.

I sighed, my hands clenching into fists at my sides as I tried to rein in my temper. Theo's presence always had a way of making my emotions spiral out of control. He made me want to both kiss him and punch him.

"No matter how often we argue or hurt each other," I said, my voice trembling with emotion, "all I have ever wanted, and all I want now is for us to work together to find the woman we both love."

"Not a day goes by that I don't desperately yearn for it," he admitted, his eyes searching mine with a mix of darkness, hope, and deep desire.

We stood there, locked in a silent battle of wills, until he finally moved closer to me. The heat radiating from his body left me weak-kneed and breathless. Without breaking eye contact, he reached up and gripped the back of my head, pulling me forward into a fierce kiss. His lips were rough and demanding against mine, igniting a wildfire of passion between us. Our tongues tangled and explored each other's mouths as we gasped for air, lost in the intensity of our connection.

But as always, the moment was fleeting. Theo pulled away, his lips swollen and wet, his eyes wild with desire.

"Truce," he growled, his hand still tangled in my hair as he stared at me with a fierce hunger.

My body trembled with longing, and my heart raced with emotion. Yet, despite our physical attraction, we needed to find common ground and work together if we ever wanted to locate Nerine again.

The word "truce" hung in the air between us, our eyes locked as we leaned in for another heated kiss. My hand rose to gently caress his cheek before pulling him closer.

"I want your mouth," he growled, his voice thick with lust and desire. He reached down, his hand rubbing against the bulge in his jeans, a clear indication of just how much he wanted me.

I sank to my knees before him, my eyes tracing over his body as I reached up to unfasten his jeans. With a swift flick of my fingers, I popped the button and slowly lowered the zipper, revealing his thick, hard cock that was already throbbing with need.

My mouth watered at the sight, and I licked my lips, longing to taste him. Leaning forward, I dragged my tongue across the tip of his cock before wrapping my lips around him, taking him deep into my mouth.

"Fucking hell," Theo moaned loudly, gripping the back of my head tightly as I moved my mouth up and down his shaft.

I could feel my arousal building in my pants as I pleasured him, but I pushed it aside for now. This was about giving him pleasure in this moment, making sure he lost control and surrendered to me.

My hand moved in sync with my mouth, caressing him as I licked and sucked on him from base to tip. His groans grew louder and more urgent, driving me on.

Theo loved to take the lead in everything, definitely when it came to sex. But not here. Not with my mouth working him into a frenzy.

As I took him deeper into my mouth, hitting the back of my throat, he tried to take control by thrusting forward and guiding my head. But I wouldn't let him. Not when it came to this—using my mouth to bring him pleasure.

I continued to lead this dance, relishing in the sounds escaping his lips and the way his cock throbbed under my skilled touch. He couldn't resist me when it came to this— his desire for me consumed him completely.

I widened my mouth, wanting to take every inch of him

in, and he eagerly obliged, thrusting with more urgency. His hips moved faster, seeking the heat of my mouth and driving himself closer to the edge.

"You do that so fucking good, Xander," he moaned, his voice filled with pleasure and need. "Yes, just like that!"

He cried out as I flicked my tongue against the sensitive ridge of his cockhead.

"Fuck yes! Harder!" he demanded, trying once again to guide my head.

But this time, he pushed my hand away and took control.

He tightened his grip on my head, and through gritted teeth, he warned, "Don't test me, Xander."

Our eyes locked, and the storm of emotions swirling in him captivated me. His dick pounded against the back of my throat. He fucked into my mouth faster and faster, telling me he sat on the verge of exploding hard and hot. But I wanted something else.

I couldn't hold back anymore. I needed him inside me. I pushed him back slightly. A scowl formed on his face, but I spoke up before he could say anything.

"Fuck me." My words lingered between us, a mute command he couldn't refuse.

His eyes widened with unmistakable desire, a primal need radiating from his gaze. He reached for me silently, lifting me to face him with fierce strength. He spun me around and roughly pushed me down onto the sofa, my body responding instinctively to his authoritative touch.

He quickly unbuttoned my jeans and slid them down over my hips, exposing my bare skin to the cool air. I could sense his gaze lingering on my exposed backside and hear the distinct jingle of his belt buckle as he lowered his jeans. A rush of air accompanied the sound as he pushed them down, revealing his throbbing arousal.

Desire surged within me, every nerve ending tingling with the anticipation of what was to come. My body trembled as he spread my cheeks and applied a cool, slick substance between them. My heart seemed to pound in my head as I awaited the first touch of his cock.

"This is mine," his voice rumbled with possessiveness and desire, sending shivers down my spine.

It was a phrase I had heard in countless fantasies during our time apart, never expecting it to become a reality again.

As he slid inside me, I gasped at the exquisite burn of pleasure mixed with pain. My body yielded to him eagerly, molding around his perfect shaft. I reached for my erection, stroking it furiously as he thrust into me with abandon.

He held onto my hips tightly, each powerful thrust eliciting a moan from deep within me. I allowed him to take control, letting him use me for his pleasure just as much as I needed it for mine. Our bodies moved in sync, the friction building and building until waves of intense pleasure overcame me.

My heart raced as our ragged breaths echoed through the room.

His hands dug into my hips almost painfully, fueling his movements as he drove himself deeper and harder into me. I arched my back and pressed my hips back to meet his thrusts, lost in blissful delirium.

"You're so fucking tight, Xander," he growled with each forceful thrust, his words only adding to the intensity of our connection. I clenched around him uncontrollably, drawing him closer and urging him on.

He reached around to stroke my arousal, matching his pace to mine as we built toward a shared climax. My body pulsed with pleasure, every nerve ending buzzing with anticipation.

But just as I was about to reach the edge, he slowed down, reveling in my struggle for release.

"Theo! Oh, God!" I cried out in frustration as he taunted me.

"You like that, don't you?" he asked with a sadistic grin.

"I fucking love it," I couldn't help but admit that I was loving every moment of it, my eyes rolling back in my head from the intense pleasure.

We stroked my cock together as he fucked me, a perfect combination of sensations overwhelming my body. But I didn't want him to stop, not until I reached the climax I so desperately craved.

"Don't stop. Keep going until I blow," I demanded, my voice strained with need.

"Stopping would defeat my plan to pump my load deep inside this sweet ass." His response was almost a growl, and then he pulled out and thrust into me with a fierce intensity. "As for you, you can't come until I give you permission."

"I'll come when I damn well want to," I argued, though I knew it was only a matter of time before I couldn't hold back any longer.

But then he pushed my hand away and took control, gripping me tightly at the base. The pleasure-filled pains ricocheting through my body were almost too much to bear.

"That's not how things work between us, Xander. It never has, and it never will." He pumped me the way he knew would push me closer to the edge. "You're mine. You understand that, right?"

My mind was racing with the desperate need to come.

"I'll be whatever you want; just keep fucking me!"

Of course, that asshole laughed in response before resuming his relentless rhythm.

"Take it! Take this fucking cock!"

I could tell by the rapid movement of his hips and his quickening breaths that he was as close to losing control as I was. And in the next moment, he swelled and, with one final explosive thrust, released himself deep inside me.

"Yes! Fuck!" he shouted, his voice echoing through the air.

I wanted to scream with frustration as Theo continued to grip my dick tightly, denying me the relief I so desperately craved.

"You bastard."

"I won't deny it." He pulled out and turned me around, pushing me back onto the couch before taking hold of my cock again.

And then, before I even had a chance to understand what he was planning, his lips engulfed me, taking me deep into the warm cavern of his mouth. It only took a few swift strokes from that wicked tongue for me to explode, waves of intense pleasure coursing through every nerve in my body.

He drew out my release with his hand, and once I could think straight again, I opened my eyes to find him smirking at me with a triumphant glint in his gray eyes.

"Still think I'm a bastard?"

"Yes."

Theo shrugged and joined me on the sofa. "Too bad you're stuck with me."

He meant those words as a joke, but they also carried a sense of truth that eased our tension. We sat there in silence, half-naked and still catching our breaths, but now the tension from earlier no longer hung heavy in the air like a suffocating fog. Instead, the intimacy and connection of our bond pulsed between us. The only thing missing in these moments was our angel—our third partner who completed us.

The three of us fit together perfectly. We fully understood and accepted each other. Our dynamic functioned smoothly, whether we were all together or just two. There was never any confusion or jealousy. We recognized the depth and strength of our love for one another.

The truth was that Theo and I shared a deep love for each other, but without Nerine, a part of our souls felt incomplete. We attempted to fill that void with our physical relationship, but no matter how hard we tried, we couldn't erase the pain of her absence from our lives.

"I'm sorry for pushing you," I whispered, my voice heavy with emotion. "I can't stand the idea of losing you, Theo."

"Walking away isn't an option for either of us, Xander." His words were firm and resolute, reminding me once again that we were in this together.

His hands turned my face toward him, his strong fingers gently caressing my cheeks before his mouth captured mine in a slow, indulgent kiss. The taste of mint and whiskey lingered on his lips, a striking contrast to his usual gruffness. I melted into it, savoring the warmth and intimacy of the moment.

At that moment, I needed him more than ever. I needed his touch, his comfort, his love. And damn, we needed to find Nerine so everything in our world would be whole again. Without her, nothing felt right. Without her, we would never find peace.

I turned to face him, wrapping my arms around his broad shoulders as I deepened the kiss until my cock twitched back to life. He reached down between us, his fingers wrapping around my shaft and stroking it with practiced ease.

We'd just come together not long ago, but sex was a welcome distraction from our problems, and I was happy to know he was eager for another romp. I reciprocated by reaching down and wrapping my fingers around his rapidly growing shaft, enjoying the feel of him in my hand.

But our passionate moment was interrupted by the persistent vibration of my phone. With a groan, I reached for it, reluctantly pulling away from Theo's embrace.

"It's a text," I said, wrinkling my brow as I read the message.

"By the look on your face, I'm guessing it's bad news?"

Theo muttered. I glanced up at him, worried and anxious to rush back as my initial desire quickly faded into concern.

"It's from one of the guys inside with Gusto Aetos," I explained. "He said they have a lead on Nerine. She might be in Atlantic City."

"Another city of sin?" Theo asked with a sigh.

"Then that means they saw the book, too," I added, my mind racing with all the possible implications.

"Fuck. Our enemies are closing in."

"What if they find her first?" I asked, unable to shake the fear and dread creeping into my thoughts.

"We can't let that happen. If anyone finds Nerine, we will be lucky to find a body."

"No. That's not an option," I said firmly, shaking my head.

I gazed out the plane's window, wishing it would fly even faster as my heart raced with worry and anticipation. "This shit is pissing me off," Theo growled, his face contorted in an angry sneer. "I swear, if Nerine did this on purpose, I'll never forgive her."

I scoffed at his words, shaking my head in disbelief. "You'd forgive her for anything if you saw she was still alive."

He growled in frustration, his only response to my brutal honesty.

"I'm going to pour us a drink," Theo announced suddenly, getting up from the couch and pulling his pants up before walking over to the small bar in the corner of the room.

Our moment of intimacy and vulnerability from a few

minutes ago felt like a distant memory now. The only version of Theo available for view was the usual tough, stoic, and calculating one, in full force and ready for whatever might come our way.

Oh well, I thought with a hint of disappointment. At least it was nice while it lasted.

Time to put on my enforcer persona.

Six

N ERINE

My heart raced as I exited the elevator and entered the bustling lobby. The scent of expensive perfumes mingled with the drifting fragrance of cigarette smoke, creating a captivating yet overwhelming aroma that assaulted my senses. I discreetly scanned the ever-present crowd for signs of danger, carefully examining each face for potential threats. My nerves were on edge, and I couldn't shake my uneasiness.

"I can't believe I agreed to this," I muttered, trying to calm my racing thoughts. Taking a deep breath, I braced myself for what was to come.

I hated that I always found it nearly impossible to say no to Penny. If I had been more assertive when dealing with her, maybe I wouldn't be in this situation. Instead of being safely tucked away in my little apartment upstairs, I was in a crowded hotel lobby surrounded by strangers.

But Penny had convinced me to meet her for lunch, determined to prevent me from becoming a recluse shut away in my apartment. While I appreciated my solitude and quiet moments, there was nothing wrong with staying in and avoiding unnecessary interactions.

Logically, I understood that Penny's intentions were pure and stemmed from concern for a friend. However, my life was beyond chaotic, and I couldn't summon even a tiny appreciation for her efforts. My mind was filled with worry and fear, leaving no space for socializing or enjoyment.

As I navigated through the bustling crowd of tourists, sidestepping luggage and energetic children, I attempted to ignore the persistent noise and chaos surrounding me. The blend of chatter and laughter combined with the sporadic cries of a baby produced a clamor that grated on my already frayed nerves.

Despite Devani's assurance that I would be safe here, I never felt at ease. Living in a constant state of caution, I tried my best to blend in and avoid attracting any attention to myself. One wrong move or a single person recognizing me could put my family in grave danger.

And on top of all that anxiety, I couldn't shake off the overwhelming heartbreak of being away from my loved ones. While I cherished moments of solitude, the isolation from my family created an emptiness that nothing could fill.

The idea of unplanned visits to see them was out of the

question, especially now that Fiona's book captivated the world. I couldn't risk bringing danger to their doorstep. Therefore, for their safety, I canceled all scheduled visits for the foreseeable future.

It was a sacrifice I had to make to protect them.

But it didn't make it any less painful.

My upcoming visit to see Mama was the only thing that had kept me going these last few months. But with it no longer on the horizon, there was nothing else to look forward to. There was no lifeline or light at the end of this endless tunnel of misery that consumed my life. All I had were memories.

Some were joyful and delightful, filling my heart with warmth and happiness. Others were bittersweet reminders of a past life I could never return to. Unfortunately, many were hauntingly horrific, replaying in my mind like a never-ending nightmare.

My hand instinctively landed on my lower abdomen, my fingers gently pressing against the jagged scar etched into my skin. A familiar sliver of unkempt rage slithered down my spine, a venomous serpent that had taken up permanent residence within me. It had been over two years since I finally escaped the hellish prison I had lived in with Andraius. Yet, whenever my thoughts lingered on him or the despicable things he had done to me, my hatred for the man bubbled up as if it had happened only yesterday.

But at least I'd killed the fucker, and I wouldn't have to endure his abuse ever again. His filthy hands would never touch me again. His repulsive mouth could no longer speak the vile names he'd called me. He would never use me as a pawn, his ideal stepping stone to achieve his ambitions.

Letting his life's blood drip from my fingers healed more wounds than I would have believed when the act actually took place.

Reflecting back now, I regretted nothing. A sense of satisfaction flowed through me, knowing that the woman the bastard considered weak and insignificant had literally gutted him.

He deserved the cut of my knife and the end of his worthless life. That night taught me two lessons: the monster couldn't defeat me, but Theo and Xander could.

I shook off thoughts of death and destruction as I spotted Penny in the elegant restaurant waiting for me. Gracefully, she rose as I approached, wrapping her arms around me in a hug and kissing me on each cheek.

"I'm so glad you decided to leave your little hole!"

"It wasn't as if you would accept no for an answer." I sat across from her, and an attendant quickly poured wine for us both.

"I don't shy away from using every trick up my sleeve to get what I want," Penny said playfully, lifting her glass. "Here's to getting the lady who keeps us organized out of her cave."

I shook my head with a small smile, touched my glass to hers, and sipped the rich, burgundy liquid. Its smoothness soothed my jangled nerves as it entered my system. A light floral scent floated through the space, calming me further.

Perhaps Penny was onto something with her air idea. Her

husband, Hagen, must possess a magic touch to pump happy pheromones throughout the hotel and help people relax.

The restaurant had a botanical vibe, with delicate blooming flowers arranged in garden-like sections throughout the room. The luxuriously plush red velvet booths and mirrored walls added a touch of elegance and indulgence. It perfectly embodied the aesthetic of the couple who owned the hotel—Penny, all about nature, light, and air; Hagen, dark, brooding, and indulgent in every way.

A miniature version of the stained-glass ceiling in the lobby floated above. In the center of the restaurant stood a large marble statue of a voluptuous Greek goddess that I couldn't help but admire. She held a massive basket of plants balanced on one hand and raised the other toward the sky in triumph. Confidence radiated from her face as if she were ready to take on the world.

With a wistful gaze at her, I recalled feeling that same way once. There was a time when I stood as the Godmother of the Night for the Angelos Syndicate, with Xander and Theo by my side, and I knew I could achieve anything.

I was ruthless.

Cunning.

Unforgiving and coldly calculating.

But now, those feelings seemed so distant that I some-times questioned whether they had ever been real. Had that truly been my life? Or had I just imagined it all?

"I wouldn't have left for anyone else." I laughed, taking another hearty sip of the well-aged wine.

The deep, rich flavor danced on my tongue, warming me

from the inside out. But as the alcohol settled, a slow, intoxicating haze dulled the edges of my mind. I should take it easy, having barely eaten anything today. The last thing I needed was to get drunk so early in the day.

Penny's proposition lingered between us like a tantalizing promise. A night out with her and her sisters-in-law sounded appealing, but my social energy was definitely depleted. Demonstrating my strength by attending lunch had exhausted me, and now Penny was urging another outing.

No way.

"Don't say no! Think it over! I'll get us a driver. We can hop from bar to bar if you want." Penny's eyes sparkled with excitement.

"That sounds awful," I replied honestly.

"Why? You're young and gorgeous! A beautiful woman like you should go out and enjoy life a little! Hey! Maybe you'll meet a cute guy. It would do you good to shake that frown off your face for a bit," she said, winking at me before finishing her wine and pouring another glass. "You need to let loose."

I shook my head, unconvinced. Meeting some random guy didn't make this outing any more appealing. In fact, it made it even less desirable.

"Hello, ladies. Are you ready to order?" The voice of our waiter interrupted our conversation.

I felt heat rise to my cheeks as I looked up at him. He was young, handsome, and tall, with dark features that vaguely reminded me of Theo. His smile was warm and inviting, evoking thoughts of Xander.

I sighed, realizing that the only men I desired were both unattainable. The idea of being touched by anyone else repulsed me. Even this attractive waiter didn't persuade me to change my mind.

Penny winked at me and ordered another bottle of wine, a Cobb salad, and a burger with crispy sweet potato fries on the side. I shook my head at her choice. This woman truly lived life to the fullest. She ate what she wanted without apology, and I felt like a slacker for being so uptight. I often saw how Hagen adored her curvy body, which reminded me of how Xander and Theo enjoyed my figure.

Nope, I wouldn't let my thoughts wander in that direction.

Instead, I joined her and ordered a bacon cheeseburger with fries.

Penny's eyes widened.

I shrugged and said, "If I can't have sex, I might as well indulge in something else delicious,"

"I see you've come over to the dark side," Penny smirked.

I shrugged nonchalantly. "Why not? You look very happy and well-fed. I should give it a try."

"Exactly." Penny beamed with pride.

Once the waiter walked away, Penny continued to nudge me to go out with her.

"I'm serious, you know. Come on; it'll be fun! I promise! You can't stay cooped up in that apartment for the rest of your life. It's not good for you, frankly."

I sighed again, knowing she was right.

"All right, fine. I'll go," I conceded, quickly adding a critical stipulation. "But dinner and drinks only! No hooking up."

"You say that now." She winked playfully. "Just wait until you see the bartenders at Hagen's new club. They'll gladly offer you something beyond a stiff drink if you catch my drift."

She gave me another cheeky wink, and I rolled my eyes good-naturedly.

She was always so brazen and direct, which was one of the things I loved most about her.

"Subtle as ever, Penny," I smirked, unable to resist teasing her. "I can only imagine what would happen if you had a daughter mixed in with your boys."

"Oh, I would corrupt her just like I have my nieces," she laughed, sipping her wine. "Thanks for agreeing to come out tonight. If I don't push you, who will?"

Her question resonated deeply, reminding me of how painfully lonely I truly felt. I pretended everything was fine to survive, yet I felt hollow and empty inside. How could any woman choose to run from the loves of her life? Why was I constantly building walls around myself, preventing any real connections or friendships from forming?

Perhaps this outing with Penny could be a small step toward reconnecting with others.

"We're going to have an amazing time tonight," Penny assured, with excitement shining in her eyes.

I wanted to believe her. I wanted to let go and have fun like she did. But I knew returning to the carefree days before everything fell apart was impossible. Too much had happened. Too much had changed. I had chosen to stay away, but at what point did I need to let go completely? When should I stop hoping to be with Xander and Theo again? It felt like an impossible task.

Tears threatened to spill from my eyes at the thought of never seeing them again, but I quickly blinked them away. What we shared was real and special. Could I ever find that kind of love and connection with someone else? The idea seemed unfathomable. Xander and Theo were one of a kind, irreplaceable.

But I had to let go of that dream and move on with my life; that was the only way forward. As I ate my lunch, grateful for a moment of peace while Penny picked at her salad, I struggled with the urge to stay home tonight. Every instinct told me to remain vigilant and prepared for whatever might come my way. Skipping going out and heading to the gym to train with the other Solon agents would be better. Keeping my skills sharp and honed was crucial now, more than ever.

"You know, Hagen has a friend who might interest you," Penny said, her eyes bright and eager. "Handsome, rich, and a monstrous cock."

I couldn't help but raise an eyebrow at her words. "Handsome, rich, and a monstrous ... cock?" I repeated, raising my voice in shock.

"Or so I've been told," Penny quickly corrected herself, prompting us to laugh.

I shook my head but felt grateful for her friendship and concern. "Penny, you're incorrigible."

"I just want to see you happy and fulfilled," she shrugged nonchalantly before taking another sip of wine.

"My happiness doesn't depend on my love life," I reminded her firmly.

"Your pussy begs to differ," she quipped playfully, causing me to blush and scold her once again.

But deep down inside, I knew she was right.

My heart yearned for a deep connection, but only with Xander and Theo. But I also knew those thoughts couldn't consume me. Fiona's actions had thrust us all into dangerous territory, and I needed to stay focused and keep everyone safe.

I silently vowed to do just that as we continued our lunch, laughing and chatting like old times. And maybe, just maybe, Penny's matchmaking would help me take a small step toward moving on and finding happiness again.

In the back of my mind, I couldn't deny that Penny was right. Before I left, Theo and Xander had satisfied every one of my sexual desires. Our chemistry as a throuple was a constant, living force pulsing with desire and lust. It seemed almost unquenchable most of the time.

Thinking of them made my body tremble, recalling how I felt so alive, satisfied, and completely filled with love. Without Theo and Xander, my life felt empty and lacking affection.

Penny raised an eyebrow, challenging me. "Tell me I'm wrong."

I sighed and rolled my eyes, refusing to admit her truth. But I couldn't stop my pussy from throbbing at the memory of them.

Ignoring Penny's knowing gaze, I turned my attention to devouring my cheeseburger. Maybe she would drop the subject if I focused hard enough on this greasy indulgence.

But she saw right through me. "The way you're devouring that cheeseburger says it all," she teased.

I groaned inwardly, reluctant to engage in this conversation. "Please, Penny. I said I'd go out tonight. Don't make me hook up with some random stranger."

"Just be open to possibilities," Penny urged, leaning in closer and gazing into my eyes with pleading intensity.

I gave in, realizing it was simpler to go along with her than to argue. "Fine, I can do that."

It was a harmless white lie to please Penny. Deep down, I knew no one else could compare to what Theo and Xander offered me. It was pointless even to try to find someone like them again.

SEVEN

T HEO

My heart raced at the sight of her, Nerine.

She was alive.

She believed she could hide behind that disguise, but I recognized her face anywhere. Every inch of skin, every curve of her body, was engraved in my memory. Even with a blindfold on, I would have known it was her with just one touch.

Nerine Angelos. No one in the world could ever compare to her. And now here she was, sitting at a table in the hotel restaurant with a wealthy and lively woman.

I immediately noticed the security team surrounding them—three men at one table and two at another, all trying to blend in but failing miserably.

However, I noticed their tells immediately.

The dark suits, the bulge of their weapons at their sides, and the way their eyes darted around while they pretended to converse. It was obvious.

I sat at the bar, positioned slightly behind Nerine and out of her view but close enough to catch their enlightening conversation. My heart lifted when I heard her decline her friend's offer to match her with a man. Could it be that she had stayed untouched by others? I couldn't help but wish for that possibility.

But by the tone of her voice, Nerine seemed completely uninterested in pursuing the "dick" her friend joked about.

Although I was glad about her lack of interest, it saddened me to witness the visible distress on her face. Her whole demeanor expressed a feeling of defeated sorrow. Her shoulders drooped, and her eyes appeared heavy with sadness.

This wasn't like any Nerine I had seen before.

Where was the fiery temptress who loved to argue with me? The woman who insisted she alone knew what was right from wrong? Where was the goddess whom I was both obsessed with and maddened by?

My first instinct upon spotting her was to lift her over my shoulder, carry her somewhere private and safe, interrogate her, and obtain the answers I'd desperately needed over the past few years.

When I saw she was safe, I held back. What I needed now was information. If I knew anything about Nerine, it was that she wouldn't provide answers willingly. If I wanted to understand why she'd disappeared, I'd have to figure it out on my own first.

Now, she called herself Rina, not just changing her appearance but also her name. And here she was in the middle of the fucking desert, looking perfectly groomed with no visible injuries.

As if the wound in my soul wasn't enough, it tore open, festering with the knowledge that whatever had happened, she had left willingly. No one had taken her or compelled her to go. She had decided to vanish without saying anything to Xander or me. It was painful to realize that she could have called us at any point over the past two years.

I tightened my jaw to control my feelings and consider the situation rationally. There was more to this story, as there often is. I scrutinized her closely, observing every part of her as she moved through the world with a blend of freedom and persistent caution.

Her contacts couldn't hide the misery and fear swirling in her eyes. I couldn't help but feel a wave of protectiveness for her, wondering if someone had pressured her into this situation.

Impatient and restless, I listened to Nerine's friend speak, fighting the urge to interrupt. The security around them was imposing, but the element of surprise was our best chance of getting out of this unscathed.

I quickly pulled out my phone to text Xander about my discovery. Once he heard the news, he'd regret staying cooped up in our hotel room instead of coming down to grab a bite to eat, as I suggested. But for now, I needed his expertise in this situation.

ME: I found her.

XANDER: WTF? Where?

ME: In the bistro closest to the high roller's tower, she's going by the name 'Rina.' She looks completely different.

XANDER: Unbelievable! I'm on my way down.

ME: No. Wait. She doesn't know I saw her, and I want it to stay that way. Hack into Ida's hotel database to learn more about her.

XANDER: That's harder than you think. Places like this are locked down tighter than Fort Knox.

ME: I have faith in your abilities.

XANDER: Asshole. Tell me more while I search.

A feeling of unease settled in my stomach as I typed my response to Xander. Something wasn't right about this whole situation.

ME: She's having lunch with another woman—someone wealthy and influential, considering the security team surrounding them. They are discussing going out, and the lady is trying to persuade Nerine to find someone to fuck.

XANDER: Over my dead body! You better stop it, or I will kick your ass.

ME: Keep dreaming. I'm the one person whose ass you can't kick. Lucky for you, she doesn't seem too keen on the idea.

XANDER: Of course not. She knows she belongs to us.

But even as Xander mentioned this, I couldn't shake the feeling that something was off.

XANDER: I found her. Rina Leto. She's leasing an apartment in the hotel's residential tower. Apartment 1106. Can I leave our room now and see her for myself?

ME: No, keep digging. We need to know everything we can find out about this Rina Leto cover.

A few minutes later, he replied with more details.

XANDER: Rina Leto is the only child of Herbert and Tonya Leto, born and raised in Kansas City. Her parents died during her second year at Missouri State in a car hydroplaning accident. She studied business and project management and has no criminal record. She embodies the perfect girl next door, as clean as a whistle.

I clenched my jaw. Devani lied to me and hadn't given two shits about it.

ME: This whole identity is airtight, which means only one group could have orchestrated this. Fucking Solon.

XANDER: Shit. We need to prove it.

ME: It confirms that Nerine didn't leave us of her own free will. She wouldn't have been able to conceal an operation like her kidnapping from us.

XANDER: Shit. This keeps getting worse. What now?

ME: Meet me in the lobby.

XANDER: On my way.

I left Nerine to continue her conversation with her friend. I headed toward the elevator banks leading to the main hotel corridor. A sense of dread settled over me. If Solon were involved in all this, things would become much more complicated and dangerous.

As I waited, I saw Xander exiting a lift and striding confidently toward a distant corner of the bustling casino, not acknowledging me.

Keeping my distance, I discreetly followed him and then slipped into a seat at one of the electronic gaming booths.

As I inserted a card, I waited for the machine to show my available balance. I began playing a round while watching Xander amid the flashing lights and sounds of the machines. A crease marred his usually smooth brow, and the tight set of his jaw revealed his urgent need to act now and think later.

"Is she in there?" Xander's voice cut through the noise as he finally turned to face me between two machines on the opposite side.

I nodded, keeping my eyes on him despite the temptation to sneak glances at the woman we were both looking for. "Yes, but we can't confront her until she's alone."

His frustration was palpable as he ran a hand through his hair.

"Keep it together. Remember, I'm the one she fights with. You are the peacemaker, gentle and sweet. Don't unleash your beast here."

Xander wore a mask of cold-hearted ruthlessness in his enforcer role. His methods were calculatedly vicious. He rarely, if ever, raised his voice, but when he did, his deadly monster emerged, and he showed no mercy.

On the other hand, I was known for being cold and calculating—a manipulator and diplomat. I never truly allowed my emotions to influence my actions, except when inflicting my punishments, which were vicious and fucked up, especially since I enjoyed instruments or two during those times.

When it came to Nerine, Xander and I were totally opposite.

The woman knew exactly how to push my buttons to the point where I wasn't sure if I wanted to fuck her or hang her off the side of a building. Meanwhile, Xander knew how to calm her down. He was her confidant and the one who smoothed her jagged edges.

"Does she look healthy?" he asked, attempting to hide his concern with sarcasm.

"Aside from her unfortunate choice of goldish dark blonde hair and brown contacts, she seems miserable," I replied. "But it's definitely her."

Xander let out a deep sigh. "Couldn't she have chosen a name that wasn't basically a shortened version of her own?"

My irritation grew at the question. "Honestly, it shocked me to see her here in plain sight. How could she think that changing her appearance would fool people who know her?"

"I thought she was smarter than that," Xander muttered.

We focused on two men hanging around outside a nearby restaurant, and my gaze sharpened as I recognized them instantly. "Stratos's guys."

"Yep," Xander confirmed with a nod. "With his men in Atlantic City and these bastards in Vegas, they're clearly searching for her, too. This isn't good."

"No kidding," I growled. "Do you think these fuckers saw her?"

"Not sure," he shrugged. "We won't know until Nerine walks out."

"That damn book," Xander cursed under his breath, "it led all of us right to her."

"And now the other idiots will figure it out, too," I finished grimly.

"She has no idea how much danger she's in," Xander said through clenched teeth.

"And she's just planning on having a night out to hook up," I added, recalling her earlier conversation with her friend.

"You said she wasn't interested," Xander said with a hint of frustration. "Why are you pissed?"

"She must have at least considered it if she's here instead of with us. But enough about that," I said, trying to refocus on the task. "We need to act fast. We can't wait."

"Fine. I'll handle this personally," Xander declared, his body tense with anticipation of finally confronting Nerine.

"Tonight," I agreed with determination. "Let's hang back and see if anyone follows her when she leaves."

"You know I won't hesitate to eliminate any threats," Xander stated firmly, reaching inside his coat and resting his hand on his gun.

"I know, Xander," I reassured him, looking into his determined eyes with understanding. "I trust you more than anyone."

"Just saying," he grumbled, refocusing on the restaurant entrance as we waited for Nerine to emerge.

"Remember, keep it cool," I reminded him. "We're almost there."

"It's about damn time," Xander muttered under his breath. "I'm ready to end this once and for all."

A surge of determination swept through me at his words. We were finally on the verge of getting Nerine back and ending this dangerous game.

My heart raced with anticipation at the thought of finally seeing Nerine again. A restlessness pricked every nerve in my body as I focused on keeping Xander calm. However, I was too preoccupied to notice it.

I worried about my self-control when I was alone with her—the intense desire to both kiss and punish her raced through my veins. The conflicting emotions battled within me, leaving me uncertain about which would prevail when we were face to face.

But one thing was sure: Xander and I would unleash our fury on Nerine for the hurt and pain she had caused us.

I wondered if she could sense us getting closer. Once strong and nurtured, our bond might still exist despite her absence. Was the hair on the back of her neck standing up in warning? Did her body instinctively know that danger was drawing near?

EIGHT

N ERINE

As I stood by my apartment window, raindrops pounding against the glass drowned out the noise from the bustling Las Vegas Strip below. It was an unusual sight—rarely did it rain in this desert city. But today, the weather seemed to mirror my mood: gray and gloomy.

I wrapped my robe tighter around me, seeking comfort and warmth in its soft fabric. My gaze swept over the blurred view outside as the raindrops created a hazy curtain that distorted the vibrant lights of the Strip.

I sighed and wondered, "Do I have to go out in this?"

But I already knew the answer. Penny's insistence on a girls' night out had been relentless, and now I regretted ever agreeing to it. All I wanted was to stay in the safety of my tiny home, far away from clubs and Penny's attempts to set me up with her hand-picked hot men.

Yet, here I was, torn between my dread of the evening ahead and the chaos of Fiona's damn book that consumed my thoughts.

Part of me hoped Penny would cancel our plans due to the freak storm raging through the city. But as luck would have it, she seemed determined to go ahead with our outing.

So, on top of everything else, I now had to worry about someone recognizing me in public. What would I do if someone spotted me? What if it put Penny and her family in danger? Just the thought sent shivers down my spine.

I wanted to tell Penny the truth but knew it wasn't an option. Not yet.

A wave of nostalgia washed over me as I gazed at my reflection in the bathroom mirror after my shower. Without my contacts, I resembled the old Nerine Angelos, a strong and confident woman who stood up for herself and those she cherished.

But now, as Rina Leto, I was trying to blend in and remain unnoticed.

I hated this identity. It felt like a betrayal to the strong woman I once was. But to protect those I loved, nothing was too much of a sacrifice.

A sudden wave of guilt struck me as I recalled my sacrifices for their sake.

I sighed as I glanced at the microwave clock, recognizing that I had allowed my thoughts to drift away.

I turned my attention to the cell phone on the counter. I could always call Mama. After all, that's what good Greek girls did on the weekends. Plus, it would give me a valid excuse to skip the night out with Penny.

"*Kóri mou!*" My mother's voice echoed through the phone on the first ring.

"Yes, this is your daughter. But you have three others, so the odds are in your favor with that greeting," I said in Greek, laughing at her for answering the phone with 'my daughter.'

The girls and I always spoke to Mama in our family's native language. It was our way of keeping our cultural traditions alive and making her happy. She loved to say that Greeks had words for everything, which helped us understand a person's feelings and intentions. However, even in English, one word often had multiple meanings—like "light," which could refer to a candle, weight, color, or illumination.

"How are you, sweetheart?"

"I'm okay." I wasn't ready to spill my guts.

First, I needed some simple updates about life to ease the tension on my shoulders.

"Is it raining there?" she asked incredulously. "I checked the weather, and it said you might have storms."

"It is," I confirmed. "Strange, right? When it rains, it pours."

"I see you've talked to your sister," she mused.

"Unfortunately," I muttered under my breath before asking, "But how is everyone else doing? How are the twins?"

"Your sisters are doing well, adjusting to college life with ease. Although, I do miss having them close by. It worries me about their safety when they're so far away."

"I know," I replied, my heart heavy with concern for my younger siblings, who now lived in different cities.

It had been on my mind lately, but I hadn't found the courage to bring it up with them. They deserved this freedom, and the thought of taking it away filled me with guilt.

The concern in Mama's voice tugged at my heartstrings. As she mentioned Fiona's book, I could hear the fear and worry woven into her words. I couldn't understand how careless Fiona had been; it seemed like Mama felt the same way.

"I have no idea," I replied with a deep sigh, unable to conceal the resignation in my voice. "If only she had shared a copy with one of us before publishing it. But now, it's out in the world, and there's no way to take it back."

"So, are you saying all we can do is pray to St. Sophia and St. Joseph?" Mama asked, her faith in the saints often being her go-to solution for problems.

"No, Mama," I said firmly. "We need to stay vigilant and safe. Keep an eye on the boys, and don't let them out of your sight."

"You know I wouldn't," she reassured me. "But I'll be praying anyway."

"Of course," I chuckled, knowing it was part of her routine. "Mama, I miss them so much it hurts." A sharp pang shot through my heart as I thought about not being able to see my boys every day. They grew so quickly at eighteen months old, and canceling my visit with them tore me apart.

No mother should be without her children, my precious terrors who gave their *Yai Yai* such a hard time.

"Let's switch to a video call so you can talk to them," Mama suggested.

"Yes, please," I eagerly replied as I tapped the buttons on my phone. Her face appeared on my screen within seconds. "There you are."

"*Yassou*, Nerine," she greeted me with a wave as if we hadn't been talking just moments ago.

"Hi, Mama," I said, shaking my head.

I watched her enter her living room, and my two boys appeared. Both were sitting in their play area, happily engaged with their toys.

"Hello, my babies! I'm so happy to see you," I exclaimed with a smile.

They both looked up, and their faces brightened at the sound of my voice, instantly melting my heart. They were the most beautiful beings in the world, and loving them was like nothing I had ever experienced. They held a special place in my heart that I didn't know was there, and I would do anything for them.

Even if my current circumstance made me feel as if I was walking through hell to protect them from harm, I wouldn't change it. They were the priority.

The guilt weighing on my conscience from tearing our family apart destroyed parts of my soul, and the fact that they resembled their fathers added to the burden.

"Ma-ma!" Hayes mumbled excitedly, squirming in his seat.

Charis clapped his tiny hands together and reached out toward the camera, his big gray eyes shining joyfully. Tears filled my eyes at the sight of them.

I had named them after their paternal grandmothers, giving Hayes, Xander's mother, Brenna's maiden name, and Charis Theo's mother's maiden name.

In terms of appearance, they were a perfect blend of their parents, with Hayes inheriting all of Xander's features except for my blue eyes and Charis resembling a male version of me with Theo's striking gray irises.

"They're growing up so fast, Mama," I said, my voice shaking with emotion. "I feel so guilty for not being there with them."

"Don't you dare hold onto that guilt, Nerine," Mama gently scolded. "You're doing what you need to do to protect them. It's for the best. And I promise, I'm taking good care of them."

"I know, Mama," I sniffled. "I'm just so thankful for your help."

"They will never forget you," she assured me. "I won't let that happen. And it won't be forever. They'll be back in your arms before you know it!"

"You've already raised your children, and now you have to raise mine too. I'm so sorry, Mama."

"Nonsense." She waved away my apology. "This isn't your fault. You must let go of this burden and concentrate on overcoming this tough time. Holding onto guilt won't change anything. You make it sound like you expected the kidnapping or to find out you were pregnant, especially with your unique brand of twins."

Her words hit me like a wave, washing over me and leaving me relieved and exposed. She was right. I hadn't expected any of this. The pregnancy was a complete shock, although having twins wasn't entirely unexpected, considering it ran in my family. But what truly astonished me was that I had somehow given birth to heteropaternal superfecundation twins, siblings with different fathers.

When my doctor first revealed the truth about their parentage, I nearly fainted. I had fantasized about it as a teenager, falling in love with Xander and Theo and wishing for them to father my children. But I never imagined it could happen.

Not only had I run from the loves of my life, but I also carried within me fraternal twins, each fathered by a different man. My body took part in this rare occurrence, releasing two eggs and enabling my lovers to fertilize one.

DNA testing conducted after birth confirmed what we had suspected all along.

It took me a year and a half to come to terms with all of this, and even now, it still felt surreal. But one thing was certain: I was beyond thrilled to have sons from both Xander and Theo. It was a wild and unexpected turn of events that I wouldn't trade for anything in the world.

I longed for the comfort of my mother's presence. "I'm lonely, Mama," I confessed. "I want to be there with you. I want to be the one to hold my children when they cry and put them to bed." "Soon," she reassured me. "No, it isn't possible," I sighed heavily, pinching the bridge of my nose in frustration. "Not with Fiona's book out in the world." The weight of the situation settled heavily on my shoulders.

"I hoped it wouldn't come to that." I heard the disappointment in Mama's words. "But you are doing what is best for everyone. You always do, Nerine. Never doubt when I say I know you sacrifice to put the rest of us first."

"But... I don't know how to fix the mess Fiona created," I admitted. Fear gripped me as I considered the potential danger her actions could bring to my doorstep. "I'm scared."

Only with Mama could I let down my guard and show my vulnerable side. She had witnessed the horrors I'd endured and never turned away. She had stood by me, encouraging me to fight through the trauma inflicted upon me by Andraius when he forced me into marriage.

Even now, she supported me in every way possible.

"I hope it blows over soon and becomes just a passing fad, like many other things," she said, trying to offer some sense of optimism.

"So do I," I replied, wishing this nightmare would end.

"In the meantime," Mama hummed, signaling that she intended to change the subject and steer my thoughts away from wallowing in self-pity. "What are you doing to pass the time?"

I couldn't help but scoff at her question. "Umm, work. That's about it." I shrugged. "My boss, Penny, thinks I live like a hermit and invited me to go out tonight."

"What did you decide? I know you like her," Mama prodded.

"I said yes," I admitted, "but I can't shake this feeling that someone will recognize me."

"Where would you go?" she inquired.

"Dinner and then some clubs afterward," I replied reluctantly. "Honestly, it sounds awful. But turning Penny down is nearly impossible. She's so kind and genuinely wants what's best for me. Plus, she keeps bringing up the idea of setting me up with someone, which is the last thing I need right now."

"It might do you some good to meet a nice man," Mama suggested, her tone gentle and understanding.

"Really?" I couldn't hide my annoyance. "Did you forget that I have two baby daddies? The thought of anyone touching me besides Xander or Theo is repulsive."

Mama paused momentarily before replying softly, "I never forget things, especially with my wonderful grandsons nearby. But I want you to enjoy yourself and relieve the stress on your mind. It's important to take care of yourself, Nerine. You've been through a lot."

Her words made me pause as I realized she was right. "Thank you for saying that, Mama. I needed to hear it."

"The issues with Fiona's book aren't yours to bear alone. We have resources. Use them."

It was time to call in Devani. She had caused this mess, and she could help solve it.

"I will, Mama," I promised, a sense of relief washing over me. "So, I've decided something."

She hummed in response, encouraging me to continue. "Let me hear it."

"Instead of going out tonight, I'm going to have an at-home self-care spa night with all my favorite products, order some delicious food, and enjoy a bottle of wine while watching a romantic comedy."

"No men on that list. I hear you loud and clear," Mama chuckled.

I couldn't help but laugh along with her, feeling lighter and more at ease.

"I love you, Mama. You always know how to make me feel better."

"I love you too, sweetheart," she beamed through the screen.

"Give the boys a kiss for me, okay?" I asked with a gentle smile.

"Of course," Mama said before we exchanged our good-byes and ended the video call.

I sank into the plush cushions of my couch, releasing a deep sigh. After sending a quick text to Penny, I canceled our plans for the evening. I could already picture her teasing remarks when we spoke next, but that was a concern for another day.

Feeling relieved and free, I ordered from my favorite Greek restaurant in the hotel. As a proud Greek girl, knowing that the property owners shared my heritage and understood the nuances of our culture's cuisine was comforting. Finding authentic Greek food was rare, but the Lykaioses had perfected it.

Slipping into my coziest nightgown and fluffy robe, I sank onto the couch with a glass of pinot noir and switched on the television. In the haven of my apartment, I didn't have to worry about being recognized or judged. My mind was racing with thoughts and worries, but at least I could unwind and feel comfortable in my skin.

Just as I finished preparing my bathroom for a luxurious spa session, there was a heavy knock on my door, causing me to frown. A moment later, the doorbell rang. Why couldn't they use that instead of pounding on the door and disturbing the neighbors?

For a split second, panic coursed through me until I glanced at the clock and remembered it was dinner time. I had completely forgotten about it in my rush to unwind and take care of myself.

Taking a deep breath, I approached the door. A tingling sensation spread up my neck, causing me to pause. Then, I noticed that the air in the hallway was unusually still and silent.

My pulse quickened as my fingers hesitated on the lock. A cold chill ran down my spine, my throat went dry, and fear gripped me.

There was no point in looking through the peephole.

They had found me.

But instead of staying safe inside and using logic to protect myself, I turned the latch and swung open the door, freezing in my tracks.

They were here.

Xander stood in the doorway like a tempest, his imposing figure dominating the small space.

His dark eyes pierced through mine with an intensity

that sent shivers down my spine. He wore a sharp, predatory smile, making my heart race and my knees weaken.

Behind him, Theo stood like a menacing shadow, his steel-gray eyes penetrating me with chilling precision. The tension radiating from him struck me like a wave, suffocating and electrifying.

"Hello, Angel," Xander growled, his voice deep and seething with malice. He lifted a bag with the food I'd ordered. "We brought you dinner."

My throat tightened as unwelcome and overwhelming memories flooded back. The sound of their voices, the touch of their hands, the way they had consumed me, body and soul. The name Angel, carved into my heart by their lips, now cut through me like a sharp blade.

"You shouldn't be here," I managed to say, though my words trembled as much as my knees.

Xander's smile widened, his dark eyes glinting with something unsettling. "Funny. I was just about to say the same thing."

Before I could react, he pushed past me with enough force to make me stumble. Heat rolled off him in powerful waves, searing through the thin fabric of my robe and sending an unwelcome jolt straight through me. I turned, stunned, as he strode into my apartment as if he owned the place, his sharp gaze scanning every corner.

Theo walked behind him, quieter yet just as intimidating. He closed the door with a purposeful click and locked it, sending a shiver down my spine.

I was trapped. Completely trapped.

"What are you doing here?" I demanded, attempting to summon some semblance of strength in my voice. Yet, it came out thin and breathless, and I loathed myself for it.

"What do you think?" Xander snapped as he turned to face me.

Fury blazed in his eyes like a wildfire. Still, I could sense something else lurking beneath it—something darker and more unsettling. It twisted my stomach and quickened my pulse.

He dropped the takeout bag to the ground and gestured around the room, his lip curling in disgust. "This? This is where you've been? Living it up while we've been tearing the world apart for you?"

"I'm not living it up," I shot back, though my voice lacked the intensity I desired. "And I didn't ask you to—"

"No." Theo's voice sliced through the air like a sharp blade, cold and unyielding. "You didn't ask us. You just vanished. You made us think—" He paused, his jaw tightening as he stepped closer to me. "You made us think you were dead."

"I had no choice," I whispered, instinctively retreating. But there was no escaping them.

Xander moved in on one side of me. At the same time, Theo positioned himself on the other, trapping me between their imposing figures.

"No choice?" Xander snarled, his voice dripping with venom. "Bullshit."

Before I could respond, his hand shot out and gripped my jaw tightly enough to make me gasp. His calloused fingers pressed into my skin, holding me firm as his dark eyes penetrated mine.

"You think you can just vanish? Leave us to suffer while you play house?" His voice was low and menacing. He tightened his grip, and a sharp jolt of pain caused my breath to hitch. "Do you have any idea what we've been through? What I've done for you?"

I attempted to pull away, but his hold was intense. His thumb grazed the edge of my bottom lip, sending a rush of heat through my body. I loathed how my body betrayed me, responding to a touch I should have feared.

"I—" The words caught in my throat as Theo's hands came to rest heavily on my shoulders from behind.

His breath was warm against my ear, his voice low and threatening. "You don't get to run, Nerine. Not from us."

NINE

X ANDER

I leaned in close, my breath mingling with hers in the charged space between us. I could feel her shallow exhales against my skin, each a reminder of her presence and vulnerability.

Her lips quivered, and for a moment, I hated how much I wanted to consume her, to claim her as my own. But this wasn't about pleasure; it was about uncovering the truth.

"You're going to confess everything, Angel," I whispered, my voice low and dangerous. "Every last detail."

Theo tightened his grip on her arms, holding her still as she looked back and forth between us, frantic and desperate.

A flicker of defiance shone in her eyes despite the fear.

She still had some fight left in her. Good. Let her try.

Because there was no escaping us this time.

"You abandoned us," I growled, my voice sinking into a guttural snarl. "Now you will experience that feeling."

Her chest heaved as she geared up to respond, but it didn't matter. Nothing she could say would alter the truth.

Theo's grasp on her shifted, and he leaned in close, his lips grazing her ear. "We're not letting you go, Nerine. Not now. Not ever."

Our words hung heavily in the air, final and unforgiving.

Nerine trembled between us, her body betraying her even as her mind fought against us.

She was where she belonged for the first time in two years.

And we were never going to let her forget it.

Her lips trembled under my grasp, the blush on her cheeks spreading to her neck and chest. It drove me insane how she fought against us with every ounce of defiance she had left while her body betrayed her with every ragged breath. I wanted to break her, to make her feel the same pain and betrayal that consumed me, but at the same time, I couldn't help wanting to worship her.

I tightened my grip on her, my thumb tracing her quivering bottom lip.

"Do you have any idea what you've done to us?" I snarled, my voice filled with anger and longing. "What you made me do? Every damn night, I thought you were dead. I thought I would never touch you again."

Her breath caught, and her eyes widened as she looked up at me with fear and arousal in equal measure.

The mix was intoxicating, sharp and heady, and I couldn't help but resent her for making me crave her even now when all I wanted to do was punish her.

"I—" Her voice broke before she pressed her lips together and shook her head. Yet, her defiance only stoked the fire burning within me.

"You left us," I said, pulling her closer until our bodies pressed together. "You fucking abandoned us. And you think you get to stand here and pretend it never happened?"

"I had no choice!" she spat back, her voice rising with the flicker of the fire that had always drawn me to her—and pushed me away. "You don't understand..."

"Then make me understand," I snapped, interrupting her. "Go on, Angel. Explain why you ran. Explain why you let us think you were dead while you played house in this fucking city."

She attempted to pull away, but my grip remained firm. I wasn't letting go this time. My other hand reached out, grasping her hip and drawing her close against me. She gasped as she felt my hard cock pressing into her softness.

"Xander, stop—" Her words faltered as her gaze darted toward Theo, searching for some salvation, but he merely smirked.

He wasn't going to save her. Neither of us was.

"Stop?" I asked, leaning in until our noses nearly touched. "Is that really what you want?"

The silence between us was deafening, a heavy weight hanging in the air, making breathing difficult. Heat radiated from our bodies, building and intensifying with every passing second. I could feel her trembling beneath my touch, her body betraying her desire despite her attempts to resist.

My hands moved slowly on her shoulders, tracing down her arms with deliberate intent.

Theo's lips brushed against her ear as he whispered in a low, seductive voice, "You can't hide your true feelings from us, Nerine. You've always been a terrible liar."

She shuddered at his words, her lips parting on a sharp inhale. I watched as she swallowed hard, the pulse in her neck visibly throbbing. Trapped between us and surrounded by our presence, she couldn't deny the truth any longer.

Her lashes fluttered, and her breath hitched as I shifted my hand from her hip to her waist, sliding just under the edge of her robe. Her skin was warm and soft beneath my touch, and when my fingers brushed against bare flesh, she arched instinctively toward me.

"You're ours, Angel," I said, my voice rough and low. "You've always been ours. No matter how far you run or how hard you fight, you'll never belong to anyone else."

Theo chuckled darkly and gripped her arms tightly as he pulled her back against him. She gasped at the sudden movement, her head tilting slightly as he trailed his lips along the curve of her neck. "You can keep fighting," he murmured in a dangerous tone. "But it won't change the truth."

She trembled between us, her eyes tightly shut as she fought to regain control. "This isn't fair," she whispered hoarsely.

"Fair?" I smirked, sliding my hand farther up her thigh,

brushing dangerously close to the heat I knew would be waiting for me. "You think this is about fairness?"

Her breath hitched, and her hips jerked involuntarily as I teased the edge of her panties. Theo's lips traveled lower, his teeth brushing against her collarbone, and a soft moan slipped from her lips before she could contain it.

"Stop fighting us," I growled, my voice heavy with desire and possessiveness. "Stop lying to yourself."

Her head fell against Theo's shoulder as her body slowly surrendered to our touch. She didn't respond with words, but the way her hips shifted and her chest arched against mine spoke volumes.

"That's it," Theo purred, his voice smooth as silk. "There's our Angel."

I gripped her chin again, forcing her to look at me. Her lips parted, eyes wide and hazy, and it took everything in me not to press my mouth to hers right then. I wanted her to feel this moment, to understand that this was what she'd been running from. Us. The only two men who had ever truly owned her.

"You're going to tell us everything," I said huskily, my thumb brushing against her plump lip again. "But first..."

I let my words fade away, my gaze fixed on her mouth as Theo's hands slid down to grip her waist tightly, silently challenging her to resist. Her lips trembled, and her breath blended with mine, shallow and shaky.

"First, you're going to remember whom you belong to."

TEN

NERINE

Xander's first kiss sent me into a waking dream, a tantalizing tease that set my senses ablaze. His taste was familiar and intoxicating, igniting a long-simmering flame.

"Xander," I couldn't help but whimper.

"What do you want, Angel?" he asked, holding my gaze with his intense dark brown eyes. "Did you crave my kiss?"

I couldn't deny it. "Yes."

"And my touch?"

"Yeah."

"What about my cock?" He licked his tongue along my bottom lip, sending shivers down my spine. "Did you miss how Theo and I fucked you, filled you?"

All I could do was whimper in response.

Every day since I'd left, I had envisioned this moment. The chaotic scenarios of our fiery reunions played out in my mind, filled with questions and accusations that I knew they would throw at me.

I anticipated tears and anger. I believed they would be cold, unforgiving, and even violent.

But what occurred was something I could never have predicted.

The two arrived at my door together, knocking as if dropping by for afternoon tea. It shocked me to the core. In all my fantasies and fears, I never imagined something so simple or easy.

Seeing them again took me straight back to the past in an instant. The feelings, the memories, the unbreakable bond that had pulsated between us was still there. But now, it was tarnished, bruised, and battered from years of pain and regret.

"Do you want us to fuck you right now? Right here?" Theo's voice was soft and filled with longing as he lightly brushed his lips against my neck.

All the longing and loneliness I had felt over the past few years vanished instantly, replaced by the intense passion that had always flowed between us.

My soul ached for their embrace, pleading for the pleasure they alone could provide.

These two men understood me and my body like no one else could. I was theirs, body and soul.

"Yes. Please. I need you both so much," I whispered,

barely able to form the words before Theo's hands tangled in my hair as he kissed my lips fiercely. Every emotion and desire I had forced into hibernation broke free, sending a wave of arousal through me that pooled between my legs.

I arched my back, pressing against Xander's chest as Theo's hands roamed over my body. They had every right to kill me, to seek revenge for the pain and destruction I had caused in their lives. Yet here I was, trapped between them, their hands igniting sparks of pleasure wherever they touched.

Xander's hands roamed over my body, pushing my robe from my shoulders to expose the silk slip I wore underneath. A deep growl reverberated in his chest as he gripped my throat, compelling me to meet his gaze.

"Who the hell were you wearing this for?" His voice was thick with possessiveness, his eyes clouded by jealousy.

Fear intertwined with arousal as a shiver ran down my spine. This wasn't the Xander I remembered. Jealousy typically belonged to Theo. Something had shifted between the two of them while I was away.

The outside world viewed Xander as a monster, but for me, he was a gentle giant. Or at least, he used to be.

"I wore it for myself," I replied defiantly. He leaned in closer, his face inches from mine. "Do you expect me to believe that when you were planning to go out and find someone to fuck?"

"How did you find out about that?" I asked, feeling a surge of panic.

"We have our ways," Xander said coolly, though his eyes still burned with desire.

Before I could say anything else, Theo leaned close to my ear. "I heard you talking about your evening plans. Your reaction to dating someone was fascinating. Is there a reason why the idea repulsed you?"

The words caught in my throat as if the intensity of my emotions strangled them. I could feel the creases forming between Xander's brows as he looked at me with a mix of confusion and frustration.

"Is it because of us?" His voice was low and husky. "Because we are the only men you want, the only men you can picture touching you?"

I took a deep breath, trying to steady myself. "I've already told you why."

But then Theo's lips were against me, nipping at my earlobe and sending shivers down my spine. "And yet you still left us," he whispered.

"I didn't have a choice," I responded, feeling their hands moving over my body.

"You always had a choice," Xander said, his grip on me tightening.

I moaned as Theo's hand cupped me between my legs, sending waves of pleasure through me. "It wasn't possible for me to contact you after what happened."

"Of course, it was." Xander tilted my chin and kissed me gently, the contrast between his soft lips and anger almost dizzying.

Here, between them, surrendering to their touch and

kisses, I knew the huge risk I was taking. They could have easily killed me in their rage and hurt over my betrayal. But deep down, I couldn't imagine being with anyone else but them one last time before facing whatever consequences awaited me.

Maybe they were still planning to kill me after tonight. Perhaps our love had soured, and this was their way of controlling me. Still, I would rather die by their hands than anyone else's.

Sensing my thoughts, Theo cupped my breast and asked, "Angel, do you think we plan on killing you after we finish fucking you? Is that why you aren't fighting us?"

Xander lifted his head to look at me expectantly, waiting for my response.

I took a deep breath, understanding that regardless of my beliefs or desires, I would have to confront the consequences of my actions.

"It doesn't matter what I believe. I betrayed you both, and I must accept whatever punishment you deem appropriate."

Their gazes met in a silent conversation before returning to me. Theo moved around to stand next to Xander, their bodies nearly touching as they loomed over me.

"Tsk tsk, Angel," Theo scolded, his tone dripping with disappointment. "You won't die by our hands tonight. We have other plans for you." He leaned down and claimed my lips in a hot, demanding kiss that left me breathless.

My heartbeat jumped, and in the next second, Theo's mouth consumed mine.

Whereas Xander's kiss was soft and gentle, Theo exploded over me like a tidal wave. Hot, demanding, and unforgiving.

Every part of me reacted. This was my Theo, the ruthless, unrelenting, dominant lover. His tongue tangled with mine, hot, hungry, exploring, tasting, devouring. He knew how to coax out the desires and needs I'd locked deep inside, the passions and emotions I'd forced into the deepest crevices of my mind for the past few years.

With his lips against mine, the door burst open, and it was impossible to close it again. Then, it was Xander's turn. Grabbing my chin roughly, he pulled me closer and kissed me intensely, his tongue exploring every corner of my mouth. This was not the same gentle kiss from before. This kiss was filled with desperation and anger, mirroring the pain I had caused him.

But I embraced it all, sharing their passion and hunger. We were all caught in the same storm of emotions and desires.

I couldn't fully explain to them the depth of my suffering during our time apart. The words felt inadequate compared to the overwhelming intensity of our reunion. Instead, I let my body express my needs, demonstrating how much I needed them, just as much as they needed each other.

As we lost ourselves in touch and kisses, it was clear that none of us were truly complete without the others. For one night, we could forget about everything else and revel in our shared passion. Even as the storm raged on, I couldn't ignore the nagging feeling that I was the one who truly felt alone in this.

They felt insincere and desperate in my mind, so I let them die on my tongue.

My body trembled as I attempted to convey my love for them through every movement. My need and desire for them still burned fiercely, consuming me. Their touch ignited a chain reaction of hungry kisses and grasping hands, leaving my skin tingling with electricity.

Theo's lips found my neck, trailing kisses down to the straps of my slip, pulling them down my shoulders and baring my body to him. My slip pooled at my feet, leaving me standing before them in only my underwear.

A wave of insecurity washed over me as I stood bare, my body showing the scars of childbirth. But any doubts vanished as they took in every inch of my fuller breasts, rounder belly, and curvier hips. Would they ask about it? Would they hate me for keeping this secret from them?

I couldn't bear the thought of their anger or rejection. But at that moment, with their hands roaming over my bare skin, I couldn't resist their touch. The danger no longer mattered. I needed them like I needed oxygen.

I fucking needed it.

I was aware it was selfish.

I understood it was callous.

I recognized it was wrong.

Guilt and shame tugged at my conscience, but I pushed them away as they skillfully intertwined like expert lovers, creating a symphony of ecstasy from my trembling form.

Desire mingled with fear until I could no longer tell whose hands were whose, but all that mattered was surrendering to the intense pleasure they offered me.

The danger no longer mattered.

I wanted this.

I wanted them.

Just one more time.

Just one more night.

Standing bare and breathless before them, I opened my arms, welcoming the electric, white-hot heat of their touch.

Xander scooped me up and carried me to the bedroom. Theo quickly followed behind. My eyes widened as I watched Theo reach behind him and pull his shirt over his head and quickly unfastened and pushed down his pants until they stood towering over me, side by side like two naked sex gods finally looking over at me like a long-lost dream.

I couldn't move.

Or blink.

Or speak.

I soaked in the sight of them as if I were finally tasting water after a lifetime in the desert. It was just a fleeting, frozen moment in time, but I engraved the vision of them deep into my mind—so sexy, so hungry, so passionate.

They stood next to each other, two flawless figures exuding warmth and desire. In that still moment, I understood this could be the final instance I witnessed them like this. Once I revealed the truth, they may never again look at me with such intense longing.

But for now, I savored their gaze, storing it in my

memory like a cherished treasure. I sank to my knees before them, my eyes locked on their throbbing cocks as I reached for them with trembling hands.

A smile spread across my face as my fingers wrapped around their shafts, stroking them slowly and deliberately. Their synchronized moans filled my ears, igniting a fire within me. The anger remained overshadowed by their primal need and hunger for me.

And in that moment, despite all that would come after, this vision of us would be engraved in my mind and heart forever.

Slowly, I bent my head, savoring the anticipation of tasting Xander's cock. The velvety shaft slid between my lips, and his hips twitched in response to my touch. A deep groan escaped his lips as I took him in completely, and his fingers tangled in my hair.

"Fuck!" he exclaimed, the thrill of pleasure evident in his voice as he pushed deeper into my mouth.

"That's it. Take his cock inside that pretty mouth of yours." Watching intently, Theo muttered words of encouragement, his desire palpable and sending shivers of pleasure straight to my pussy.

My tongue twirled around Xander's shaft as I sucked hard, bobbing my head in rhythm with my movements. His grip on my hair grew tighter, guiding me as he thrust into my mouth. As I felt him getting closer to climax, I slowed down and pulled away, turning toward Theo and engulfing his cock instead.

"Oh, god," he moaned as I took him into my mouth,

feeling the heat and hardness of him against my tongue. "Nerine, fuck!"

I swirled my tongue around the head of his cock, meeting his gaze with a playful look before returning to my task. My pussy throbbed at the sight of them above me like this, Xander stroking himself while watching Theo's cock slide in and out of my mouth.

"You were made for this, Angel," Xander growled with pleasure.

"Your mouth was made for our cocks," Theo corrected with a groan, pushing further into my mouth until he reached the back of my throat. "Don't stop!"

Fueled by their desire and delighted in giving them both so much pleasure, I continued with even more fervor. Pleasuring them with my mouth and hands always gave me a sense of power and strength that was intoxicating.

I had always loved sucking their cocks since the first time I had done it. The taste, the feel, the sounds all drove me wild. And this time was no different.

I pushed that thought away and focused on the pleasure, feeling my pussy grow wetter with every stroke of their cocks in my mouth.

Sure, I loved making them feel good, but knowing that I could reduce these two strong men to quivering messes with my mouth and hands always left me buzzing with a sense of strength.

I loved the taste of them, the feel of their shafts sliding against my tongue, the feel of their white-hot heat exploding in my mouth. I loved the sounds they made. The way they guided my head up and down on their beautiful cocks.

This time, just like before, I enjoyed it as much as I always have. Setting aside the possibility that I might never experience this again, I reveled in that powerful feeling, my pussy growing slicker with every stroke of their cocks.

"Fuck," Theo growled as I flicked my tongue hard over the head of his cock. "You're going to make me come, Angel."

As much as I loved his taste, I didn't want this to end. I had no idea if they would fuck me once they'd come, and I was pretty sure I'd die if they didn't. I pulled Theo's cock from my mouth and switched again, sliding Xander's cock between my lips once more.

"You beautiful vixen," Xander growled, his voice heavy with desire. "How the hell are you so good at this?"

I let out a playful pop before glancing at him with a mischievous smile.

"I learned from the best," I replied before taking him back into my mouth. A soft chuckle escaped Theo, and Xander responded with another deep growl.

"She's not lying," Theo confirmed, his gaze on mine. A storm of desire raged in his eyes, and I couldn't help but feel overwhelmed by the intense pleasure and joy swelling in my heart.

Xander's cock swelled in my mouth, and he suddenly pulled away from me.

I whimpered again, but he shook his head with determination.

"I'm not coming in your mouth," he stated firmly, his voice dripping with arousal. "I need your pussy."

"Our pussy," Theo reminded him with a hungry look in his eyes.

The truth was, I wanted to be theirs again. I had never tried to leave them.

I had no idea if they understood how much I missed them, how much my body longed for them, without me expressing it in words.

Maybe they'd still be confused afterward.

I wasn't going to stop trying to show them how much I loved them until the day I died.

I looked up at them anxiously, my heart racing as I knelt before them. The soft lamplight cast shadows across their rugged features, and I couldn't take my eyes away from their intense gazes.

"On the bed," Xander's voice was low and commanding, sending a shiver down my spine. With trembling hands, I reached behind me and pulled myself onto the soft mattress, sitting there with bated breath.

The next moment, they joined me on the bed, lying on either side. Their hands roamed my skin feverishly, causing my flesh to tingle with anticipation.

I gazed at them with hungry eyes.

"Kiss," I demanded, unable to contain my desire any longer.

They looked down at me, surprise etched on their faces.

"You want us to kiss?" Theo asked, his eyebrows knitting together in confusion.

"Yes," I replied eagerly. "It's the three of us, not just me with the two of you."

The energy in the room shifted, becoming almost electric as if a dam had broken within us.

Their gazes met mine, and then they turned to each other. Their lips collided in a passionate kiss that ignited sparks of desire within me. Theo and Xander's mouths moved hungrily against each other, rough and demanding. Seeing them lost in passion only intensified the fire inside me.

"God, yes," I moaned, reaching for them and pulling them closer to me.

Our lips met in a passionate embrace, pressing eagerly against one another as we explored and savored every inch of skin.

As we devoured each other hungrily, Theo's voice pierced through the haze of pleasure. "I need to see you come," he stated, his tone commanding and filled with desire. He pushed me back onto the bed, trailing hot kisses down my body until he reached my throbbing core. "You smell so good, Nerine. I've missed your scent."

Goosebumps rose on my skin as Xander took one of my nipples into his mouth and sucked on it possessively.

Theo positioned himself between my legs and brought his face to my slick folds, teasing me with his hot breath before finally giving in and tasting me with his tongue. My legs trembled with each circle and flicked on my sensitive clit, driving me closer to the edge.

At the same time, Xander continued to pleasure my

breast, causing a delicious mixture of pain and pleasure to course through me.

I could feel myself teetering on the edge of ecstasy, my body craving release. "Dammit," I ordered. "Make me come."

"There she is," Theo growled with satisfaction. "I knew you were in there." He blew against my swollen bud, sending shivers down my spine. "The fire in you only adds to how incredible you taste."

At that moment, I wanted nothing more than to give myself to them completely. I reached down and tangled my fingers in Theo's hair, urging him closer to my center.

But he pulled back, his dark eyes ravenous as he gazed up at me. "That doesn't mean you have any say in how this goes," he warned before diving back in with his tongue.

My world was a blur of primal sensations as Xander's mouth silenced my moans while Theo's skilled tongue delved deep into my slick heat. I spread my legs wider, opening myself fully to their touch.

When Theo slipped two fingers inside me, curling them just right to hit all the right spots, I couldn't hold back any longer.

My body exploded in a mind-blowing climax, pleasure radiating from every inch of skin as I arched off the bed and cried out their names. "God, yes, Theo, Xander, yes!"

Through it all, Theo held onto my hips tightly, keeping me grounded as waves of pleasure pulsed through me. They understood precisely what my body needed and exactly how to push me to the brink, sending me spiraling into ecstasy.

They had always known. It was instinctual for them, but

they also spent countless hours learning and perfecting every movement and touch, knowing exactly how I would react and responding accordingly. They understood every tiny adjustment that would drive me wild and never failed to leave me breathless and wanting more.

The wildfire roaring within me erupted repeatedly at their touch. The heat of their fingers against my skin, the warmth of their breath on my neck, and the fire in their eyes all fueled the intense sensation coursing through my body. When Xander pulled his mouth from mine and captured my pebbled nipple once again, biting it gently at first and then harder and harder, Theo moaned and nibbled at my clit, their dual assault sending me crashing over the edge a second time.

My body was writhing uncontrollably under their synchronized moves, every nerve ending on high alert as they continued to pleasure me.

"That's it," Xander murmured, moving to my other nipple and biting down.

I cried out, my fingers sinking into his hair as he pleasured me with expert precision. The feel of his body next to mine was intoxicating, his strong muscles pressing against me as Theo's mouth still sucked and nibbled at my clit through my orgasm, leaving me lost in bliss.

They knew I was coming but kept going, never letting up for a second. Theo's fingers slid in and out of my soaked pussy while he continued sucking, licking, nibbling at my tender flesh. His familiar fingers pushed deep inside me, intuitively finding the right spot to keep me flying.

As I struggled to catch my breath, Theo stated matter-of-factly, "One more."

And with that, he fucked into me hard and fast, quickly sweeping me into another release.

I cried out again, my body pulsing and seizing with the sweetest ecstasy as immense rolling waves of pleasure ricocheted through me. My hips rolled up instinctively to meet his mouth as he gripped my ass tightly, holding me in place as I writhed under his delicious assault.

But just as I thought I couldn't handle any more pleasure, I felt his mouth go away, and his hands gripped my hips, pulling me up.

"I need your pussy now, Angel," Theo muttered urgently.

My eyes fluttered open to see him lining up his thick cock and pushing it inside me.

I was so wet, my pussy pulsing with pleasure, that it was easy for him to bury himself deep within me. His eyes were wild and savage and primal as he peered down at his cock sliding into me.

"God, yes, I missed this pussy," he growled, his voice thick with desire.

I whimpered as the feeling of his cock inside me after all this time left me weak and soft. I opened my thighs as wide as possible, welcoming him in as far as he could go.

"Fuck me, Theo," I cried out desperately. "Please fuck me hard. I need your cock so badly!"

A flush of pleasure washed over me once again, taking all coherent thoughts away. All that mattered at that moment was the intense pleasure coursing through my body and the two men who were providing it.

"You're mine," Theo growled possessively, slamming into me with even more force. The thick length of his cock throbbed hotly against my spasming pussy as he thrust into me repeatedly, harder and harder.

"Theo! Oh, God!" I cried out uncontrollably, my eyes locking with his as he fucked me deeply.

"Fuck, Nerine," he growled through gritted teeth, his voice thick with emotion.

I wrapped my legs around his hips, drawing him in deeper and allowing him to take complete control. "Fuck! You feel so fucking good! Your pussy is so tight and wet!"

"Fuck," Xander groaned beside us, his hot gaze trained on Theo's cock pushing into my pussy. "I love watching the two of you."

The expression on his face was one of sheer hunger and lust, mirroring Theo's own. I wasn't out of danger yet, though, and many questions still exist. But none of that mattered as I lost myself in the intense pleasure of having these two men inside me.

As their stormy eyes held shadows that threatened to push me over the edge again, I felt a twisted mixture of fear and desire. The intensity of their anger only served to excite me further, making me crave their touch even more.

My soaked pussy pulsed around Theo's thick shaft, eager to endure the full extent of his wrath as long as he never stopped fucking me. Xander reached up to Theo, his hand falling on his neck as he pulled him close. Watching with pure lust, I couldn't tear my gaze away as their mouths crashed together in a fiery, passionate kiss. Theo's cock twitched inside me, swelling as he thrust harder into my wetness.

My heart skipped a beat at the sight of them together, their tongues tangling as they moaned in unison. It hit me like a ton of bricks—once, they were mine. But now, they belonged to each other.

The connection between them was palpable, radiating from them like electricity. It seemed somehow stronger now than it ever had been. The way they moved together, almost as if they had a psychic connection and communicated without words, was all so intense and beautiful to witness.

And then they showed up at my door together, like two peas in a pod—a pang of sadness and longing for what we used to have burned deep within my soul.

But watching them kiss as if they were soulmates was heartbreaking and undeniably sexy. When they finally pulled apart, the glance shared between them didn't escape my notice. Would they ever look at me like that again?

Theo's cock swelled inside me as they looked down at me again. Xander reached down between us, his fingers landing on my clit and rubbing in hard circles.

"Oh my God!" I cried out, entirely under their control.

Theo slammed into me with even more force, his hips meeting mine in a frenzied rhythm.

"Fuck her harder, Theo!" Xander demanded, working my clit with an intensity that sent shivers down my spine. "I want to watch her come again."

"Xander," I whimpered, searching his eyes for any sign of the earlier anger he had shown toward me when he had wrapped his fingers around my throat.

But it was still there, simmering beneath the surface. And as much as it frightened me, it also excited me in a twisted way.

I didn't want this to end, but I was also afraid of what would happen after it ended.

If I could have resisted, I would have tried to prolong things and prevent myself from coming. But they knew my body too well; there was no point in resisting. We all wanted —no, needed—this release.

As I melted into the sensations coursing through my body, my head fell back, and I drowned in the sea of pleasure that surged within us. I crashed over the edge as Theo's cock relentlessly fucked into me until I was screaming and writhing beneath them. When Xander removed his fingers from my clit, I whimpered with disappointment.

But then he positioned himself beside me, his cock pressing against my lips.

"Angel," he growled low but demanding.

I eagerly opened my mouth, welcoming him as he slid between my lips. Lifting my gaze to meet his stormy dark eyes, I took him into my mouth and sucked him in greedily. My tongue swirled around the tip of his cock as I relished in the deep, guttural groans that escaped from his lips. I knew exactly how to please him. Theo had taught me how to do it, and Xander's reaction only confirmed that I was doing it right.

It was his favorite trick, and I was determined to show him how much I had learned from Theo.

Theo relentlessly thrust into me, his eyes fixed on the sight of Xander's cock sliding in and out of my mouth. His taste enveloped my senses—salty, musky, alluring, and addictive.

Theo's pace quickened with each passing moment, and I could feel the familiar swell building inside me. I eagerly increased my suction and rhythm, knowing that it was driving him closer to his climax.

When he finally released his load into my mouth, I welcomed the warm, sticky sensation and savored every drop. Knowing that I could bring such pleasure to someone like Xander, who was usually gruff and guarded, was powerful.

As Xander pulled away and looked down at me, I smiled up at him with satisfaction. His initial anger had faded, replaced by amazement and longing.

He gently cupped my cheek, shaking his head in disbelief. I licked my lips teasingly and whispered, "Your beautiful cock always tastes so delicious, Xander."

His expression intensified as he murmured my name under his breath while shaking his head again.

Our attention then shifted back to Theo, whose arousal had not lessened in the slightest. His dark hair flowed around his chiseled face as he panted heavily, his eyes ablaze with deep desire.

With each forceful thrust into my body, he showed no signs of slowing down. His grip on my hips tightened as he continued to piston deeper and harder with each satisfying stroke.

I watched with desire as Theo grabbed Xander's head and pulled him forward for another passionate kiss. Then, taking Xander's hand in his, he guided it toward his balls without needing any words.

This was the dynamic between us. Theo asserted dominance in all things sexual, and Xander and I were all more than willing to give in to his desires.

A surge of arousal flooded through me as I watched the two of them together, their bodies moving in perfect synchrony. My body responded by tightening around Theo's thick cock, urging him on as he drove into me with a relentless rhythm.

As my mind cleared, I suddenly realized we weren't using protection. The logical part of my brain screamed at me to remember the past consequences of birth control failures. But at that moment, with Theo inside me, I couldn't bring myself to stop him. It felt too good, too right, even if it made me the most foolish woman on earth.

He pulled away from Xander's mouth and leaned down over me, his body still thrusting vigorously. With each powerful movement, he let out a deep groan before capturing my lips with his own. Our tongues entwined urgently as our bodies moved in perfect unison.

My breasts heaved against his chest as our skin slid deliciously against each other. I tightened my thighs around his hips, pouring all of the love and passion I felt for him into every movement and kiss.

And when Xander joined in our embrace, our three tongues danced together feverishly until Theo finally released inside me with a guttural growl.

"Fuck!" He exclaimed as his body shuddered against mine, and he slammed into me one final time.

I cried out in pleasure as his hot release filled me and pushed me over the edge as well. Our voices mingled as we lost ourselves in the intense sensations and emotions that consumed us.

As we collapsed onto the bed in a tangled mess, I felt overwhelmed by the presence of both Xander and Theo beside me. Tears streamed down my cheeks uncontrollably as I struggled to hold onto the happiness and love from our past. Instead, a profound sense of vulnerability and apprehension washed over me.

I needed to say something: to explain why I had stayed away for so long and to apologize for my role in creating this complicated situation. However, the fear of ruining the moment and hurting them again weighed heavily on me.

They deserved answers, explanations, and, most importantly, the truth about the changes that would affect their lives. As much as it pained me, I owed it to Xander and Theo to be honest and face the consequences of my actions.

I knew better than to think they still loved me just because they'd had sex with me. I refused to give myself false hope. My past experiences repeatedly taught me that happily ever after was not in my cards. Each time it felt within my reach, something or someone would snatch it away.

But right now, I was determined to live in the moment.

Tomorrow, there was a ninety-nine percent chance Theo and Xander would see me only through eyes filled with hate.

"Even if you don't believe me, know that I never stopped loving you both. With all my heart," I whispered, tears streaming down my cheeks. "I'm so sorry for leaving."

"I love you too," they said in perfect harmony. My lips trembled as their words enveloped me, an intense desire to hold onto them forever swelling within me.

But I couldn't allow myself to hope. I wouldn't let myself hope. And yet, a small part of me couldn't help but wish to believe they could forgive me and that the hatred I expected would never come to be.

Perhaps, just perhaps, we could find a way to weather this storm together. They clung to me tightly as sleep gradually invaded my thoughts, intertwined with the persistent anxiety of the storm threatening our delicate reunion.

ELEVEN

T HEO

"Shhh!" I warned Xander as his foot struck the leg of a chair tucked in a dark corner of Nerine's bedroom.

He shot me the glare he reserved for scaring the hell out of idiots who interfered with our business. However, whenever he applied that tactic to me, I raised an eyebrow, silently telling him to back off.

"Then shine a damn light over here so I don't knock anything over and wake Nerine up," he hissed.

I glanced in her direction, tucked under a thick blanket and lost in deep sleep. The dark smudges under her eyes hinted at her exhaustion but couldn't diminish her beauty. Even the silly disguise she thought could hide her identity failed to mask the fact that she was a stunning woman. I'd love nothing more than to crawl back into bed with her and pry the answers I wanted out of her in more self-serving ways.

Plus, the intense fucking Xander and I had given her added to her need for sleep. It would surprise me if she could walk later tonight.

Hopefully, she wouldn't wake until Xander and I thoroughly swept the apartment. We needed every piece of information possible to understand what had happened with Nerine and how to protect her.

Enemies were closing in, and unless we got ahead of them, there was no way to keep Nerine safe.

"No light. She'll only get in the way if we wake her," I said.

Xander sighed and nodded, accepting the truth of my words.

Xander and I searched through Nerine's apartment for the next half hour. It was small yet cozy, adorned with luxurious blankets, pillows, and furnishings. Beautiful artwork decorated the walls, many created by local Boston artists. Outside the large windows was a clear view of the neon lights dotted the strip.

"I want to hate this place," I whispered to Xander. "But it's nice."

"I wish it were ugly," he agreed. "Even so, I can't understand why Nerine chose this damn city."

"None of this makes any sense."

It seemed so out of character for Nerine to live here, not just in this apartment but in this god-forsaken city that appeared not to have any natural trees or greenery occurring anywhere within its limits.

Nerine was a city girl, but she also loved being surrounded by nature, especially the parks and recreational areas around Boston.

Nerine's influence was why lush greenery surrounded the Angelos estate. Peter Angelos wanted his eldest child to enjoy her home and created a space for her to do so.

This view—Las Vegas itself, a city of glass, neon, smoke, and mirrors, filled with mindless zombies shoving their money into flashing machines—wasn't where I ever expected our Angel to find refuge.

Perhaps that's why she'd chosen it. Nobody would have expected a woman like Nerine to hide in an unwelcoming environment.

Despite the coziness of the small space, the most advanced security systems protected every corner of the apartment. Nerine, or whoever had brought her here, spared no expense on cameras, locks, and alarms to ensure her safety.

This was something I couldn't criticize.

However, this level of security made it painfully clear that she lived in fear.

I glanced at her sleeping figure, and the shield I had built around my heart began to crack. No matter how hard I tried, this woman had a way of infiltrating the smallest cracks and breaking through my defenses.

I wanted answers and intended to find them, but the deep-seated need to keep her safe overshadowed everything.

My anger no longer seemed important. I wouldn't lie to

myself and say it wouldn't resurface in the future, but it wasn't a priority for now.

It was clear she hadn't left because she didn't love us.

Xander continued to inspect shelves and drawers. His face revealed nothing but intense concentration, making me wonder if he felt the same chaotic emotions swirling inside me.

"Look at this," Xander whispered, beckoning me to join him near the fireplace.

As I approached, I noticed Xander was staring into a small nook entirely out of view from the central part of the apartment.

I stopped beside him, following his gaze as he examined several framed photos on one of the shelves. I recognized pictures of Nerine's mother, *Theia* Delia, and her sisters, Christina, Ariana, and Fiona—each candidly showcasing different looks, from hair to eye color.

In another photo, Nerine sat on a large armchair with two young boys in her lap. She held them close, and the smile on her face radiated complete joy and utter love.

I narrowed my eyes, first focusing on Nerine's face and then on the boys. My mind practically skipped as I recognized the resemblance. Not only did they look like Nerine, but they also resembled us.

Xander's voice hissed beside me.

"Are those kids...?" Xander swallowed hard. "Ours?"

"I don't know, I..." My voice trailed off into the darkness.

"Theo," Xander whispered, his face losing color.

The room seemed to spin as I struggled to process what I saw.

They couldn't have been more than two years old. Both bore a striking resemblance to Nerine, but the more I looked at them, the faster my heart raced.

"Theo," Xander repeated as he grabbed my hand, squeezing it in a rare gesture. Outside of the throes of passion, we rarely touched. But lately, he'd been reaching for me more.

The boy on the left stared back at me with Nerine's cobalt blue eyes, but his face was a replica of Xander's. The one on the right took my breath away. It felt like gazing into my soul. Piercing gray eyes emerged from Nerine's likeness, striking my heart like a bolt of lightning.

I squeezed Xander's hand tightly, quickly calculating in my head.

"Did this really happen?" I whispered in disbelief.

"It sure fucking looks like it." His voice sounded as distant and bewildered as I felt.

Maybe this was a dream like I had just stepped into some alternate reality. Perhaps we were still tangled up in bed with Nerine.

But the strength of Xander's hand gripping mine told me we were fully awake.

"But... how? Twins? Is that even possible?" I asked, my eyes fixed on the photo.

"Damn. I'm not sure. I think it is, but it's incredibly rare." Xander shook his head. "We talked about it once when we were teens. She brought it up as if it were a fantasy. I was curious, so I looked into it. It's only happened a few times in history. But... us? No way."

I tore my gaze away from the photo and turned to him, my eyes searching his.

"We might be jumping to conclusions," Xander shook his head and rubbed his neck, reluctant to accept what we had seen.

"Yeah, maybe," I nodded in agreement.

I turned to look into the bedroom where Nerine slept. My eyes fell on the curve of her hips beneath the blanket.

"Did you notice her hips? They're fuller."

Xander nodded. "Her breasts, too. Her nipples are a different color. Darker."

I ran my hand through my hair, continuing to watch her sleep. Her chest rose and fell as she slumbered peacefully, which was ironic. It was as if she hadn't just rocked our entire world without saying a word.

The anger I thought had calmed only moments earlier surged forward, fierce and uncontrolled.

How could she have hidden something like that from us? Xander reached for my hand again, squeezing it more tightly this time.

"I'm furious," he growled beside me.

"That's too tame a word for how I'm feeling," I said. "What the hell are we going to do?"

"To her?" he asked, scoffing and shaking his head. "I have no damn clue. But whatever we decide, it'll have to wait until we get answers. We don't have much time."

"Right." I let go of Xander's hand and turned.

My body shook under the weight of everything pressing down on it. No matter how well I concealed my emotions in response to the challenges life threw my way, in this instance, there was no way to hide anything.

I needed to pull myself together. If we were all going to survive, we had to act fast.

"Let's clean up before we wake her," I said, clenching my jaw. "Then we'll handle our Angel."

Without another word, we worked as quickly as possible, sweeping the apartment to eliminate traces of Nerine or her family.

Xander pulled several duffel bags from the closet and filled them with her photos, books, clothes, and jewelry. After we packed all the items that traced back to Nerine, we wiped down the entire place to remove any of Nerine's fingerprints.

Given our time constraints, we couldn't completely sweep the place but were as thorough as possible. If anyone came after us looking for clear signs of Nerine's presence here, it would at least slow them down.

Throughout our work, my mind was in overdrive. From all indications, Xander was the same; he hadn't said a word, only letting the occasional grunt escape his lips.

The weight of the truth pressed down on us like a boulder crushing our future. Xander and I, two reckless and unprepared men, faced the daunting challenge of becoming fathers. And Nerine, the woman we had always known to be strong and capable, was now living a lie under an assumed identity. Could she embrace the role of a mother figure?

Despite all the chaos and uncertainty, I found comfort in knowing the boys seemed happy and well-cared for. I did not doubt that Nerine's mother, the only person she truly trusted, was taking good care of them. Yet, it still didn't feel right. Children deserved to be with their parents, especially their mothers.

This was nothing but a fucked up situation.

Nerine, the Angelos Angel and the Godmother of the Night for one of the most powerful crime syndicates on the East Coast, was hiding and estranged from her family and loved ones. It wasn't fair.

Fuck this.

No matter what it took, I was determined to help Nerine reclaim her rightful place as leader of her family's empire. She had shed blood, sweat, and tears for it, and I wouldn't stop until she got back what was rightfully hers.

"We have to fix this," I told Xander as he finished packing the last duffel bag by the door.

"I know," he replied grimly. "But first, we need answers."

"Right," I nodded in agreement as we headed to see Nerine in the bedroom.

"She's going to be angry," Xander warned.

"Good," I smirked. "We can all be angry together."

He grunted and shook his head disapprovingly.

"But let's try to keep ourselves in check this time," he reminded me.

"You're the one who's already hard." I chuckled as he revealed four silk scarves from Nerine's closet and began to tie her to the bedpost. "Take it slow. We don't want her waking up too soon."

My arousal was growing, and I discreetly adjusted my swelling shaft.

"I've got it handled," Xander assured me with a smirk.

"I can't help but enjoy seeing her like this," I admitted, torn between my anger and desire for her in this vulnerable state.

"I get it." He nodded in understanding.

With skillful movements, he bound Nerine's limbs with the scarves to the bed. As he walked around to face me, I couldn't help but pull him close and kiss him passionately. His hand found its way to my cock, stroking it eagerly.

"Do you want me to handle this before we wake her?" he offered, pulling away from our kiss. "It might help ease your temper."

I firmly shook my head. "No, a little edging won't hurt anyone."

I pulled him into another kiss, feeling my cock swell even more in his hand. When he finally pulled away, he met my gaze steadily.

"We have kids," he said flatly.

"We can't be certain of that," I countered, attempting to hold on to a sense of denial.

But Xander shot me a knowing glance. "Yeah, we do."

"Shit," I muttered under my breath, unable to mask the anxiety churning within me at the idea of becoming a father. "This is happening."

"Yeah," Xander whispered in awe. "A picture speaks a

thousand words, right?" "We're fathers," I said, nodding as I tried to grasp the magnitude of it all.

"Fuck me," Xander breathed out. "This is going to change everything."

"I believe it already has," I replied, pulling him into a tight hug as we found solace in each other's embrace. This was our new reality now, whether we liked it or not.

TWELVE

Nerine

A heavy, weighted groan escaped my lips as I slowly emerged from the fog of sleep. Blinking against the dim amber light that filled the room from the small lamp on the nightstand, I urged myself to stay in bed, reluctant to face another day of loneliness and heartache.

But even with my eyes shut, I couldn't shake the awareness that it was all just a dream, a brief glimpse of happiness before the harsh reality of my life came crashing down on me.

In my dream, the men I loved touched me with a tenderness and desire I had longed for. There was no hate or resentment in their eyes; only a shared desperation and love consumed us. It was blissful and intoxicating—a feeling I never wanted to end.

But now, as I lay in bed alone once again, I was forced to confront the truth: they were not here with me, and I was still alone.

I let out a defeated sigh. "Just a dream, Nerine," I whispered to myself. "They didn't find you. You're still alone. Accept it."

"Oh, but we have," a familiar voice growled from above, causing me to jump and struggle against the restraints binding my wrists and legs.

"Theo!" I gasped as his fingers tightened around my throat. Beside him stood Xander, his expression serious and resolute.

"And we fucked you," he added bluntly. "And we plan to do it again."

A shiver ran down my spine as Theo leaned in closer. "But first, we want answers."

Panic surged through me as I attempted to sit up, only to find myself bound by ties around my wrists and legs. Confusion mingled with fear as my two lovers loomed over me with intense gazes that revealed no trace of warmth or love.

"What are you doing?" I demanded frantically.

"Making sure we get what we want," Xander replied, his voice laced with determination.

None of this made any sense. Just last night, I had felt the love and passion radiating from their eyes. But now, I only saw cold calculation and a fierce resolve to get what they wanted from me.

"So, this is your plan?" I asked, straining against my restraints. "I never fought you before."

"We're not talking about sex," Theo said. "You've never been one to deny our desires, Nerine?"

Ignoring his thinly veiled insult, I shook my head in disbelief.

"Please let me go," I pleaded, feeling irritated.

"Not until we get the truth," Xander stated firmly, his expression sharp and unforgiving.

As panic threatened to consume me, I pleaded once more for them to let me go.

"Talk," Theo demanded, his arms crossed over his chest. He and Xander stood side by side like twin interrogators, their matching expressions of fury and frustration only heightening my fear.

"What exactly do you want to know?" I asked, tugging at the ties binding my wrists in a futile effort to escape.

"Tell us about the night you left," Xander demanded through gritted teeth.

"What's the point?" I replied. "It was years ago. I can barely even remember it anymore."

But as soon as the words left my mouth, I could taste the lie on my lips. They knew it, too. My memory was sharp and detailed, and there was no way I could forget that night or the reasons I had left. My heart sank as I realized I could no longer escape the truth. Tied up and at their mercy, I would have to face the consequences of my actions from that fateful night years ago.

"Fuck," I cursed under my breath, a knot tightening in

my stomach. "I don't know what happened. I woke up in a strange house, alone in California. My mother and sisters were nowhere to be found. All I knew was that I couldn't endure another situation like the one with Andraius."

I peered up at them, determination radiating from me as I recalled how I felt when I regained consciousness in that bedroom. I had never been more scared in my life.

The memories flooded back, and a wave of fear and panic washed over me again. Even after two years, the terror still lingered within me, a constant reminder of what had occurred.

"I wasn't ever going to let someone rape me again. And if anyone tried, I would kill them just as I'd killed Andraius. Or I would die trying."

My words hung heavy in the air between us.

I had no idea what their intention was. I couldn't read their hard expressions. They'd fucked me already. Maybe now it was time to kill me. They certainly looked angry enough to do so.

But they'd told me they loved me before I drifted off. Had I dreamed that? Had all our love turned to hate because I blew up our lives? Had I damaged our relationship beyond repair?

I wouldn't trust me again if I were in their shoes.

I had no clue what they wanted, and I knew nothing about what they had endured over the past few years. All I knew was that I'd hurt them in a way that seemed beyond anything we could come back from.

Perhaps they still planned to kill me. They certainly

looked angry enough to do so. Whatever the outcome, I'd give them the truth; it was the least I owed them.

"When did you find out Solon had taken you?" Theo's voice was sharp and accusatory.

I raised an eyebrow, impressed by their deduction. It wasn't exactly a secret if anyone was paying attention.

"I didn't take long to figure it out," I admitted. "Every time I tried to escape, a member of the Solon security team caught me. But they never hurt me, which made me suspect that Solon was behind it. Later, I learned that Devani had ordered them not to harm me, or she would have killed them herself."

Silence enveloped us as they processed my words. I could see the storm brewing in their eyes as they pieced together the mystery of my disappearance.

"And when did you find out you were pregnant, Nerine?" Xander's tone was filled with anger and hurt.

Theo's piercing gray eyes drilled into mine, his expression as sharp and deadly as ever. I couldn't help but gasp in surprise; I should have anticipated this question."

My gaze flicked to the open door, noticing that most of my belongings were missing. It made it clear they knew the hidden nook where I stored my memories.

I redirected my attention to them. Their frosty expressions were disconcerting, prompting me to want to turn my gaze away. Shame and regret surged within me like a wildfire of emotion, igniting and intensifying in my heart.

Every moment away from them weighed heavily on my heart, especially when I thought about all the milestones I had missed with our twin boys. It wasn't the same without Xander and Theo by my side, and it broke my heart.

Living without them felt like having a massive hole inside me that no one else could fill. Now, confronted with their anger and disappointment, I realized the extent of the pain I had caused them by leaving.

There was no justification for my actions, and I couldn't comfort their suffering. All I could do was apologize and hope for their forgiveness.

"Two weeks after I arrived at that house, Devani came to see me. She told me I was pregnant and said I couldn't go back until after I gave birth and things were safe. Of course, I didn't believe her, but she showed me lab results from when I was in Boston. I'm not sure how she managed to get the tests done, but Devani has her ways, and the results confirmed that I was pregnant."

Tears streamed down my face like hot, heavy raindrops, and I desperately longed to wipe them away. But my hands were bound tightly, rendering me helpless as I stared into their faces, hoping they could see the regret in my eyes through the blur of tears.

"Do you finally understand?" I pleaded. "I didn't go with them willingly. I was pregnant, and that's why they took me. Solon took my mother and my sisters, too."

"I don't believe a word of it," Theo hissed.

"What aren't you telling us?" Xander demanded, his voice tense with suspicion.

I looked up at them, shaking my head in frustration. "I

am telling the truth," I insisted, praying they couldn't see through my lie.

"We know when you're lying or leaving things out," Theo said coldly, glaring at me.

"What does it matter? You're going to kill me anyway," I replied bitterly.

"Are you serious right now, Nerine?" Xander erupted as his calm facade shattered. "What aren't you telling us?"

This wasn't the Xander I knew.

He always kept his cool with me, even during moments of anger. It was Theo who frequently lost his temper with me. But now, it seemed like I had broken them both.

"What am I supposed to believe? I deserve whatever you do to me. I accept it." I managed to keep my voice steady, even though the burning in the back of my throat felt like acid, scalding, and utterly painful.

"If we had wanted you dead, we would have done it long ago," Theo stated, his tone icy. "I've already told you this. You will live a long life, Nerine. I'm going to make sure of it."

"But you intend to make me pay for hurting you."

Theo and Xander exchanged glances before Theo focused back on me and said, "We will decide your penance later. Now, speak. We want the rest of it."

I couldn't tell them everything now that they knew about Hayes and Charis. "I'm not saying another word until you let me go."

"We're in charge here, Angel," Theo reminded me.

Xander raised an eyebrow. "You're not in a position to make demands."

I rolled my eyes, annoyed that they were right. There was no point in arguing with them since they were as stubborn as mules. That was how they had always been. Why should I have expected anything different?

"I'll share what I can," I reluctantly agreed, closing my eyes and taking a deep breath before starting my story. "Devani visited me one day. I had no idea why she wanted to meet, but I trusted her."

A buzzing sound interrupted our conversation, prompting them to grab their phones simultaneously. They read their messages with increasing alarm before glancing at each other in panic.

"Shit," Xander muttered under his breath.

I asked anxiously, "What's wrong?"

Theo quickly pulled a gun from his waistband, his face filled with fear and urgency. "We need to go now."

"Right now," Xander added, his voice tense with urgency.

"What the hell is happening?" I demanded, tugging at my restraints once more. "Untie me immediately!"

But they ignored me, their gazes filled with worry and determination as they swiftly approached the door.

Theo firmly said, "Our conversation isn't over."

"Hell no, it's not," Xander growled before both of them walked out of the room, leaving me still tied up and seething with uncontrollable anger coursing through my veins.

"Come back here!" I shouted, aware they would ignore me no matter how loudly I yelled.

Thirteen

Nerine

Xander's voice was urgent as he spoke to Theo. "We need to move quickly," he said, his eyes fixed on the phone in his hand. The two hurried through my apartment, their eyes scanning every corner.

Frustration and anger surged within me. "This is completely absurd!" I yelled, struggling against the restraints that confined me. "You have no right to keep me here!"

They didn't even flinch at my outburst. "Do you even remember who I am?" I yelled, straining against the ties once again.

"As if we could ever forget," Xander muttered before dropping to his knees and peering under the bed.

"I hate you," I seethed.

But Theo lifted his head and met my gaze. "No, you love us," he said with a smirk. "You're angry because Xander's a pro at tying knots."

I clenched my jaw, attempting to push away the memories of the pleasure their ropes had brought me. There was no escape once they had bound me in place.

"You really believed me when I said I loved you?" I spat out, feeling another surge of anger rising within me.

Theo leaned in close, almost touching our lips. "Your love for us, especially our cocks, has never been the issue," he whispered. "You proved it by how quickly we were able to slide our dicks inside you after we walked through that door."

"If I could move, I'd punch you both in the face," I growled, straining against my bonds again. "You egotistical bastards! You showed up at my door."

My arms strained against the silk restraints as I imagined what to do to them once free. "Let me go! I was perfectly fine without you two. If you don't let me go, I swear I'll beat you until your eyes pop out of your head and then grind them into a bloody pulp."

"You might have stirred the beast," Xander said, a touch of amusement in his voice.

"I am not a fucking beast," I snapped back at him. "I'm a queen who will rip that dick, the one you say I like so much, off your body. Mark my words. I will turn your lives into living hells once I'm free. Don't say I didn't warn you."

"You can take the girl out of Boston," Xander joked.

"But you can't take the Boston out of the girl," Theo

added. "And when have you done anything other than make our lives hell in the past two years?"

"Do you think I wanted this life?" I asked, my voice shaking with exhaustion and defeat.

"Do you think we wanted this life?" Theo shot back, his voice heavy with pain. "We had no choice but to clear this area and erase any trace of your existence. We can argue later."

My rage simmered and then fizzled as exhaustion and utter despair overwhelmed me. I slumped against the bed, feeling defeated.

"Empty my closet," I said, too exhausted to argue any longer. "And don't forget to clean out my nightstand."

Theo briefly vanished into my closet and returned with two bulging duffel bags, tightly zipped shut.

"We've handled everything while you were asleep," he said matter-of-factly.

"Of course you did," I sighed, shaking my head in resignation.

He tossed a heap of clothes onto the bed beside me, and I looked at them skeptically.

"You need to get dressed quickly," he said, looking away from me.

I raised an eyebrow, trying not to point out the obvious. "In that?" I asked incredulously. "Do you really think I won't stick out like a sore thumb dressed as a broke college student in one of the most luxurious hotels in the city?"

"We're professionals," Theo said, now standing over me. "Don't forget that this is our livelihood. Did you forget everything while escaping your old life?"

"Whatever," I muttered, frowning and choosing not to engage with him any further.

I took deep breaths, attempting to calm the panic that had been coursing through me since I woke up to find them looming over me.

"And don't even think about trying to fight us," Theo warned as he sat beside me on the bed.

I remained silent, my body tense as Theo slowly loosened the scarves around my ankles. I could feel his intense gaze on me, ready to pounce if I made any move. But why would I? Being with him and Xander was all I wanted.

Now that I knew this wasn't merely a figment of my imagination, I couldn't bear the thought of spending another moment without them. My future may not be filled with roses and sunshine, but I trusted Theo's promise that he wouldn't kill me.

Xander and Theo both wanted me by their side. A shiver ran down my spine as Theo's fingers glided over the skin of my wrist while he untied my hands. His body heat radiated from him as he leaned over me, and I fought the urge to wrap my arms around his neck and pull him closer.

I yearned to feel his bare skin against mine once more.

Our eyes met, and I caught sight of the same storm brewing in his cloudy gray irises. It was always a battle between us when we were this close, an unspoken contest to see who would give in first and break the tension with a fiery kiss. His gaze flickered to my lips, confirming that our thoughts aligned along the same path.

"Enough!" Xander's voice sliced through our trance. "Get

up. We need to hurry. There's no time for you two to begin something you can't finish."

"He's right," Theo growled. "Stand up."

We both sprang into action, the scarves tumbling onto the bed as I hurried to my feet. Quickly, I threw on my baggy clothes: black cotton panties, oversized jeans, and a massive sweatshirt from UNLV. I barely had time to slip into white sneakers and tuck my hair under a baseball cap before they flanked me, grabbing my arms and rushing me out of the hotel room.

"Did you get all my photos?" I asked.

"Packed in here," Xander replied, holding up the duffel bag.

One hung over his shoulder while Theo carried two more. I prayed they had grabbed everything because I would never return to that apartment again.

"Put these on." Theo handed me a pair of oversized sunglasses.

I frowned, stuffing the frames into my pocket. "I'll attract attention wearing that with this outfit."

"Fine. Just keep your head down." He tugged at the rim of my hat so I could barely see.

"Like I wasn't aware of this."

Tension hung thick as we descended to the tower's ground floor. They shared subtle nods and gestures, silently signaling any potential threats nearby. We wove through the usual crowd at the resort and past the high roller section of the casino, heading toward the hotel lobby.

Thankfully, it was peak check-in time, providing plenty

of cover from clueless tourists and onlookers flooding the area.

A wave of sadness washed over me briefly as I realized I wouldn't see Penny or the friends I had made here again. But just as quickly, those emotions shifted to elation, knowing I wouldn't have to deal with all the headaches Las Vegas brought its locals.

I was done with this place. I had never truly enjoyed it in the first place.

My companions stayed as serious as ever, their guard still high as they meticulously scanned for any hidden dangers lurking in the shadows.

"Is that Tobias Stratos's consigliere?" I whispered.

Andraius and all the nightmares that came with him were born into the Stratos family. To say I blamed them for my countless scars, both physical and emotional, is an understatement. After Andraius's death, Tobias, his nephew, expected me to jump at his command and marry him with underhanded persuasion.

One Stratos was more than enough for a million lifetimes, and I clarified my position on Tobias's tactics. The Stratoses wanted revenge for the shame I had brought upon them, and their hatred for me knew no bounds.

"Good eye, Angel," Theo whispered as we hurriedly turned away from them. We maneuvered through the maze-like hallways of the bustling casino, passing rows of flashing slot machines and crowded roulette tables until we arrived at the section leading to the parking garage at the back of the property.

"Wait, I recognize that guy. The one in the corner by the bar," I said. "That's Dante Galani's nephew. I remember seeing him at a party."

"That's fucking Rico," Xander muttered as he pulled me to the side, concealing us from view. "Well, that accounts for two families who hate our guts. Why not make it three, and we'll have a complete set? Galani needs to deal with this shit with his son, not us."

The former head of the Galani family hated me on a visceral level. Aside from the fact that I had assisted his son Anthony in overthrowing him and that he viewed me as a significant threat to his power, I was a woman in a world where I didn't belong.

Oh, and there was this little issue of me stabbing him.

According to rumors, Dante named his nephew Marco as his heir. However, no one understood what he would inherit since Anthony held the position of Godfather of the Night for the Galani Family and aligned with our Angelos Syndicate.

Dante's hatred for me burned fiercely after an incident two years ago when I refused to back down from his insults and ended up stabbing him.

He'd learned the meaning of the phrase, *fuck around and find out.*

"Let's go," Xander commanded.

As we stepped outside through the revolving doors, the darkness of the parking lot surrounded us, hiding any potential danger lurking in the shadows. The tension between us remained tangible, our senses heightened and on alert.

"Where's the car?" I asked, my voice revealing my anxiety.

Xander responded with a grunt and a tug on my forearm.

We passed a long line of vehicles before turning a corner and approaching a man in a sleek black suit, quietly smoking as he scrolled through his phone. My heart skipped a beat; it was one of Aetos's men.

"Aetos, too?" The question barely left my lips before Theo covered my mouth with his hand.

He shook his head. "And we have a set."

"That doesn't comfort me."

I might be dead right now if it weren't for Xander and Theo. Those three families were so close to finding me, all because of clues in a damn book.

There was no denying that I was now with Theo and Xander after we walked through the casino and hotel together. They attracted attention wherever they went, whether they meant to or not. And with my outrageous outfit, it was impossible for anyone not to notice the tall, quirky girl strolling beside two handsome men.

"Follow me, Angel," Theo whispered, taking my hand and pulling me away as the man by the car turned his back. We rushed past the first row of vehicles, navigating through the parking garage to avoid detection before reaching Xander's car at the end of the lot.

My companions unceremoniously shoved me into the backseat among the duffel bags, making me scowl as they closed the door in my face. Theo took the passenger seat while Xander slid behind the wheel and safely drove us away.

I couldn't shake the feeling of unease as we drove away.

With so many scouts from rival families lurking around, it seemed almost sure that one of them would spot us. But to my relief, we arrived at a private hangar at McCarran Airport just a few minutes later.

"We have our own private plane now?" I asked incredulously.

"We've had some profitable ventures while you were away, Angel," Theo smirked.

As we settled into the plush seats of the luxurious plane, I felt tension rising in my chest. My two companions sat across from me, their eyes fixed on mine as if daring me to speak. Taking a deep breath, I finally mustered the courage to ask the question that had been burning in my mind.

"Can you please tell me where we're going now?" I asked, my voice trembling slightly.

Xander and Theo exchanged glances before responding, their stern expressions sending a chill down my spine.

"I guess you'll have to figure that out alone," Xander replied cryptically.

Confused and increasingly uneasy, I turned my full attention to them.

Leaning forward, they seemed to loom over me with their combined presence.

"Now you decide," Theo's voice was low and menacing. "Where have you hidden our sons, Angel?"

FOURTEEN

X ANDER

My heart raced in my chest as I perched on the edge of my seat, awaiting her answer. The photo of the two boys—our sons—had dominated my thoughts since I saw it. It shocked my system, a reality I had never thought possible.

However, amidst these swirling emotions, I had overlooked two potential threats that Nerine had perceptively noticed at the hotel. Anger bubbled up at my carelessness, fueled by the fear and anxiety that now seemed like a persistent presence in my life.

Was this to be my future? A life filled with constant danger and the unrelenting need to protect my family at all costs? The thought sent shivers down my spine, like a nightmare worse than any I had experienced in the past two years. And now, with answers to my questions finally within reach, I struggled to accept the possibility that everything I knew could change in an instant.

A part of me resisted, holding on to the past and denying the reality of my newfound fatherhood. Yet, another part of me overflowed with immense love for these two beings I had never encountered—my sons.

I turned to Nerine, taking in the sight of her as she squirmed in the seat before us. Defiance flickered in her sapphire eyes, but beneath that, I noticed her trembling fingers and quivering bottom lip. She was afraid, despite her efforts to maintain stoicism. If I touched her thigh, it would shake under my hand.

But she needed to stay composed. We all did. Lowering our guard would be deadly in this moment of uncertainty and danger.

So we pressed on, pursuing the truth and nothing but the truth. Surviving in this world required that we confront and fully expose our fears, no matter how bloody or painful they may be. Our ultimate aim was to protect those boys at all costs.

"Nerine," I said, my voice low and urgent. "We need your answer. Reveal everything. If those boys are truly ours, they will find them soon. And as we both know, they hold the key to striking at the Angelos family—a weapon our enemies would not hesitate to use against us."

"Why do you think I've kept them hidden?" she snapped, her eyes blazing with anger. "And what the hell do you mean by 'if the boys are truly ours'? Of course, they're yours."

"Nerine," Theo said her name, soothing her in a way that contrasted with his usual tendency to ignite her anger. "We know they're ours."

It seemed as if I was the actor in that role as of late.

She took a deep breath, her chest rising and falling with the weight of her words. The tension in the room was palpable as Theo raised an eyebrow, his expression skeptical. Nerine's voice quavered with anger and frustration as she spoke.

"I can assure you, they are under constant surveillance and protection," she said, her tone tight and controlled.

Theo scoffed, his jaw tightening.

"Like you were?" he asked, his sarcasm dripping with venom. "Solon didn't do a great job of that. They couldn't even stop that damn book from being published, could they? It led us here. What makes you think..."

Before he could finish his sentence, Nerine exploded in anger. "Look, I get it, okay?" she shouted, her fists clenched at her sides. "That book is a disaster."

I glanced at her, surprised by the intensity of her outburst. I had assumed she had written the scandalous book that caused all this chaos, but apparently, I was mistaken. She looked just as upset about it as we were. I caught Theo's gaze and knew he was thinking the same thing.

"I can't help but wonder what your sisters and mother thought of the book," Theo said slyly, raising an eyebrow in contemplation. "Considering some parts were rather...scandalous. And that's saying a lot coming from a fucking sexual deviant like me."

Anger ignited in Nerine's eyes at his taunt.

"Yeah, I imagine they're all embarrassed," I agreed with a sigh. "Especially Fiona, at her age."

"Fiona!" Nerine practically growled her name with pure bitterness.

I waited a moment before speaking again, gently leaning toward Nerine.

"What's up with Fiona?" I asked, my curiosity getting the best of me.

"Fiona's the one who wrote the damn book!" Nerine cried out, her voice filled with rage and frustration. "I want to strangle her!"

My jaw dropped. "You're kidding..."

Theo let out a long sigh, running a hand through his hair.

"Fuck," he muttered under his breath.

Nerine glared at us, shaking her head.

"Does this look like the face of someone who's joking?" she asked, pointing at herself.

"Fiona genuinely believed that no one but herself would read it. How the heck it went viral is beyond me."

Even though the situation was serious, Theo and I couldn't help but laugh at Nerine's words. She looked at us as if we had completely lost our minds.

"What's so funny?" she asked incredulously.

"Can you believe this?" I said to Theo, still laughing

uncontrollably. "She thought nobody would read it? That was some spicy stuff." I shook my head, chuckling.

"Do you remember that double penetration scene?" I asked, trying to catch my breath between fits of laughter.

"Oh my god, I can't believe Fiona wrote that!"

Once again, we broke into hysterical laughter, unable to control our amusement at the absurdity of it all.

"It's not funny," Nerine huffed, crossing her arms over her chest and scrunching her face into a pout. "She blew up our lives with this damn book! Why is that hilarious?"

Theo chuckled, and I couldn't help but join in. "Can you imagine Fiona's expression when she saw it climbing the charts?"

"Oh yeah," I added with a nod. "She must have been freaking out."

"Stupid kid," Theo laughed.

"You know," I said, wiping tears from my eyes, "It's a good thing."

Nerine looked at me as if I had lost my mind.

"How could you possibly think that?" her tone was one of frustration.

I turned to face her, my expression serious.

"Don't you see?" I asked. "She did us a favor. It brought us to you. We wouldn't even know we had sons if she hadn't written that book, Angel," I added. "You were keeping them from us. Or did you conveniently forget that?"

Her shoulders slumped, and guilt and shame washed over her face. For a brief moment, I almost felt sorry for her. But

then I recalled the choices she had made and the consequences of those choices we were now facing.

"Now," I growled, leaning in closer and gripping her chin
firmly, forcing her to meet my gaze. "Don't make me ask
again," I warned. "Where the hell have you hidden our sons?"

But instead of stalling or fighting back as I had expected,
Nerine sighed heavily and spoke the only word that
mattered: "Phoenix."

Fifteen

N ERINE

The steady hum of the plane engines resonated in my ears, a familiar sound that typically calmed me. But today was anything but ordinary. My body was tense, my mind a whirlwind of conflicting emotions. The usual anxiety and worry were present, but now excitement and uncertainty were intertwined. After so long, seeing my boys again filled me with both joy and apprehension for what lay ahead.

At least I no longer had to conceal the truth about Charis and Hayes. Though it was revealed unexpectedly, Theo and Xander were now aware of them. Their eyes still reflected anger and pain, and I couldn't blame them. I had taken something from them that I could never give back: memories, milestones, and experiences.

We could attempt to move on, but it felt like an unforgivable betrayal.

I sighed, gazing out the window at the passing landscape. Something captured my attention, a sense that something was off. Suddenly, it struck me.

"The plane is heading the wrong way," I blurted, feeling confused. "This isn't the route to Phoenix. What's going on?"

Both Theo and Xander turned to me in surprise. Theo raised an impressed eyebrow before questioning me.

"How do you know we're off course just by looking at clouds and mountains, Angel?"

"I picked up some new skills during my absence," I replied cryptically.

"Is that so?" Xander chimed in with a mischievous grin on his face. "Tell us more."

I narrowed my eyes at his teasing tone, resisting the urge to make a snarky comeback. Something in his dark gaze stirred a familiar tingle inside me. His playful demeanor evoked memories of the seductive enforcer who could ignite every part of me with just a look or a touch.

"Do you have an explanation for us, Angel?" Theo's voice carried a hint of authority, sending a shiver down my spine.

No matter how angry I might be with them, they always knew how to disarm me with just a few words. It was both infuriating and irresistible.

"I had a lot of time to myself," I began, trying to maintain my composure. "And as you both know, I get bored easily."

Xander chuckled. "You don't say. I remember that about you."

Ignoring his comment, I continued. "I had a clear view of the airport from my apartment. I spent hours watching the flight patterns and memorizing the direction each plane took off and at what time. We're definitely not on the right path to Arizona."

"You never fail to amaze me, Nerine," Theo said admiringly. "I'm truly impressed."

"You'll wish you hadn't said that," Xander chimed in.

"Most likely," Theo replied with a smirk. "But we'll find a way to make her pay for it."

My breath caught in my throat as the tension between us shifted from playful banter to something more serious. These men were dangerous in every sense of the word.

How could they expect me to have a normal conversation with them when they kept swinging between teasing and threatening?

"Where... Where are we going?"

Theo's eyes met mine with a calm intensity as he sat beside me. "We're headed to Los Angeles first, Angel," he explained. "Then, we'll switch jets and fly to Arizona. Just to be safe."

While their presence comforted me, it also unsettled me. They exuded power and control, making it difficult for me to think clearly.

"I suppose that's why you're the security expert," I said, trying to lighten the mood. "You think of everything." I gazed out the window as I attempted to rapidly process everything that had happened over the last twenty-four hours. I never expected Theo and Xander to find me. I didn't think I could hold my boys so soon or introduce them to their fathers.

"Thank you," I finally managed to say, breaking the tense silence. Yet my words felt weak and inadequate against the overwhelming emotions swirling inside me.

"Our job is to protect you, Angel," Xander said from across the aisle. His deep voice sent shivers down my spine.

I knew they would do whatever it took to keep me safe and out of harm's way.

"Thank you," I said softly, taking a deep breath to calm my racing heart and clear my mind.

As much as I wanted to escape their intense presence and think clearly, there was no avoiding them on this private jet. Their auras suffocated me, making it impossible to focus on anything else.

"I'm going to lie down," I declared, rising from my seat. "Is there a cabin or somewhere quiet where I can rest?"

But before I could take another step, Theo barked at me, startling me into freezing in place.

"Sit back down!" he commanded firmly.

"But I'm exhausted," I protested weakly.

"You slept like a baby earlier," Xander reminded me with a smirk.

I felt myself blush even harder at the memory of just how well I had slept, thanks to them practically fucking me unconscious. The memory of their hands gliding over every inch of my body, their mouths eagerly exploring mine, their hard cocks thrusting inside me. It all flooded my mind, sending shivers down my spine and making my heart race.

Xander's gaze locked onto mine, and I knew he remembered it. His eyes deepened with desire, and his breathing grew more ragged as he absorbed the sight of my hardened nipples straining against the fabric of my sweatshirt.

With a heavy sigh, I sat down, aware they wouldn't let me leave until I provided more information.

"Fine," I conceded reluctantly, crossing my arms defensively over my chest.

"Now, tell us everything you left out of your 'little confession' earlier, Angel," Theo demanded sternly. "And while you're at it, explain why you thought it was a good idea to stay away from home for so long without even a single phone call."

Xander crossed his arms over his broad chest, nodding firmly. "Yeah, I want to know that too."

"And how could you possibly think it was wise to give birth without us?" Theo continued. "What if something had gone wrong?"

"You're not doctors. What could you have done?" I snapped defensively.

"Careful, Angel," Theo warned in a low voice, brimming with anger.

My gaze flickered between them, searching their eyes for any trace of the love we once shared. Tears filled my eyes as I struggled to find it, spilling down my cheeks.

"You said you still loved me. Was I mistaken?" I asked through sobs.

They exchanged a look before turning back to me with sorrowful eyes.

"You betrayed us, Angel," Theo's voice was heavy with hurt.

"I accept it. I'm the villain. I understand," I said bitterly, feeling the familiar ache of longing for what we once had returned with full force. "I can't blame you."

"You need to tell us everything, Nerine," Xander said, his tone serious and commanding. Ignoring my tears and evident pain, they demanded answers. Steeling myself, I took a deep breath and wiped away the tears from my cheeks before speaking again.

"I thought I was protecting you," I said, desperately wanting them to grasp this one fact above all else. If they could see things from my perspective, maybe they would find it in their hearts to forgive me. Without that, I feared for what our future might hold.

"From what?" Theo asked, his voice softening slightly. Xander remained silent at his side, still brooding and angry but listening intently.

"The Aetos family debt," I replied with a heavy sigh. "It wouldn't exist if it weren't for your father, Theo."

The burden of this secret had been crushing me for so long, and finally, sharing it with them felt like a slight relief.

Theo's father, Mik Nephus, was one of Papa's top enforcers. The Angelos and Aetos families were in territory battles when we were younger. Thinking to negotiate a truce, Papa had given direct orders to all enforcers and soldiers not to retaliate.

But Theios Mik, wanting to induct his older sons into our way of life, decided to attack Castro Aetos's private car with a bomb. Except, it wasn't the Godfather who died, but an innocent little boy on his way to school in his daddy's car.

Theo peered at me, his eyes narrowing and waiting for me to continue.

"When Theios Mik mistakenly killed Castro Aetos's youngest son, he created a life debt for the youngest Nephus, Onassis, and Angelos families. Any deaths beyond those were unacceptable. He wanted the youngest child for his lost youngest child."

I shook my head, my mind replaying every detail I had learned since leaving.

"Gusto, Aetos's oldest son, has now taken over as the new head of the family, as you both know."

"He's a total prick," Xander growled, his disdain for Gusto evident.

"I agree. Unfortunately, he's also incredibly stubborn. He refuses to let this go and is on an unrelenting mission to avenge his brother's death."

I watched Theo closely, searching for any signs of how he was processing my words. But he remained stoic and unmoving.

"Even after the tragic loss of your mother, Theo, Gusto continues to act. He doesn't count *Theia* Viola's death as payment. The Nephus debt is still open."

"Like I said, he's a total prick," Xander chimed in again.

"It will remain that way as long as you're alive, Theo," I added gravely.

"Damn," he muttered under his breath, his anger becoming more visible with each passing moment. His stormy gaze met mine intensely, and my heart ached at the pain and torment I saw within them. "We're all in danger because of me. Is that what you're saying? Just because my heart keeps beating in my chest?"

"No, I —"

"This never-ending feud has gone on for far too long!" he roared, his frustration and anguish reverberating through the cabin. "And now I can't even have my sons in my life because of this bullshit?"

His words echoed off the walls, filling the room with a sense of despair and hopelessness. It tore me apart to see him blame himself for everything.

"It's not your fault," I insisted, my voice full of conviction. "You were born into this mess, just like the rest of us! We had no control over our bloodline, Theo."

Even though I felt pain and anguish, hearing him claim both boys as his own gave me a sense of warmth and comfort. To me, they were all part of one family now. I wasn't sure how much convincing it would take for them to see it that way, but I hoped they were already beginning to understand.

"It is ridiculous; I know," I continued. "But it's not your fault. None of us asked for this, yet we are facing it together."

"She's right, Theo," Xander added, surprising me with his rare display of affection.

He reached out and took Theo's hand, gently squeezing it before letting go. I couldn't help but smile at the sight. Maybe Xander had softened in my absence. It warmed my heart to think that perhaps they had found solace and comfort in each other's embrace while I was away.

"No, we didn't ask for any of this," Theo said, his head shaking in frustration.

A lock of dark hair fell over his eye, and I had to resist the urge to brush it away. However, he was clearly upset and on the brink of a complete breakdown. Just one touch could set him off.

"But neither did our sons, did they? We can't let this go on any longer. We can't let this feud taint their lives."

My heart skipped a beat at his words. I had always known that if they could accept the boys as their own, they would do anything to protect them, just as I had. Perhaps this fierce protectiveness toward the boys would help them understand why I made my choices.

"There's more," I said, gazing at Xander. "Unfortunately, you're also a target in this vendetta."

I hated having to continue, knowing that each word felt like a knife to their hearts. But they needed to understand the full extent of what we were facing. And if we stood together as a united front, perhaps we could finally break free from the endless cycle of violence and revenge.

Xander's brows lifted as he asked, "Me?"

I couldn't avoid the truth any longer. With a soft smile, I replied, "I'm afraid so. Your father tried to clean up *Theios* Mik's mess. *Theios* Alex shouldn't have ever gotten involved."

"What are you talking about?" Xander's voice was thick with worry.

Taking a deep breath, I prepared myself for what I had to say next. "I'm talking about Zoe's death."

Silence hung in the air as Xander absorbed my words. Finally, he leaned forward on his knees and asked, "What does my little sister have to do with this?"

"We were all told she died from a head injury when she fell off her bike, right?" I said gently.

"Yes, that's true," Xander confirmed.

"I'm so sorry, Xander. It's not true. Gusto ordered Zoe's death as a hit to hurt your family."

His eyes widened in shock and confusion as he looked at me carefully. "Nerine, are you trying to tell me that they ... they killed a six-year-old girl? In cold blood?"

I nodded sadly. "Yes, Xan. I am so sorry." Tears stung my eyes as I watched him struggle with that revelation. I could only imagine how difficult it was for him to make sense of such an unimaginable act.

Turning to Theo, he searched for answers in his expression before returning to me.

"But why?" he demanded. "I'm the oldest son. Why not come for me? Why Zoe? None of this makes sense."

"Well..." I hesitated before dropping another bombshell. "That's another interesting fact that I've discovered. And trust me, it's shocking."

"Stop beating around the bush!" Xander barked, his frustration evident.

"It turns out you aren't the oldest child in your family, Xander," I said carefully, watching his reaction closely.

Theo gasped and reached for Xander's hand, but he pulled away and shook his head. "Explain."

"Your parents had another baby as teenagers ... a little girl. They gave her up for adoption."

"Why the fuck would they do that?" Xander's anger was palpable.

"I suppose to avoid scandal," I shrugged. "It was a different time back then. Having a baby out of wedlock meant a life of shame, even if the mother eventually married the father of her child."

Xander paused again, processing this information. I yearned to comfort and show him that he wasn't alone, but I knew he wouldn't want me close while he was distancing himself from Theo's touch.

Lost in thought, Xander stared out the window before speaking again in a soft, distant voice. "I remember Mama mentioning 'her girl' when I was young. It never made sense to me at the time. One day, I walked in on her and my father arguing in the kitchen. They didn't notice me standing in the doorway, and Mama was crying. She told him she missed her girl and regretted everything."

He stopped again, transported back to that moment in the kitchen.

"She asked Pops if she could visit her, but my father refused. This made her cry even harder, and he pulled her into his arms. That's when they noticed me. As a kid, I thought she referred to an old friend when she mentioned 'her girl.' It was the only thing that made sense to me at that time. I never really thought about it again until now."

His head shook slowly, lost in the depths of his memories. "A few years later, I walked into her bedroom and found her sitting by the window with the lights off, clutching a photograph tightly in her hand. She pulled me onto her lap and held me close as if afraid to let go. She tried to hide her tears, but her swollen, red eyes gave her away. She placed the photo carefully on the table next to us, and I remember sneaking back later to try and find it, but it had vanished without a trace."

My heart ached for him.

"I'm so sorry, Xander," I whispered, my voice trembling.

He let out a deep sigh, shaking his head once more. "So you're telling me that I'm not the oldest?" His tone held a hint of surprise.

"You were the youngest when everything happened," I confirmed.

As the pieces started coming together for him, he nodded slowly. "And that's why Zoe's death couldn't settle my father's debt. Her birth occurred years after that mess." The realization struck him hard.

"Yes," I replied softly, trying to offer some comfort with my words, if not with a touch. "Xander, I know this is a lot to process. But please believe me when I say that your parents weren't intentionally trying to hurt you by keeping this truth from you. They were likely trying to protect you in their own way."

"I'm not so sure about that," he retorted bitterly. "If that was their intention, they did a shitty job."

"Maybe they weren't successful, but it could have been their motivation," Theo interjected.

Xander sighed again, running his hand through his hair before facing me. His next question hung heavy in the air.

"I hate to ask, but is there more?"

With reluctance, I nodded. "A little."

"Then spill it," he demanded.

"Gusto knew about the three of us the whole time," I revealed. "He assisted Andraius with the coup at the Angelos compound and informed him that the money was under my name. He convinced him that marrying me was the best way to access it."

"That's un-fucking-believable," Theo exclaimed. "So now we finally know. All these years of scheming, death, and violence were just revenge for the mess my father made and the actions *Theios* Peter directed *Theios* Alex to take to fix it. Did I get that right?"

"Yes," I admitted sadly, knowing this was the truth behind everything that had happened.

We sat silently for a few moments as the weight of this revelation settled upon us. I desperately hoped they could see now that I had no choice but to do what I did. I prayed that they understood why I couldn't stay with them.

"I know I don't deserve it," I finally whispered, my voice trembling with emotion. "But do the two of you think there will ever come a time when you can forgive me?" My heart clenched as I waited for their response.

Sixteen

T HEO

The transformation in Nerine's once fiery eyes was now evident. The intense blaze that had burned just hours earlier, demanding we release her from her bindings, no longer existed. In its place, her shoulders sagged with shame, and her cobalt eyes reflected nothing but remorse and anguish. It became clear to me just how heavy her burden was, along with all the dark secrets she carried.

My anger toward her vanished in an instant. How could I possibly blame her? If I were in her position, I couldn't say that I wouldn't have made the same choices.

No, any blame fell squarely on my family and Xander's. And ultimately, on Nerine's family.

Here we were, the three of us, confronting the consequences of our elders' actions. It was a cruel fate, but our enemies were unyielding in their quest for revenge. They would not rest until they achieved their goal.

And success, in their eyes, meant death.

But there was only one solution in my mind.

"The only way out of this is for me to remove myself."

"Remove yourself from what?" Xander demanded.

"From everything. From you. Our relationship," I replied, turning to face Nerine. "And from our sons' lives."

"That's absurd, Theo," Nerine protested.

"She's right," Xander growled, clearly angered by my suggestion. "You can't give up on us because of this."

"I'm not giving up on anything. I'm proposing a solution to save our lives," I countered before returning to Nerine. "And saving our sons' lives, too."

Xander's voice rose in frustration. "And how is leaving us a solution?"

"It's the only way to keep us safe," I stated firmly.

"And that's not giving up?" Xander shouted, his anger escalating. "Do you even remember your vow, Theo? Maybe you didn't make it in front of God or our families, but you made it to me."

"My vow?" I questioned, raising an eyebrow. "What does that have to do with anything?"

He scoffed, his words fueling the flames of our heated argument.

"I can't believe you would even ask that. Your vow means everything—everything—in this situation, Theo. You promised me that no matter how difficult things became or what our enemies threw at us, you would never abandon us. How could you forget something like that?"

Our voices grew louder as we stood up, facing each other with fiery gazes.

"How dare you think I need reminding," I seethed, and my anger peaked.

"I'm offering a solution to keep us safe, and you question my loyalty? Don't you see my father's actions brought us here, Xander?" I cried out. "His foolish pride, his insatiable ego! And for what? To prove to his sons that he possessed the courage to take down the leader of our enemy?"

I turned away, pacing back and forth in the small cabin of the plane. I couldn't stand still—my fury was building inside me like a raging inferno, threatening to consume me.

"And as if that wasn't enough, as if he hadn't already caused enough damage, he defied orders and chased after that car. He killed a child, for God's sake!" My voice echoed through the cabin as I continued pacing like a trapped animal. At that moment, I hated being on this plane. All I wanted was to run away. To escape from my past, my family, and the cursed blood flowing through my veins.

But I couldn't. This cursed legacy was a part of me, a weight on my shoulders that I could never shake off. No matter how much I wished to be someone else, the burden of this curse was mine.

"Theo."

"Theo," Nerine's voice sliced through my thoughts like a sharp knife, startling me and pulling me back to the reality of our current situation. Unable to meet her gaze, I turned away and focused on the clouds outside the plane window. Fluffy, white clouds drifted by, peacefully displaying purity and cleanliness, starkly contrasting the dark, twisted path that had led me here. I was tainted, marked by my family's sins, since the moment I drew my first breath as an infant.

Shaking my head, I muttered bitterly, "The sins of the father fall on the son. Isn't that how it goes?"

"Fuck that nonsense," Nerine exploded from behind me, her voice laced with anger and frustration. "How can you believe such bullshit?"

I could feel their disappointment and pain radiating from them. I was hurting them, just as I had feared I would. They shouldn't expect anything less from me.

I knew deep down that I bore the blame for this mess. It was all because of my connections to my fucked up family.

"Honestly, I don't know how the two of you can still stand to be around me." My words hung heavy in the air for what felt like an eternity before a hand suddenly landed on my forearm and pulled me around.

Nerine stood before me, her usually bright sea-blue eyes now clouded with pain and frustration. Xander watched from his seat, a mix of sadness, disappointment, and understanding playing across his face.

Without warning, Nerine punched me in the stomach with surprising strength, causing me to stumble backward.

"What the fuck?" I exclaimed, caught off guard by her sudden aggression.

"I thought you were smarter than this! When did you

become so stupid?" she demanded, hitting me again, harder this time.

I shifted away from her blows but hit the small white leather couch against the side of the plane.

"Calm the fuck down," I demanded, trying to give her a few seconds to release her anger before I grabbed her hands in an attempt to stop her constant assault.

But she wouldn't listen. "No! I'm serious, Theo!" she yelled again, pushing me so hard that I fell back onto the sofa.

She stood over me, her beautiful face contorted with anger as she shook her head in disbelief. "Are you a dumbass? Only a dumbass says the shit you just said."

I took a deep breath, trying to calm myself down as well. "Nerine—"

"Don't Nerine me. None of us are going anywhere. Is that clear?" She kept yelling, not giving me a chance to respond. "We can't just snap our fingers and become different people. I'm the prime example of how that fucking doesn't work. You will not come find me just to run away. I need you now more than ever. Do you hear me?"

She jumped on top of me and hit me again, this time pounding her fist into my chest.

I managed to capture her wrists this time, pulling her toward me and ordering, "Stop punching me."

"You aren't going anywhere until you get it through your thick skull. None of us are." Her voice was shaking now, tears streaming down her face and falling onto mine. "We're a family now."

"A family?" I repeated, unable to process her words as I held onto her tightly.

Her brow furrowed in confusion and frustration as she replied, "What did you think we were? You, me, Xander—we're family. And now we have our boys. We protect one another."

I was at a loss for words. Family, just the three of us and our little ones?

"Don't act so surprised," Nerine scolded, wiping her tears with one hand while still clinging to me with the other. "I know you're angry, and I understand. But everything I've done was to protect us, our circle, our family." Her voice broke as she continued. "And if I can't back out, you can't either."

The raw emotion storming in her eyes was like a hurricane breaking through the carefully built walls I had constructed around myself. Her forehead pressed against mine, drawing us closer together. "I'm sorry for hurting you. I know I'm not the perfect angel you thought I was. But we must figure this out for our family and the boys." The word "family" echoed in my mind as I gazed at the woman before me.

Nerine.

Xander.

Our boys.

A family.

These two simple words contained an entire world of love and possibility. As much as I tried to resist, it was time to forgive her.

In an instant, the tension inside me shattered like glass, replaced by a flood of emotions. Anger and pain washed away, leaving behind only an immense, all-encompassing love for this woman.

Releasing Nerine's wrist, I gently cupped her face and lifted it. Tenderly wiping away the tears from her cheeks with my thumb, I spoke softly, "You've made your point loud and clear, Angel."

She gave me a watery smile as I pulled her toward me. Our lips just inches apart, Xander's voice interrupted from his chair, "Are you done with your tantrum now, Theo?"

My response was immediate and filled with frustration. "Fuck off, Xan."

Ignoring his presence, I closed the distance between Nerine and me and captured her lips in a deep kiss. She melted into me, her mouth soft and inviting. A moment later, my eyes met Xander's as he crouched beside us. A familiar spark of lust shone in his gaze, charging the energy around us into a frenzy.

"I'd rather fuck her," he stated boldly.

I couldn't help but feel my cock twitch in agreement. The three of us remained still, waiting to see who would make the next move.

"I thought you said you wouldn't touch me until you got everything out of me?" Nerine whispered, daring to break the electric silence.

My desire for her only grew at her boldness. Looking up into her eyes, I could see something ethereal and transcendent in her beauty, something that surpassed words.

"We've all suffered enough pain for a lifetime," I murmured, my fingers tangling in her hair and resting at the nape of her neck. She looked down at me, searching my eyes for something unspoken.

"Nerine," I breathed, "you've given us more than we ever could have imagined."

She gasped at my words, her lips parting slightly with anticipation. It was time to put an end to this game of resistance.

Without hesitation, I pulled her back, our lips colliding together. Her mouth felt like velvet against mine, soft and pliable, yielding to my desires.

Her thighs tightened around my hips as she kissed me deeply, inviting and welcoming. As I reached down between her legs and settled my thumb against her denim-covered clit, Xander stepped up behind her, his hands cupping her breasts.

Suddenly, Xander pinched one of her nipples, causing her to break away from our kiss and cry out in pleasure.

"Oh, dear God." Her moans filled the cabin like a familiar song that had been long forgotten, sweet and comforting.

My arousal grew to almost painful levels as I watched them continue their passionate embrace.

As I circled Nerine's sensitive nub through her clothes, I reached up and grabbed Xander's shoulder, pulling him closer. He held her chin, and his lips met hers while my gaze stayed fixed on the two of them.

This was what we needed.

This was what we had been missing.

Together.

As one.

Our bodies entwined in a symphony of desire and love.

Watching them together intensified my desire. Their passion fueled my own.

Their bodies entwined, a tangle of desire and passion. The heat between them intensified as their hands roamed over each other's skin, igniting flames of need. I removed my hand from between her legs and reached for the edge of her sweatshirt. I pulled it up, deliberately letting my fingers trace along the curves of her body, causing her to shiver.

Xander took the cue, gripping her arms as we removed the garment.

With no time to spare, our angel stood before us, topless, her body a canvas of perfection. The soft curve of her breasts, highlighted by the golden glow of her skin, beckoned us like a moth to a flame.

Now that I knew she had given birth, I could see the changes in her body. Her breasts were fuller and rounder, and her nipples were darker and more pronounced. As she sat straddling me, half-naked and breathtakingly beautiful, I couldn't help but marvel at how childbirth had only enhanced her allure.

Xander grabbed her hips and pulled her away from me, turning her to face him as she stood up. His mouth captured hers again with a hunger that matched my own. He lost himself in the kiss, his hands roaming over her body, memorizing every inch.

Xander and I never lacked pleasure or affection in Nerine's absence. However, no matter how deeply we immersed ourselves in each other's bodies, there was an undeniable void without the missing piece of our souls.

Having her here filled that void and smoothed the jagged edges that marked us. Nerine was gentle in all the ways we were tough. She balanced my energies. Without her, we were a three-legged table struggling to bear the weight of the world.

With her back in our arms, we were complete again.

Xander gently pushed her back onto the couch and leaned down, popping the button of her jeans. The denim slipped down her thighs, revealing her golden skin inch by inch, like a gradual unveiling of a goddess.

The way she lay before us, embracing her sexuality and desire, was a dream come true. She revealed nothing to us when it came to sex. She couldn't even if she tried.

I rose to my feet and gestured for Xander to stand beside me. Together, we took in the sight of our naked angel and fed off the wild, insatiable lust she incited inside us.

"I missed you both so much," Nerine admitted with a shy smile. "Let me show you."

She pushed off the sofa and dropped to the floor, her knees hitting with a soft thud as she knelt before us. With a seductive smile playing on her lips, she reached for Xander's belt buckle, freeing the leather from its loop and unfastening his pants.

Her eyes locked with his as she pulled down his boxers, revealing his throbbing cock that sprang free. She held his gaze and licked her lips, giving us a glimpse of the wanton vixen she kept locked away most of the time.

Turning to me, she smiled as she noticed I had removed my clothes while she undressed Xander. My erection stood proudly before her, pulsing with need and begging for release.

Instead of diving straight into pleasure and curious to see what she had planned, I took a deep breath, trying to regain some semblance of sanity.

Except, I lost every one of my rational thoughts the moment she wrapped her fingers around both of our cocks, stroking up and down our shafts with practiced ease.

"I love how you both feel," she purred, mischief glinting in her blue irises as they met mine. "Your cock is so pretty, Theo. So thick and hard. I can barely wrap my fingers around you. Dicks aren't supposed to be pretty, but yours is."

I shuddered as her grip tightened, sending a jolt of electricity down my spine. With a mischievous smile adorned on her lips, she leaned forward and engulfed the head of my cock between them.

"Fuck me!" I cried out, feeling a wave of pleasure wash over me as her warm tongue slid across my weeping shaft.

She sucked me in with eager determination, causing tension to swirl inside my body and leaving me breathless. Up and down, her lips slipped over my pulsing cock, creating a mesmerizing rhythm.

Xander reached over to me, grabbed my face, and covered my mouth with his. Our tongues danced together as he devoured me, adding another layer of intense sensation to the already overwhelming pleasure. A moan escaped from deep in my throat as I felt the pulsing pleasure of sensations rocketing throughout my body, pushing me closer to the edge of climax.

And then, the beautiful, wicked temptress pulled away from my twitching cock only to turn and engulf Xander's cock with her velvety lips.

He jerked, his tongue freezing for a second in my mouth, telling me that he was experiencing the same torture I had just endured. But just like me, he couldn't resist the alluring pull she held over us.

I held onto the back of his head and pulled him closer, our kiss now charged with primal desire and need. It starkly contrasted with how we had been devouring Nerine just moments earlier.

Xander groaned into my mouth before suddenly pulling away, his gaze darting down to Nerine as she worked her magic on his throbbing dick. She was beyond sexy, her wet lips wrapped tightly around his hardness.

She hummed, reveling in the feel of him filling her mouth. Her eyes were closed in ecstasy as she slid up and down his engorged shaft.

"My god, Angel," I hissed, unable to tear my gaze away from the erotic scene in front of us. "You are the most beautiful sight I've ever seen."

Her lashes fluttered open as she released Xander's cock from her mouth.

She started to lean over to grab me again, but Xander ordered, "No."

She stopped with a whimper, "Please."

That damn plea was going to drive me insane.

"I have other plans for you." He sat on the low couch and reached for her.

The hunger in her cobalt irises and the goosebumps prickling her skin made it abundantly clear she had no objections to the change in plans.

She rose, taking his offered hand. Then he took hold of her hips and lifted her over him, settling her with one knee on either side of his thighs.

"Sit on my cock, Angel," he demanded, his voice thick with desire and urgency. "Now."

Without a protest, she smiled and positioned, letting the head of his cock brush against her sopping pussy before guiding him inside.

The tattoo etched down her spine, symbolizing the three of us glistened with sweat, as she threw her head back and moaned loudly, "Oh, Xander. You feel so good."

God, she was so fucking beautiful.

"That's it," he said through gritted teeth, his brow furrowed with primal need. "Yes. Fuck, yes!"

She moved slowly at first, but Xander wanted more. He took hold of her ass and brought her down hard, burying himself completely inside her.

She bowed her back at the invasion, and I couldn't help but grab hold of my cock as it wept with precum.

I loved seeing this side of Xander's untamed, primal need that came out when he was overwhelmed by pleasure.

With Nerine, he was always gentle and attentive, like a

true gentleman. But rarely, if ever, did he allow his inner beast to surface in such a fierce, dominant, and unapologetically savage manner—perhaps the brutal, ruthless enforcer he was made him soften for our woman.

Then there were times like this when he rode the edge between control and surrender, times when Nerine had pushed him too far, and his beast emerged without restraint.

He thirsted for Nerine's pussy like he needed water to survive. Her full breasts bounced in the air as Xander fucked into her hard, their bodies moving together like well-oiled machines. I loved watching them, seeing how Xander fisted Nerine's hair in an unforgiving hold that looked almost painful. He dug his fingers into the tender flesh of her hip, leaving his mark on her skin.

His eyes glimmered with a possessive desire to conquer, to possess, to ensure she submitted to him entirely.

Her eyes were closed as she threw her head back. She released soft shallow breaths through her slightly opened lips, swollen from sucking our cocks.

The pleasure on her face was undeniable.

This woman was desire-incarnate, and she belonged to Xander and me.

She rolled her hips sensually and expertly, milking Xander's cock with her pussy and bringing us all closer to the brink of ecstasy.

"Are you going to play voyeur or join us?" Nerine asked through panted gasps, teasing me with the offer of pleasurable release.

Seeing Xander and Nerine together was enough to push

me over the edge like a teenager. But I wouldn't allow that to happen. I wanted to savor every moment of this experience.

"I'll be joining you soon enough," I said, watching as Xander channeled my dominant nature when it came to Nerine.

I was not a gentle lover in any way. Nerine desired my intensity and the pleasure that pushed boundaries. I gave her everything she desired, carefully pushing her to the brink of ecstasy before sending her spiraling into pure bliss.

"Oh please, Theo. I need you so much," Nerine pleaded, her body writhing against Xander's as he continued to thrust into her roughly.

"You beg so beautifully, Angel. How can I resist?" I stepped closer, placing my hands on top of Xander's as we both touched and pleasured Nerine.

"I don't beg," she gasped, meeting my gaze with a defiant look.

Xander and I exchanged smirks, knowing full well that she did indeed beg in her way.

"Of course not," I said with amusement, trailing my fingers up her naked body until they wrapped around her slender throat. "You only ask with your moans and pleas."

My engorged throbbing dick lay heavy along Nerine's backside, begging for attention. Her body moved against mine, teasing me and driving me wild with desire.

Leaning close to her ear, I whispered, "Want to know a secret?"

"Yes." Her head rolled back with a moan.

"I need you just as much as Xander does," I admitted,

sliding my hand from her throat to cup the back of her neck. "We both do. Don't ever leave us again."

She reached back and tangled her fingers in my hair.

"Or what?" she challenged, a mischievous glint in her eye.

I nipped at her earlobe and let Xander take over the conversation.

"It's simple," he said, pausing his movements and holding her still on his cock. "We will kill you."

Nerine's grip on my hair tightened as if she were about to pull it out. "Well then, we understand what will happen if either of you decides to leave me."

"I guess we are," Xander smirked, leaning forward to nip at her lower lip before shifting his gaze to mine. "And what about you, Theo?"

The playful atmosphere grew more serious as he sought reassurance from me.

"We're clear," I assured him, biting down on Nerine's neck and then asking, "Now can we get back to fucking her?"

"Yes," Nerine moaned. "Can we please get back to fucking me?"

The mood shifted once again, our breaths growing heavy with arousal once more. Xander and I pulled Nerine into a heated kiss. Each took turns exploring her mouth with our tongues. Our hands roamed over her smooth skin as she resumed gliding along Xander's thick cock.

My erection dripped with need, craving its turn in the action.

"It's time for me to join in," I announced, placing my

hand on Nerine's lower back and urging her forward onto Xander's length.

She looked incredible in that moment, completely open and ready for us. Reaching for the armrest of the sofa, I grabbed a packet of lube and quickly tore it open, slicking up my shaft.

Moving into position behind her, I rubbed the head of my cock along their bodies. Xander's breathing quickened as I started at his balls and slid toward Nerine's tight entrance. She was already dripping wet, her juices coating Xander's cock and teasing me.

I aligned myself with her puckered hole and gave her the signal, "Now, Angel."

She slowly pressed down, her ass swallowing up my cock inch by delicious, hot inch. The heat of her surrounding me and the feel of Xander's massive girth throbbing against my shaft through the thin skin separating us almost sent me crashing over the edge.

I took a deep breath, determined to hold on until we were ready.

"My God, my God," Nerine called out as I completely buried myself inside her. "It's so good. Oh fuck, Theo."

We let her lead in the beginning, watching as she rocked back and forth to grow accustomed to the sensations of the two of us inside her. Once we knew she was ready, we took control.

Xander slid into her sweet pussy, pulling out just as I pushed into her tight ass until we moved in a primal dance that sent the three of us into a trance of pure pleasure.

Connected like this, nothing else existed.

Nerine, Xander, and Theo. The bond we'd created in adolescence was still a living, breathing thing as adults.

The pleasure was overwhelming and not enough. It would never be enough. I wanted to gorge myself on it forever.

Our bodies worked together with precision, drawing pleasure from every cell of my body, my cock hot and swollen inside my love. I caught Xander's eye over her shoulder and held his hot gaze. He was on fire with lust, panting and groaning, lost in passion, just like me, and as we slammed into Nerine together, I knew nothing in the world would ever get between us again.

Xander.

Nerine.

Me.

We were one. We always had been. And we always would be.

The look of pure, unadulterated desire and love in Xander's eyes, mixed with the intoxicating feel of his cock sliding against mine and the white-hot heat of Nerine's ass, sent me crashing over the edge cascading into pure ecstasy.

"I'm coming," I groaned, gasping and thrusting hard into the depths of her body.

Her pussy spasmed and quivered as she cried out, and Xander groaned loudly. His dick twitched against mine, and our voices echoed through the plane as our bodies exploded into a symphony of beautiful pleasure, the three of us exactly where we needed to remain, in each other's embrace.

Seventeen

NERINE

As the plane descended toward LAX, I felt a mix of exhaustion and adrenaline coursing through my body. My mind was still reeling from the chaotic events of my life, and I could feel the weight of it all dragging me down.

On a positive note, Theo and Xander seemed to forgive me for my mistakes. While I understood that things wouldn't magically become perfect, having them listen to my side of the story was more than I had expected. The three of us had reached a tense truce, but the wounds were still fresh, and we were all trying to navigate our emotions.

As we prepared to land, I couldn't help but wonder if there were better ways to handle the aftermath of everything.

Perhaps jumping on Theo and trying to hurt him wasn't rational. Still, somehow, it led to an intense physical encounter between the three of us that left us all breathless and satisfied.

The chemistry that Theo, Xander, and I shared was a living, breathing entity, something undeniable. It transcended physical attraction, reaching deep into our souls and leaving us feeling incomplete when we were apart.

Still, it wouldn't fix the damage I caused to our relationship. That would take time.

After twenty minutes, our private jet touched down at LAX and taxied into a hangar. As we were about to leave the comfort of the luxurious plane, I couldn't help but sigh—the prospect of moving after my earlier activities wasn't ideal. At least the flight to Phoenix gave me an hour and a half to recover.

"I take it you're sore," Xander said with a satisfied grin.

I winced, taking his hand and letting him pull me to my feet. "You could say that."

"Good. Get used to it. We have two years of unsatisfied lust to take out on you."

"As if you wouldn't have fucked me senseless on the regular if I never left."

Theo shrugged as he made his way to the door. "You're not wrong."

In one swift motion, he pulled out his gun and phone. "Wait until I check the hangar and the jet to move."

Xander nodded, and Theo exited.

After a brief moment, Theo signaled that it was secure,

and we made our way down the stairs from the jet. However, Theo and Xander were cautious. They positioned me securely between them, weapons at the ready and their eyes carefully surveying the surroundings.

Once we reached the new aircraft, it took several minutes for them to consider it safe enough for us to board with our crew.

As we settled into our seats and took off again, two flight attendants emerged with a large platter of hot Thai food. The aroma filled the cabin, and I shook my head as I watched Theo and Xander rush to the table to pile their plates high, as if they had been starving for weeks, before returning to their seats.

"They've always eaten like this since we were teenagers," I remarked to the attendants standing in the corner.

Neither replied. Instead, they pressed their lips together as if trying to hold back laughter.

"They know our quirks and habits," Xander said between bites of food.

I rolled my eyes and shrugged. "Sorry about that. They do have a lot of quirks, don't they?"

This time, one of the attendants turned away to hide a smile and busied himself with restocking the drink cart.

"Stop talking about us," Theo chimed in playfully. "They're professionals. Don't expect them to agree with you or speak poorly of their bosses."

"Technically, I'm your boss, too," I teased. "So I can say whatever I want about everyone."

Both of their heads snapped up, surprised by my comment.

"Are you claiming it then, Angel?" Theo's intense gaze bore into mine. "I'm more than ready to hand it over."

My heart thundered in my chest. The pounding was so loud I was certain those around me could hear it. Emotions swelled like a tidal wave, and I fought to keep them in check.

"Even if I wanted to, I can't," I replied honestly, feeling the weight of responsibility crushing me as the Angelos.

Xander set his dish on a side table with a clatter and leaned forward, his gaze intense. "Why not? You are the Godmother of the Night for the Angelos Family. The right to the seat runs through your blood, solidified by our victory over Andraius and reaffirmed by your handling of those assholes at the meeting. Tell me, what is stopping you from being the Angelos?"

I sighed heavily, knowing they wouldn't accept my answer, even though I knew I wasn't worthy or deserving of the role they expected me to fill.

"I disappeared. I no longer hold the power."

"Who said you disappeared?" Theo chimed in, continuing to eat despite the tension in the air. "To the outside world, you simply went into hiding when you found out about your pregnancy. A protective mother, especially one who leads a powerful family with a target on her back, would do anything for her children."

These men were insane.

"Are you kidding me?" I exclaimed, springing up from my seat. Everything was spiraling out of control, and I had little power over it. "It's not that simple. Where do you come up with this shit?"

"He's right, Angel," Xander interjected calmly, taking a sip of water before continuing. "In our world, danger lurks at every corner, and our sons are heirs to an extraordinary legacy of power and wealth."

I threw my hands up and paced back and forth.

"Men! This is what happens when a girl falls for not just one, but two men who both believe they hold all the solutions to the world's issues." I scanned the cabin, searching for the flight attendants who had disappeared. "Great. Now, I can't tell them to stop giving you food nonstop at this altitude. All that food is having negative effects on your brain."

Taking a few deep breaths, I attempted to calm myself and find logical ways to reach the two idiots I love so damn much. But when I opened my eyes, Theo stood inches away from me, his gray irises burning with annoyance and anger.

My immediate reaction was to step back, but his strong arms wrapped around me and held me firmly in place.

"You can't give anyone orders unless you accept that you are the Angelos," he growled, looming over me as if trying to intimidate me into submission.

"I don't need to be the Angelos to give orders." I glared up at him defiantly. "I was born an Angelos, you idiot. My father was Peter Angelos, Godfather of the Night. He made me his heir at birth. The blood in my veins says I give orders."

"Then act like it," he retorted sharply, his grip on my waist tightening as he spoke. "You're not a little girl anymore.

It's time to get your act together and accept your responsibility, whether you want it or not."

"Don't call me a little girl!" I seethed, pushing against his chest with all my strength. But he hardly moved. "Let me go, or I'll punch you in the face."

He looked down at me with a smirk and pointed to his chin. "Go ahead. Hit me if it makes you feel better. Just remember there will be consequences."

"Oh please, what consequences could you possibly come up with?" I spat back, my frustration reaching its peak.

Without warning, he grabbed onto my throat and pinned me against the wall of the cabin.

"I might be 'acting Godfather of the Night,' but I'm still the same old Theo, Angel," he whispered, his hot breath brushing against my lips. "Two years apart haven't changed anything about our dynamic."

Heat flooded through my body as arousal coursed through me, causing my nipples to harden and a coil of desire to form between my legs. "What does that have to do with this situation?"

"You already know," he growled, his breath hot against my lips. "Nothing will stop me from turning your ass red, fucking you senseless, and leaving you begging for more."

"I don't need you," I countered, my voice shaking with anger and desire. "Xander will take care of me."

"Can we please leave me out of this?" Xander interjected from behind us.

Theo pressed his nose against mine, sending shivers down my spine as he spoke in a low, seductive tone. "Even

Xander can't satisfy that need inside you when I put it there. Only I can make you scream, cry, and beg for mercy."

"You're such an asshole," I shot back, attempting to take control of the situation.

Theo's grip on my throat tightened slightly, yet his eyes sparkled with desire.

"It doesn't change the fact that you want me to make you scream, cry, and whimper," he said in a low, husky voice.

My breath caught in my throat as his words sank in, and all I could do was stare at him with wide eyes filled with a mix of need and frustration. My skin burned with this new, darker arousal coursing through me. My nipples ached, and my pussy throbbed.

"Am I wrong?" he asked, his voice low and husky.

I couldn't deny the physical reaction my body had to him. "I hate how you can use my body against me. It's not fair."

"When did I ever suggest I was a reasonable man?" He pressed his body against mine, pinning me between him and the cold metal wall of the jet. "You fought for the role of the Angelos. You nearly died for it. So why are you fleeing from it now? Give me the truth, Angel."

My lips trembled as I struggled to find the words. "Why can't I lie to you? It would make everything so much easier if I could."

"Because that's not how we operate," he said firmly. "Now tell me the truth. Give me the real reason you can't be the Angelos."

I wanted to turn away, hide my shame, and pretend that

my weaknesses didn't exist. But Theo held me in place, refusing to let me escape.

Then Xander stepped into view next to Theo. "We're here with you," he said softly. "You're not alone anymore."

"That's exactly it!" I exclaimed, unable to hide my frustration. "Neither of you see it. It's not that I can't be the Angelos. I don't deserve the power. You two do. Even if I come back, what role will I have? A figurehead, as useless as Andraius was."

"Don't compare yourself to that piece of shit," Xander's tone brooked no argument. "You are nothing like him."

"But it's the truth," I insisted. "How can I just take over again?"

Theo narrowed his eyes at me. "You're still holding back. What is it that scares you so much?"

I stared at him, struggling to find the words. They couldn't possibly understand that this wasn't something we could fix with a snap of our fingers.

A lump formed in my throat as my mind raced, unable to articulate my thoughts.

"Theo, move," Xander commanded. "You're only making things worse for her."

Frowning, Theo stepped aside and asked, "What do you mean?"

"This." In one swift motion, Xander lifted me into his arms and carried me to the couch like a small ragdoll instead of a tall woman.

"Is this necessary?" I protested as he settled me on his lap and tucked my head against his shoulder.

"Just relax," Xander murmured. "The conversation is over for now. We'll figure it out later."

My first instinct was to resist, to push him away and reject the comfort he offered. But with Xander's strong arms around me, I felt safe, protected, and loved. It had always been this way with him since we were teenagers.

He was my gentle giant, the ruthless enforcer who softened only for me. I could tell him anything without fear of judgment. It didn't matter how often I messed up. He was always there for me.

Theo and I fought fiercely and loved just as passionately. However, Xander and I shared a different kind of bond, one filled with easy conversations and deep emotions. It was effortless to open up to him.

We sat silently for what seemed like hours, listening to the hum of the jet's engines filling the space between us.

Finally, gathering my courage, I spoke up. "What if I mess everything up again?"

"What did you do wrong the first time?" Xander brushed a strand of hair from my forehead and gently kissed my brow. "I don't remember you doing anything wrong."

"I broke our family," I whispered, tears pricking at my eyes. "And now you want me to lead the organization?"

"Who said we have a broken family?" he asked. "In fact, it has only grown stronger."

"I kept you from our boys," I choked out. "How can any of you trust me again?"

Theo moved beside us, gently placing my feet on his lap. "Angel, how many times have you said everything was for our protection since we walked through your apartment door? You put your life on the line for us. That's what a leader does."

The weight of the situation pressed down on me, but I couldn't push it away.

"Can we please table this for now? We have bigger concerns at the moment. I promise we can address it once we've secured our boys, mama, and the girls."

Xander wrapped his arms around me, holding me tightly against him, and I closed my eyes, hoping to find some relief from the chaos surrounding us.

Unfortunately, Theo wasn't as willing to let it go.

"There is no avoiding it," he declared, his tone firm. "You are the Angelos. It's only a matter of time before you reclaim your rightful place."

Before I could respond, Xander stepped in. "For God's sake, she asked us to stop. Can we drop it?"

My encrypted cellphone buzzed, interrupting the tense conversation. A cold shiver ran down my spine. Only one person used that device, Devani.

Which meant she'd activated a Solon operation.

"What's wrong?" Xander asked, sensing my unease.

"I don't know yet," I replied, quickly grabbing my bag and pulling out my phone to read the message.

"Oh, shit," I muttered, looking up at them with wide eyes.

Immediately, Theo got to his feet. "What does it say?"

"Solon... They're waiting for us," I whispered, pointing out the window toward the hangar below.

"Damn it," Xander cursed under his breath. "That can't be good."

"Did they say anything else?" Theo prodded.

"No, just that," I said, showing him the message on my phone.

Dread settled heavily in my stomach as I raced through all the possible scenarios. Fear clutched at my heart as I considered the worst-case scenarios.

I met Xander and Theo's worried gazes. "Something's not right here. What if it involves the boys?"

"First, let's not jump to conclusions," Theo reasoned.

Xander got up and began to pace back and forth in the small cabin.

I also stood up, but my legs felt like jelly. Slowly, I sank back into my seat, gripping the armrests tightly as my heart pounded with anxiety.

"Don't do that thing," Xander scolded, shaking his head.

"What thing?" I asked, furrowing my brow in confusion.

"The thing where you immediately think the most horrendous thing possible happened and panic."

"I'm not panicking," I protested, even though I knew my voice gave away the terror I felt inside.

He raised an eyebrow and pulled out his mobile.

"I'm going to check in with our team on the ground," he announced before heading to the back of the plane.

I sat there, my hands trembling as I considered the various possibilities of why Solon would suddenly show up.

First, they were here to explain their actions from two years ago to Xander and Theo. However, that seemed highly unlikely. Solon operated as a "do what we want" organization that never clarified their decisions to anyone.

Secondly, one of the twins might have got into trouble at school. A college mishap was something manageable. What could be worse than Fiona publishing a romanticized version of my life without my consent?

But then there was the third option that terrified me the most. What if something had happened to the boys? They were our biggest vulnerability, the strongest leverage against us. My mind reeled at the thought of anyone reaching them before we could ensure their safety.

Xander stopped pacing to make a call and immediately shouted orders to whoever was on the other end. His urgency pushed me into action. We were close enough to Phoenix that I could call Mama.

With trembling fingers, I dialed her number and held my breath as it rang. However, it went to voicemail, and my heart sank. I tried two more times with the same outcome before ultimately leaving a desperate message.

"Mama, please call me back as soon as possible. It's an emergency."

Next, I reached out to Fiona with the same result. Chills ran down my whole body as pure, unadulterated fear seeped into every single one of my nerves.

Fiona always kept her phone on her and knew to respond with at least a text no matter where she was, even if it was a one-word message.

"Think, Nerine. Think," I whispered, my head spinning. "Oh, fuck. The security system."

I pulled up the app on my cell and logged onto the secured server monitoring cameras around Mama's house.

"Shit, come on," I muttered.

Why was it taking so long to load? I had Mama's house equipped with a state-of-the-art system run over fiber optic wiring with a backup power source to keep everything active during a power outage for seventy-two hours.

"No, no, no, no, no," I muttered when the signal pulled up and showed the word "offline."

That fucking was impossible unless someone had tampered with my setup.

Solon installed it, dammit.

Nausea engulfed my stomach, and my heart pounded erratically and uncontrollably in my chest.

"I can't log into the system at Mama's house. My security is compromised. Everything is offline," I said.

The stark expressions on both Theo and Xander's faces told me they understood my concern. Xander relayed my information to the person on the phone, and they began a back-and-forth about the position of soldiers and calling in allies.

How could my entire family disappear like this?

I called Mama and Fiona again, but there was still no answer. Tears sprang to my eyes as my heart filled with worry.

"Fuck," I muttered, shaking my head, searching my brain.

If Solon was involved, it meant someone figured out where we were quickly and easily. Devani and her team spent countless hours and more money than I could imagine orchestrating this new life she'd forced on me to ever compromise me.

Fiona's book may have helped our enemies locate me, but it made no mention of the boys or where they lived with Mama. Fortunately, she also excluded any reference to my pregnancy or information about the twins' colleges. None of this added up.

Solon preferred to stay in the shadows, and very few people knew the group's existence. Their message clearly indicated that they intended to undermine any plans Theo and Xander had to protect me, the boys, Mama, and my sisters.

I still couldn't wrap my head around how they figured out something had gone wrong when no one knew we were going to Phoenix.

I reflected on everything from when I opened the door to find Theo and Xander standing there until just a few moments ago, reviewing all that had transpired.

Then it hit me.

"It was the fucking flight manifest!" I shouted to Xander. "At least that's a possibility."

He cocked his head to the side as if not understanding what I was talking about. "I'm not following?"

"Remember when I told you I studied flight patterns from my apartment?"

He nodded.

"I used flight manifests to help me track the directions of different flights. They are easy to look up. I never told you to file a false one for our trip."

"Shit," Xander nodded. "What was the point of changing aircraft if we left a paper trail?"

Theo walked out of the bedroom in the back of the plane with a tight, drawn expression of worry.

Xander explained my theory, and he nodded in agreement.

"Right. Just one more thing to add to our list." He paused, a crease forming between his brows. "Wait. That still doesn't explain how Solon has information we don't. It still doesn't explain who alerted anyone to look for a second manifest out of LAX. We covered our tracks. I ensured that decoys resembling us left the hangar in a car and headed to a nearby hotel."

"I know Devani wouldn't betray me. She wouldn't go as far as she has if she were just going to turn around and stab me in the back." I had to defend her.

None of us would have survived the last two years if it wasn't for her.

"She's trustworthy, but what about her team? Do you know who she has on you? From how it looks to me, they've done a piss poor job of protecting you."

I'd never questioned any of it before, but now it made me feel like a fool.

"Someone who works for her organization isn't loyal." It hurt my heart to see this. "They are setting us up for something."

I had to contact Devani, but how could I know if my phone was safe?

"I'm over Solon fucking with my life," Theo stated, his

anger unmistakable. "Here are the facts: Solon contacted you, saying they are waiting for us to arrive. They refused to give you any details about what they want. At the same time, three enemies of the Angelos family have arrived in Vegas searching for you. Fiona's book stirred up trouble, but some must have been in town long before the novel went viral."

"I see that now," I agreed. "Months ago, I kept feeling like people were watching me. At first, I thought it was just my paranoia, but it kept happening repeatedly. It wasn't until I recognized some of Stratos's men that I realized something was off."

"And you didn't think to protect yourself?" Xander asked with an edge of irritation.

"As I mentioned, I thought I was letting my imagination run wild. It's not like I was going out to hang with my girls every night or anything. My routine consisted of waking up, going to work, coming home, making dinner, eating, and sleeping."

"We don't know what we will face when we land." Xander gripped the back of his neck. "We need to prepare for anything."

"If they meant to kill us, we'd never see them coming, let alone receive a call to expect them upon our arrival. The organization's purpose is assassinations."

"I'd rather prepare than find myself holding my dick." Theo sprang into action, pulling a few duffel bags from the overhead bins and laying them on the floor.

When he unzipped the first one, dozens of firearms came into view.

"Are we going to war?" I exclaimed as he started pulling them out and laying them on the floor.

"Yes," was all Theo said as he tossed weapons to Xander, and both of them equipped themselves with as much gear as possible without looking overly bulky with firearms.

"Buckle your seatbelt, Angel. We'll land in a few minutes." Xander positioned himself across from me and tossed my way a pistol, two blades, and a thigh rig. "I believe these belong to you."

I grasped the hilt of one of the daggers, unable to tear my gaze away from the decorative handle that made the stiletto-style knife seem deceptively delicate.

Memories from two years ago overwhelmed me. I found myself in the library of my family home, consumed by anger, vengeance, and a deep hatred for the man I married to save my mother and sisters.

There was pain, so much pain.

And the blood, hot and sticky. It covered my body. All of it belonged to the monster who'd tried to destroy me.

I touched the tip of the double-edged knife and smirked. Andraius learned his lesson when I sliced his belly from one side to the other.

I opened my hand and spun the blade over my palm, and for the first time in so long, the sense of control, the power I once felt, bloomed inside me.

"This saved me that night. It allowed me to reclaim my life."

"No," Theo countered. "You saved yourself that night. That was just the tool you used to regain your life."

I met his stormy gaze. "Don't forget that you and Xander cleaned up my mess."

"We protected our queen, as we're supposed to."

I couldn't help but swallow, feeling the back of my throat burn with emotion.

"Aren't you tired of fixing all the messes I make?"

"In which organization do the Seconds sit around and do nothing?" Theo asked. "It's our job to clean up whatever situation the family head puts us in that week. Your situation with Andraius was nothing compared to what *Theios* Alex handled with your dad."

"From the stories, Pops told me," Xander said. "When *Theios* Peter took over the organization, he got into territory wars over stupid shit, caused rifts with allies, and even killed the wrong asshole or two. As his second, Pops had his hands full cleaning up the situations and ensuring all was right with the world."

I shook my head. "It's difficult to view Papa as anything other than the calm, rational man I remember."

"We've got your back, Angel."

The cabin pressure fluctuated, signaling our arrival at the airport.

"Can we pause this for now and focus on what's going on with our family?"

"For now," both men said in unison, and I sighed in relief.

A few moments later, the plane landed and slowly taxied down the runway toward the hangar. With each second that brought us closer, my heart raced faster and faster.

We all looked out the window as the plane glided into the hangar, the light streaming inside gradually fading to darkness as the building blocked the sun.

I searched the hangar and initially saw nothing until a swarm of people in black military fatigues surrounded the plane.

"Here we go," I muttered, letting out an exasperated sigh. "Stay calm."

Theo and Xander followed my gaze.

"I can't make out that little logo. What is it?" Xander asked.

I replied, having seen the uniforms up close and personal more than once. "Red scorpion. Solon's insignia worn on the upper left arm."

The group stood in formation, waiting for the stairs to descend. They didn't try to hide the fact that they were armed to the teeth with automatic weapons.

I studied them as uneasiness settled in my stomach.

"This isn't my usual Solan team. I don't recognize any of them."

"Well, let's find out what they want, shall we?" Theo raised his eyebrow and stepped toward the door.

He signaled for the attendants to release the latch. Gradually, the stairs unfolded until they reached the ground.

In a flurry of movement, the cabin filled with agents. They shoved Theo back, positioning him next to me.

I tried to jump up, but Xander kept me in place.

"Stay right here," he commanded. "I didn't find you just to lose you again."

My heart raced in my chest, and I could only hope we would survive whatever happened next.

"Is Devani here?" I asked.

No one replied.

I attempted to stand again, but Theo and Xander restrained me this time, staying by my side.

"What's going on? I want to know why you're here," I demanded. "Where is Devani?"

They responded by dividing and at the very back stood Mama.

It wasn't just Mama, but Charis and Hayes were in her arms.

"Oh my God." I rushed to her, unsure if I was imagining what I saw, until I wrapped my arms around them. "Mama."

Relief washed over me, and the next moment, both boys grabbed onto me, eager for my attention. "Mama, Mama, Mama."

I took them from my mother's arms, holding them close. Their tiny bodies felt so warm, and they smelled amazing.

"You're safe," I whispered, kissing their foreheads.

Mama ran her hand down the back of my hair. "They're safe."

Tears streamed down my cheeks. There was no way I could repay her for always protecting my babies. This woman had sacrificed everything for me.

"Thank you, Mama. Are you okay?"

She nodded, smiling at me. She pulled me to the nearby sofa, pushing me and the boys down. She brushed my hair from my forehead, tucked it behind my ear, and then cupped my cheek to wipe away my tears.

I couldn't help but find solace in her mothering, even while I held my children.

I shifted my attention to Theo and Xander.

They stayed in their original spots, even though I knew they wanted to get closer to me and the boys.

I wouldn't keep them waiting long. "I tried to call you," I told Mama. "I tried to call Fiona, too." My mother's eyes darkened at the mention of my sister's name, and her expression fell.

"What's wrong?" I asked, as the relief from moments ago vanished and dread resurfaced, hot and raging.

She shook her head, the bleakness in her blue eyes reflecting sheer devastation.

Before Mama could say anything, a woman about my height stepped forward. "Ms. Angelos, we need to talk. I'm Agent Davenport. Director Devani Patel-King said you would understand the message."

"I see," I said, placing the boys on the ground, where they immediately clung to my legs and stood up.

Devani never used her official title. Technically, she was retired and had relinquished her director position. However, in her world, no one really left the job. For her to invoke her position and dispatch a team with an agent meant we were in an extraction protocol.

She prepared us for this, but I never expected it actually to happen. Something occurred, but what exactly? "Thank you for bringing my family back to me."

"Certainly, ma'am. We've made additional arrangements, which include Mr. Nephus and Mr. Onassis."

"What the fuck is going on, Angel?" Theo asked. "Updating us would be a great idea."

"First, I need to know why Fiona isn't with Mom and the boys." I fixed my gaze on the agent.

From my peripheral vision, I saw Mama wipe tears from her eyes, and I realized that someone had taken her.

"Your sister's whereabouts are unknown. We believe the Aetos family has taken her."

Everything inside me froze. No, no, no.

"I don't understand," I said, shaking my head. "Why Fiona?"

"To pay the debt they think your father owes them for his inability to control his men," Mama said.

"That's absurd." There was no logic to any of this.

Mama nodded. "I didn't say it made any sense."

My heart broke at the thought of Fiona with our enemies.

"We have to find her before they put her through the same nightmares I endured with Andraius." White-hot anger surged through my blood, replacing my fear.

I vowed revenge on the Aetos family for this bullshit. I would destroy them.

They touched my family. I sacrificed so much, and now these fuckers used some convoluted beliefs to justify their actions. I planned to gut them just like Andraius.

"I want their blood," I stated, knowing how unhinged I sounded.

"So do I. I'm sick and tired of these bastards hurting my babies. I'm a respectable grandmother now. Otherwise, I'd tell you to bring me one to test if my skills have gotten rusty."

I blinked, seeing my mother in a completely different light.

"What?" Mama tilted her head to the side. "Do you think you're the only one who went into the Caves during interrogations or knows how to use a blade?"

Papa taught me everything I could about interrogation and discipline in the room of his facilities, which he called the Caves. There were rooms for everything, from training areas to interrogation and extraction spaces. Xander was the king of the Caves. No one wanted a visit from him while locked in a cell, but Theo was the truly unhinged one. When he visited a prisoner, it was always a mess.

"You helped Papa in the Caves?" I couldn't hide my confusion. "Why didn't I know about this?"

"It wasn't any of your business. A husband and wife can have secrets. You inherited your blade skills from me. Peter was better with his fists, and of course, he loved his firearms. Theo wasn't the only calm one people feared back in the day."

I glanced up at Theo, who pressed his lips together, trying not to smile. This was information overload, and I wasn't sure I could handle it at the moment. I placed a hand on my chest, my mind spinning. "Mama, we need to set this topic aside because I'm not sure I know you right now."

"Bring me back, my baby girl, Nerine." The intensity of Mama's gaze made me nod.

As if Theo and Xander could read my mind, we said in unison, "We will."

For months, I'd felt the weight of the world on my shoulders, carrying it all by myself. I'd spent two years protecting everyone I loved, expecting the worst to happen.

Now, we were in that situation, but everything was different. I wasn't alone.

Theo and Xander were with me. We would fight this battle together.

Fiona was the priority.

And if it all worked out, I would bring Mama a gift to test her old skills.

EIGHTEEN

X ANDER

After learning about *Theia* Delia's surprising skills with blades, Nerine, Theo, and I flooded Agent Davenport with questions about Fiona's kidnapping.

"What about my other sisters?" Nerine asked. "Christina and Ariana?"

"They're safe, as far as we know. We have a team keeping a close watch on them."

"How did they manage to take Fiona?" Theo asked.

"We have people looking into how her location was compromised."

"Fiona should have had a personal security team," I said,

barely concealing my anger at their incompetence. "Where the fuck were they?"

"That's what we're trying to figure out," Nerine said. "Someone assisted the Aetos family in coordinating this from the inside. It's the only way the cameras I set up at her place stopped working, just like they did at Mama's."

Nerine picked up one of the boys and effortlessly settled him on her hip. He immediately snuggled into her neck, and she stroked his back.

Fucking hell. I had to focus on the issues and ensure we covered every base. However, the two boys before me were the only things on my mind. Their love for and bond with Nerine was clearly evident.

The desperate urge to reach out and stroke their cheeks pushed at me.

The other little one clung to Nerine's leg. Sensing my interest, he turned and stared wide-eyed at Theo and me, a crease forming between his brows. Then, the toddler in Nerine's arms redirected his attention to us.

God, they looked so much like us. They were perfect replicas of the three of us.

We were giants compared to them. Yet, despite the tense, chaotic energy surrounding them, neither seemed the least scared.

It was Nerine's presence, I realized. With her, they felt safe and secure. Accomplishing such a feat within the confines of our world was astounding.

The two of them glanced at each other and then back to Theo and me as if they were trying to figure something out.

They were so fucking beautiful. My heart cracked wide open just seeing them. I wanted to gather them both in my arms but knew it would frighten them. So, I resisted that urge and allowed these feelings I never expected to fill my heart.

I couldn't help but smile when the boys mimicked how my head tilted as if it were a game.

The next thing I heard was Nerine's command. "I need everyone out. Please exit the plane. Now."

"Ms. Angelos, we have transportation waiting for you outside. Our instructions are to take you and your family to the designated safe house outside Phoenix. From there, we will coordinate the next phase of the plan."

"Excellent, thank you," Nerine said with an air of authority, disregarding their plans. "We will be down in a few moments. Mama, please go with these men, and the boys and I will join you shortly."

"Okay, honey," *Theia* Delia said with an understanding smile. The plane cleared, leaving only the five of us on board alone.

Nerine sat the little one on the floor beside his brother and kneeled by them. "Boys, I want you two to meet some important people."

They looked up at us curiously, intently.

My heart skipped a beat as I drank them in without the chaos of the others surrounding us. Theo inhaled deeply, and I knew he was as overwhelmed with emotion as I was.

"Do you recognize them?" Nerine asked, her voice so soft

it could have been a whisper. "I showed you pictures of them. They are your Papas."

They each nodded as the crease between their brows returned. It reminded me so much of Nerine when she concentrated.

They were so fucking beautiful.

"Theo, this is Charis," Nerine said, gently pushing the boy toward us.

Theo gasped at hearing the boy's name, his mother's maiden name.

"Xander, this is Hayes."

My eyes widened as I realized what she'd done. She'd honored our mothers by giving the boys our mothers' maiden names.

She couldn't understand how much it meant to me, and I loved her for it. Tears burned the backs of my eyes, but this was no time for crying.

Hayes gave me the same curious inspection as before.

"Hey there," I said in a gentle tone. "It's nice to meet you."

Theo knelt beside us, watching the boys carefully.

"Hi." Theo gingerly reached out his hand.

Hayes looked over at him, studying Theo's palm, and then stepped toward him, throwing his arms around Theo's neck. Theo's eyes widened in surprise.

"Hayes looks like you, Xander, but his personality is a lot like yours, Theo," Nerine spoke softly. "I'm not surprised he's gravitating toward you."

Theo wrapped his arms around Hayes and held him close.

Charis turned to me, flashed me a grin, and then giggled, "Papa!"

He raised his arms and waited for me to lift him. The complete, unguarded acceptance sent a bolt of lightning straight to my heart. Unable to control my overflowing emotions further, I hugged him tightly.

He was so little. His tiny body so fragile.

"Yes, I'm your Papa," I said, thick with emotion.

I looked up at Nerine over his shoulder and saw her eyes shining with tears.

"Thank you," I mouthed to her silently.

She nodded in understanding and gave us a few moments to embrace, watching from a short distance away. After a moment, the boys pulled back, and Theo and I switched places, embracing our other son with just as much emotion.

"We should talk," Nerine interjected, breaking the spell of the intimate moment. "We don't have much time."

Theo and I agreed and sat down while our sons played quietly at our feet.

"Do you see why I needed to keep them out of sight? They look just like the two of you."

"Yes," I agreed. "There's no denying whose children they are."

"I hate that we have to hide them," Nerine admitted. "But their safety comes first."

"You're right," I agreed. "The world needs to see what

our love created. But not yet. I never want them to believe we hid them because we didn't love them."

"They know that they're loved," Nerine said. "Hiding them isn't doing them any harm right now."

"But we can't hide them forever," Theo insisted. "Eventually, that will be impossible."

"I know," Nerine said. "Nothing can change until we have our rival families under control and Fiona back, safe and sound. I'm so worried about her. The Aetos family is ruthless. I'm worried what they might be doing to her."

"We'll find her," Theo insisted, reaching over and grabbing her hand.

He leaned into her, comforting her. My head spun as I tried to figure out our next move. Hayes and Charis stopped playing to watch Theo comfort their mama.

"You two need to get married."

Their heads snapped up, and they both frowned and thought I'd lost my mind.

"Immediately," I insisted.

"Are you serious, Xander?" Nerine asked. "That's the last thing on the agenda right now."

"No, it's not. It's preemptive."

Nerine scowled. "Explain before our sons see a violent side of their mother."

"I have a feeling they inherited some of that temper," Theo interjected. "Xander, straighten this out. I'm not following this logic either."

"Pause for a second and think. If the two of you marry,

then it will avoid another Andraius situation. No one can force Nerine to marry anyone."

"I see your point." She nodded. "Except you forget one thing."

I leaned forward. "That is?"

"I will never allow anyone to put me in that situation again," she glared at me, fire blazing in her cobalt irises. Nobody, and I mean nobody, will ever force me into a situation like that again. I will fight until my last breath. I made a vow to myself, and I will keep it."

The impact of her words washed over me as if it were a physical bomb of energy.

She was my warrior queen who'd survived hell and back and refused to allow anyone to destroy her.

I nodded and said, "I'm suggesting it for other reasons, too."

"Like what?" She asked.

"Well, for starters, it'll keep him from ever contemplating that running is an option," I said, jutting my chin toward Theo.

Instantly, anger flared in his eyes. But then Hayes tugged on his pant leg and crawled into his lap, melting away his fury. I couldn't help but smirk. No. Theo wasn't going anywhere.

"Theo, you might as well change your name to Angelos. That way, you'll match with the boys." I smirked and then thought about my suggestion.

It wasn't a bad idea. Theo hated his name and everything

it stood for. He was the last of his line, and our sons were the heirs to the Angelos Syndicate.

I was a fucking genius.

Theo squinted, looking at me as if he planned to clock me. However, Hayes kept him from following through, grabbed a few strands of Theo's beard, and pulled.

"Ow!" Theo cried out, laughing and untangling his fingers.

Hayes laughed and clapped his hands. He was definitely my kid. He liked to fuck with Theo as much as I did.

"I suppose you're right, Xander," Theo replied. "I don't have much attachment to my family name anyway. Why the fuck would I keep Nephus when all it means is death and destruction?"

"I can't believe the two of you." Nerine shook her head. "Men."

"What?" I asked.

"It's quite egotistical to plan our futures without asking for my input," she sighed. "Ask me, and I might say yes. Tell me, and it's a definite no."

Completely ignoring anything Nerine said, Theo suggested, "You should change your name too, Xander."

"Might as well," I agreed with a careless shrug.

My parents' faces flashed in my mind. They had always wanted me to carry on the family name, hoping for many generations to come. Still, I knew they would understand if I changed it to reflect my growing family.

"I swear the two of you are complete jerks."

"We are stating obvious facts about things that need to happen," I explained.

"I see..." She shrugged. "Well, let me give you a fact. I'm not marrying anyone who doesn't propose to me first."

"Propose?" Theo asked, his eyes widening.

I couldn't help but laugh at their exchange. Naturally, our angel would want things done in a precise order.

"It's a done deal, Nerine," Theo said.

And Theo's typical reaction was to push back.

"No, it isn't!" she insisted.

I smirked and sat back to watch the entertaining back-and-forth typical of Nerine and Theo's foreplay.

"Stop acting like this is some big revelation. Your mother made this decision, and you went along with it," Theo said. "I'm not going to ask for your hand in marriage when we were already engaged. You're mine, Angel. Nothing will ever change that."

Her eyes widened, and a fire burned in her cobalt gaze. After all, she was the Godmother of the Angelos Mafia. No one instructed a queen on how to manage her affairs or business.

She leaned forward, a crease between her brows. "I don't think you know who you're dealing with! I'm—"

Before she could proceed, Agent Davenport stepped back onto the plane with several team members trailing behind her.

"Excuse me, Ms. Angelos? I'm sorry to interrupt, but we need to move—right now. We have information about a possible location for Fiona."

"You have?" she exclaimed, jumping to her feet with us following suit.

"Yes, ma'am," she replied. "Your car is waiting."

Theo and I scooped up the boys, and Nerine grabbed her things.

"Let's go," I said, and we all headed for the exit, our little family completely intact, safely together, and well on its way to becoming a bonded unit.

Nineteen

I sat at the head of the large wooden table in the safe house, with Theo and Xander beside me, absorbing everything Solon discovered about Fiona's abduction.

Nothing seemed to make sense about the information coming in, and perhaps the exhaustion creeping into my mind made it difficult to concentrate.

Forty-eight hours of nonstop stress fucked up a girl's ability to function.

I glanced at my sides, taking in the room around me and shaking my head. We were in a fucking mansion. I couldn't understand how this was considered a secure location.

After leaving the airport hangar, it took a little over an

hour to reach a small, sleepy town outside Phoenix. The property designated as the safe house seemed like just a small single-family home on a vast expanse of farmland.

However, as we navigated the long, winding road leading to the house, a large, sprawling farmhouse emerged, hidden behind a canopy of dense trees and an iron gate.

I quickly realized Solon's definition of a safe house was vague. We were at a camouflaged estate, pretending it was a safe house.

As if sensing my unrest, Theo picked up my hand and kissed my knuckles, and Xander repeated the gesture with the other hand.

I was incredibly grateful for these two men. It took having them back in my life to realize how well we fit together and how much of a unit we really were. We were a team that thrived on each other's energy.

"It's going to be okay," Theo reassured.

I wasn't so sure, but I nodded.

Behind us, Solon agents stood guarding the large living room, and though it should have felt reassuring, a traitor stood among them, so the comfort wasn't there.

Mama and the boys were in a nearby wing of the house, under the watchful protection of Angelos's soldiers, who had arrived in Phoenix shortly after us. The people Theo and Xander called in were the group I refer to as the Originals. They were part of the guard who had protected me and kept my secrets during my years with Andraius. I trusted them and knew they would risk their lives for my family.

"I promise we are doing everything possible to get your sister back."

I narrowed my gaze, not caring if I came off rude or not. "Agent Davenport, considering one of your people handed my sister over to our enemy, I find your words less than reassuring."

"Understood." She gave no outward reaction to my response and continued her report. "We made a second sweep of your mother and sister's homes. We found both ransacked. Everything indicates they are looking for your mother."

My heartbeat kicked up.

"They're protected, Angel," Theo whispered.

Xander squeezed my fingers. "Your Originals are with them. They won't let you down."

"I want to kill everyone involved in this mess. Not a single one of those fuckers deserves to live."

"We understand. You'll have your revenge, but first, we need to bring Fiona back." Theo placed my hand on his thigh and leaned forward with his elbows resting on the table. "You still haven't updated us on your search for Fiona. You mentioned a lead. Can I assume it didn't work out?"

"The first one wasn't as fruitful as we had hoped," replied Davenport's assistant, Agent Deluca. "However, my team is pursuing a few other leads."

The two agents sat side by side, embodying complete opposites in build and demeanor. Agent Davenport reminded me of a tall, graceful ballerina poised for performance. Everything about her was meticulously arranged, from her dark blonde hair styled in a no-nonsense bun to the crisp, wrinkle-free fatigues draping her frame. Her expression remained neutral throughout each interaction. Yet, her delicate, petite stature and features seemed to overshadow her serious personality. No one would ever suspect she posed a threat to anyone.

On the other hand, Agent Deluca smiled warmly, disarming everyone around him. He was a large, rugged man with dark brown eyes and a thick, gray goatee. His voice was low and soothing, cutting through the seriousness of the situation, much like an uncle aiming to reassure those near him.

As I reflected on it more, I realized he was such a nice person that no one would consider him a threat. The fact that I knew they were both deadly assassins, despite their underestimated appearances, made them the perfect sleeper agents.

Suddenly, my thoughts returned to the information about Mama's house. "Please tell me you swept the house before Aetos's people entered."

"No, we never had the chance to finish that part of the plan." His brow furrowed with concern. "We discovered the break-in when the operatives arrived to carry out their footprint elimination protocol. We have already spoken with your mother. She confirmed our suspicions. They took personal documents, family memorabilia, photos, and other identifying information. Since Fiona's apartment was in the same condition, we assume the same happened there."

I swallowed the acid bubbling in the back of my throat.

"The Aetoses want to clarify that they know about our boys."

"It appears so, Ms. Angelos."

"I see," I said, my head spinning.

Despite receiving this information from the Solon agents and the fact that they had saved my mother and the boys before anyone else could arrive, something felt off.

What were they holding back?

My gut screamed I was missing a large piece of the puzzle.

I knew that someone involved in this operation was currently working with Aetos. However, the Angelos soldiers here provided an extra layer of protection for my babies. Yes, they were all assassins, but many of my people had the same skills.

Aside from Devani and me, only a few agents knew of my family's presence in Phoenix. I recognized just one or two of the agents present today. What happened to the others? I couldn't afford to trust any of these unfamiliar faces. Solon's training focused on turning recruits into master manipulators and deceivers. This was how they blended in and integrated seamlessly into any group worldwide.

For now, they seemed to be on my side. But all I had to rely on was their word. At this point, I had no idea whom to trust, which was unsettling.

Theo, Xander, and Mama were the only people I could count on.

At this point, my faith in Devani wavered.

"There's more," Davenport said, placing a tablet before us. "You need to take a look at this."

"What is it?" Theo asked.

"Surveillance photos," she said, tapping the screen. "This first one shows the Stratos estate in Chicago. Do you recognize this gentleman? That driver is a long-time employee of the Aetos family."

I examined the image. Parked in front of the stunning mansion was a massive armored SUV. Outside stood an older man in a dark suit, his salt-and-pepper hair contrasting with the very visible sidearm tucked beneath his jacket.

He looked familiar, but I couldn't place him.

Then, from my side, Xander said, "That's Jayco Pakos, Gusto Aetos's driver. He's worked directly for him since he was a kid."

The agent flicked her finger across the screen to show another picture.

I immediately recognized the place from a blueprint tucked away in Papa's desk years ago.

"That's the Aetos estate."

Next to my ear, Xander whispered, "How do you know this? You've never been there."

"I'm nosy and love to snoop," I said, pointing to a vehicle before asking, "Whose car is that?"

"It belongs to Tobias Stratos."

I clenched my jaw. "Asshole refused to take no for an answer and now is going to pretend it's about family honor or some other bullshit."

"He is Andraius's nephew. You can't expect anything but a similar response to rejection," Theo reminded me. "Both are sore losers and play dirty."

I cocked my head to the side and asked, "Does that still mean the two of you plan to serve him up on a platter for me to enjoy?"

"Yes," Theo stated. "In my opinion, you deserve every Stratos bowing at your feet for what they allowed to happen to you."

"I couldn't agree more," Xander smirked, then shifted his attention to the agent. "When were these taken?"

"Last week."

The agent's eye no longer displayed the complete look of professionalism. They had softened, and if I noticed correctly, there was an amused glint.

Interesting; she found the ridiculous banter with Xander, Theo, and me humorous.

"Is there anything else we need to know?" I asked.

"Yes. The tail we have on Gusto Aetos photographed him at dinner."

She swiped the tablet again, and the exterior of Vinnie's Greek restaurant, an old favorite haunt of my father's, appeared.

"I love the food there," I said. "They make the best desserts."

I zoomed in on one of the restaurant windows. Nothing had changed in the two years since I'd left. I wasn't sure why I thought it would when it looked just as it had since I was a little girl.

The decorations remained the same, from the red and white tablecloths and fake grapes hanging from the ceiling to the giant wine bottles perched in the corner, with those little red glass candle holders flickering on each table and bowls of olives ready for guests when they arrived at the tables.

In my mind, I made a note to take the boys there when they were a bit older and could sit for a meal without a meltdown.

A pang of grief washed over me as I realized Papa would never get to meet my boys, and Linus wouldn't ever get to run around with his nephews.

I refused to allow their memories to fade away. I planned to do whatever I could to teach my boys about the two people who'd sacrificed so much for our family.

I peered down at the photograph. Gusto and Tobias dined together. "They sure look friendly. I can almost guess what they are celebrating a toast to."

"Assholes," Theo stated. "Well, this confirms they've banded together against us."

I looked over at the agents. "Is there more?"

"This is the latest for now."

"Thank you for the information. It's invaluable." I glanced toward Theo and Xander, waiting for them to speak.

"My estate—our estate, the Angelos estate—is on high alert. My teams have prepared for every eventuality. We'll stay safe if we return there," Xander's words conveyed confidence, indicating he'd implemented protections that far exceeded what was in place before my kidnapping.

Given that Solon orchestrated my abduction, I doubted anyone anticipated Xander or Theo sharing information about the security and protection upgrades implemented for our organization and property.

Xander and Theo had never trusted Solon. This sentiment was evident during my training with Devani two years ago. I expected their suspicions of the organization to lean more toward corruption than trustworthiness, especially now.

"Once we're safe and sound back home," Xander continued, "I recommend storming the compounds owned by the Stratos and Aetos families."

"Seriously?" I spun around sharply and glared.

"Yes. Fuck yes. End this shit, once and for all. It's gone on way too long," Xander replied, his eyes fiery with violent passion. "We have too much to lose to keep putting up with their threats and violence. Especially now."

"I agree, one hundred fifty percent," Theo said, nodding solemnly. "Everything has changed now. The stakes are a million times higher with the boys involved. We will protect our future. They are our future."

"So that's the plan? Storm both compounds simultaneously?" Davenport asked with a definitive nod. "I can have my men in place in days. It won't take long."

"We can take them out simultaneously, so they won't be able to warn each other," Deluca said.

I looked over at them, wanting to punch all of them in the face.

First of all, they hadn't considered my input. And second, their plan was fucking ridiculous.

They carelessly threw around half-baked solutions without considering their actions could have catastrophic effects.

Naturally, I wanted to conclude this game that had lasted for decades. We all wanted it to end, especially me. The thought of living in peace and raising our boys without constantly worrying every time we left the estate felt like a dream.

It wasn't possible with a strategy like this. Oh, it was so simple to go in guns blazing.

Sure, why not? Let's go storm the castle and have our heads shot off.

Idiots. Idiots with guns and no sense surrounded me.

Had any of them considered what would happen if Fiona was there? She could become collateral damage.

I refused to allow any of them to fuck this up.

Plus, there was a matter of knowing if we could trust Solon.

Right now, I wasn't so sure.

But everything in me screamed that Devani was the last person to betray me. She had gone out of her way to protect me and keep me safe. She had taken me under her wing and treated me like a sister. Then there were the countless hours she spent training me, molding me into what she liked to call a "ruthless assassin."

If it hadn't been for her, I wouldn't have survived the night, Andraius attacked me. No, Devani wouldn't betray me. There was genuine loyalty and trust between us.

However, I wasn't comfortable with the Solon team before me.

I needed to find a way to contact Devani. I had to find a way. There was no other choice.

Xander looked over at me, and I narrowed my gaze. He lifted his hands in surrender.

He cleared his throat. "The Angelos has something to say."

Everyone grew quiet as the energy of my agitation filled the space.

"It's interesting how you're making decisions for my family." I stood, placing my hands on the table, and glared at the agents across from me, including Xander and Theo. "Let's get this straight—nothing happens without my approval. These are my sons. It's my sister who is missing. I have the final say on any plans that are put in place."

"Are you objecting to what we have laid out?" Deluca asked. "We are trying to find your sister."

"I object for several reasons. First and foremost, you have no idea where Fiona is. Storming anyone's compound puts too many people at risk and increases the chance of innocent casualties. Second, we want to maintain our allies, not drive them to our enemies. Strategy is the way to defeat Aetos and Stratos. Is that understood?"

"What action do you suggest we take, Angel?" Xander asked.

I held Agent Davenport's gaze. "I think it's time to talk with your spies in the Aetos and Stratos families. Once you confirm Fiona's whereabouts, we'll decide on a solid course of action."

"What makes you think we have anyone on the inside?"

"All you've done since we met is trickle information to us. That's basic Solon 101." My phone vibrated in my pocket, but I ignored it, knowing only one person called me on that device. And the only way to read the message was to finish this discussion with Agent Davenport.

"And that tells you we have someone inside other families?"

"No, it tells me you are stringing us along as you gather your intel. I spent a lot of time with your director. She's taught me a thing or two."

Davenport's lips tightened a fraction. "Give me one hour."

"Thank you. I am going to stretch my legs and check on the boys." I pushed back from my chair and strode toward the hallway leading to Mama and my babies.

As soon as I turned the corner, I lifted my phone to glance at the incoming message.

DEVANI: Fiona isn't on either estate but in Boston. Find a way to get back home without being detected. Keep your family close, especially the boys.

I took a deep breath and replied, trying to keep my racing heart from bursting out of my chest.

ME: Want to expand on that last part? It's not like I'm stressed or anything.

I already anticipated what she would say. Just messaging me on the encrypted phone confirmed it. The hair on my neck stood up, and a wave of unease washed over me.

DEVANI: A few bad apples spoil the whole barrel, so I need to clean it.

Well, good luck to whoever fucked her over. They were going to have a painful end-of-life experience. Devani wasn't the forgiving type. And if they ran, it would only get worse. From the things I'd learned, Devani cleared her first assassination assignment at fourteen by sneaking into a military compound and slicing a general's throat.

If she could do that as a teenager, God knew what she could do as a seasoned director for a whole continent.

An unsettling thought crossed my mind. I hoped she never considered recruiting one or both of my boys for her organization. That was the last thing I needed to worry about.

I approached the room with Mama and the boys. The six soldiers stationed outside inclined their heads.

Seeing them eased some of my tension, and then I felt Theo and Xander's presence behind me.

"Let's go inside, and you tell us what's wrong." Theo settled a palm against my lower back.

Quietly, I opened the bedroom door and stepped inside.

I found Mama and the boys sound asleep on the king-sized bed. Charis slept with his head on Mama's belly, and Hayes napped against her other side, curled up in a little ball.

I couldn't help but sigh, seeing them so peaceful. Theo and Xander seemed to have the same sense of calm as they stood next to me, taking them in.

After a few seconds, Xander nudged us further into the room. "Let's go to the other side. Who messaged you, and what did it say?"

"You felt the vibration?"

"Your butt was right at my face. It's hard to miss."

Once we reached the far end of the room, I scanned the

area and took a deep breath before saying in Greek, "*We need to go back to Boston immediately.*"

Their gazes bore into mine with my language change, and then they nodded their understanding of the need to keep things private.

"*Are we taking Theia Delia and the boys with us, Angel?*" Theo asked, also in Greek.

I took a deep breath, frustration filling my soul. I wanted to keep Mama and my babies far away from Boston, but at this point, it was safer to have them with us.

"*We don't have any other choice. The only people we can trust are each other.*"

"*Understood. I'll get everything packed up,*" Xander said, walking away.

"*Wait,*" I said, putting out a hand to stop him, lowering my voice to a whisper. "*We can't let anyone know our plans. Keep it to yourself.*"

"*Yes, Angel,*" Xander assured me. "*You don't trust them either. I saw it in your eyes earlier. One of them is a mole.*"

I nodded.

Theo took my hand and kissed my palm, his eyes peering into mine. "*Are you okay?*"

"*I will be,*" I nodded. "*Eventually. Once I know we're safe.*"

"*We'd never let anyone hurt you or our sons,*" he whispered, planting another kiss on my palm.

It was a rare moment of gentle affection that was more precious than he could know. Everything was changing between us, but he was a constant. The dynamic we'd lived with for so long—the bickering, the electric tension, the push and pull mixed in with a tender, pure, unadulterated love.

"I know, Theo," I nodded, offering him a soft smile.

We turned to look at the sleeping boys together, and he put his arm around me, pulling me close.

"You made some beautiful babies."

"The three of us made them together," I whispered, leaning into his chest.

The boys' small chests rose and fell as they slept. They were completely at peace, unaware of the chaos surrounding them and the life they had been born into.

I desperately wanted them to have a life of safety and warmth, not chaos and competition. Unlike Theo's dread and regret regarding his heritage, I wanted them to grow up feeling deep affection for their family.

Papa and Mama had given me and my sisters everything I dreamt of for my babies. But nothing was guaranteed in our world, especially with its violence and rivalry. The best I could do was give them a normal upbringing for as long as possible.

I shook my head at that thought.

"What are you thinking?" Theo rested his chin on the top of my head.

"How impossible it will be to give Charis and Hayes a normal childhood when they have two enforcer fathers and a mother who is the Godmother of the Night for the Angelos Syndicate."

"It's not as if some suburban mother and an accountant

father raised you. Your parents brought you up in the middle of territory battles and all kinds of fuckery."

"Are you using me as the example of a model child?" I tilted my head to the side to peer up at him. *"If I recall, you hated my guts and would have thrown me off the nearest bridge if there was any way to get away with it."*

"It was hate-love, and once you weren't jailbait, I could fuck you into behaving."

"You're not even four years older than me. Jailbait, my ass."

All of a sudden, my mood shifted, and my heart clenched. *"Theo, I'm worried about Fiona."*

"Don't forget. She's the meanest and smartest one out of all four of you. If there is a way to fuck with someone, she'll do it."

"But what if they..." I trailed off, not wanting to describe the horror I imagined.

"Then we collect each of them and serve them to her in the Caves to exercise her rage."

I turned to face him, lifted onto my toes, and kissed him.

When we pulled back, Theo said, *"We have to prepare. Davenport will come looking for us soon."*

I nodded, and Theo exited the room.

I stayed in place for a few more seconds, aware that I couldn't escape my legacy or role in the family.

For those boys, Fiona, and my future with Theo and Xander, it was time to reclaim my role as the Angelos, Godmother of the syndicate. I'd destroyed my enemies once through calm, cold calculation and would do it again.

But this time, I would claim their power as collateral.

TWENTY

N ERINE

I was seriously demented.

Those are the only words to describe my mental state at this moment. Instead of feeling anxiety or fear, like any normal person would, all I wanted to do was jump on Xander and lick him all over.

Watching him handle Agents Davenport and Deluca was a masterclass in being an asshole.

Why I found it so damn sexy, I wasn't sure.

Perhaps it was because I seldom saw him in action. Whatever the reason, the wave of desire flowing through me felt inappropriate, given our circumstances.

Focus Nerine.

I tried to suppress my lust and remind myself that we were in a perilous situation, surrounded by enemies who could strike when we least expected it.

Usually, handling this type of thing landed on Theo with his unique calm and diplomacy skill set. However, we decided that Xander's bulldozer-enforcer demeanor was exactly what we needed to make our exit from this safe house. Theo's role in this production was more about pushing the agenda of leaving, while my large, unyielding man let his mean side out.

Once given the green light, all I had to do was stand back and watch Xander in action. In a split second, he shifted into his enforcer role, stalked into the kitchen where everyone was snacking, and informed Davenport that someone had compromised our location.

I couldn't deny observing the contrasting aspects of Theo and Xander's personalities in play was hot as hell. While Theo remained calm and collected in his public role, Xander was a force to be reckoned with, an asshole who didn't hesitate to get in the face of anyone who dared stand in his way.

It was funny how they were complete opposites when it came to me.

Deep down, a small part of me worried and hoped this confrontation wouldn't end in violence.

"What do you mean compromised?" Davenport asked in disbelief,

"What do you not understand?" Xander's voice dripped with anger and frustration as he explained, "You have a traitor, and they leaked the location of this safe house."

"That's impossible," Davenport said, waving her hand dismissively. "I know my people. They are loyal. Who told you this?"

"My sources," Xander replied through gritted teeth. "Just like you have yours, mine keep me informed of any threats to my business or my family's safety."

"I can assure you—" Deluca started.

But Xander interrupted him, his anger boiling over. "Say whatever the hell you want. But it doesn't change the fact that this place isn't safe anymore."

"Sir, this is the safest place for your family," Deluca insisted.

"Unfortunately, I disagree," Xander said. "We followed your rules, and now my family is in danger. It's time to follow mine."

"I'm not sure what you mean," Davenport said cautiously.

"We appreciate your help. However, it's time for us to go," Theo stepped toward them, taking on his role as peacemaker. "We've arranged for our own safe house."

"I see." Davenport nodded. "That's understandable. My men can arrange transportation for you if you give me a moment to gather them."

"No." Xander shook his head firmly. "We prefer to keep our location confidential. As Theo stated, we already have transportation on the way."

"With all due respect, sir, we have been assigned to protect you and your family." Deluca stepped forward, a determined look on his face.

Xander wasn't backing down, either. He closed the distance between them, getting right in Deluca's face.

"With all due respect, Deluca, we don't need your protection," Xander growled. He then turned his attention to Davenport and added, "Back down and let me protect my family."

Well fuck, this was getting out of hand and going to a level that wasn't necessary.

Tension hung thick in the air as Xander and the agent confronted each other.

I glanced at Theo. This was an ideal moment for him to step in or provide support.

Sensing my thoughts, he raised his gaze and shook his head.

I clenched my jaw. When did pushing Solon to the brink of explosion become part of the plan? We were dealing with a rogue assassin group with flexible morals. Had they forgotten this?

These men were going to push me to my breaking point. Now, all my warm and fuzzy feelings were gone completely.

I tried to calm my breath and prayed we made it out alive.

After a few tense seconds, Theo finally spoke up again. "We meant no disrespect, Agent Davenport. The news we received was unexpected and left us feeling vulnerable and uneasy. We believe that leaving is the best course of action to ensure our safety."

"We appreciate all of your efforts and support," I added, wanting to diffuse the tension. "Your team's protection was invaluable, and we are grateful for everything you have done for us. However, we will manage our own protection from this point forward."

"Very well. We will accept your decision despite our concerns." Davenport gave a curt nod, her eyes flickering between Xander and Deluca as if she anticipated a confrontation. "Let's clear our equipment and take our leave."

Deluca stepped back, his gaze still locked on Xander, who returned the intense stare.

"Thank you for your assistance," I said, trying to calm any remaining tension.

Davenport and her team began packing their equipment, and the sounds of zippers and Velcro filled the room.

Theo, Xander, and I made our way to our part of the house. Once we entered the living room of our suite and closed the door securely, I sighed, letting my body relax for the first time in hours.

"Great job," I said, shooting a sharp glance at Xander. "But you, hothead, could definitely improve your delivery."

He scoffed, "Whatever. That was part of the plan. Besides, you were eager for it, which got the job done."

I pursed my lips, recalling how his aggression had dulled my senses during the questioning. "Yes, until you crossed the line. Then all the tingles vanished because I thought you and Deluca were about to throw punches."

"I don't like it when anyone questions me," he muttered, running a hand through his messy hair and offering me an apologetic grin.

"Understandable." Theo chuckled. "But there's this thing called diplomacy. Maybe you've heard of it?"

Xander rolled his eyes and walked over to grab some bags. "I never claimed to be smooth."

"No, you did not." I laughed. "Okay, let's focus on getting out of here now that we've dealt with that obstacle."

"The car and driver are ready," Theo reported. "The decoys will join us as planned. Great idea, Angel."

"I've learned a few things from being around these agents," I replied before heading into the next bedroom, where Mama was waiting with the boys. "It's time to go."

She lifted Hayes into her arms, and I took Charis in mine. After getting into the car and speeding down the highway, I pulled out my phone and texted Devani to update her on our progress.

It was a long journey, with over three hours of driving and two vehicle changes, before we finally boarded a private plane bound for Boston. This time, I made sure to double-check that the pilot had filed a false manifest to throw off any unwanted attention.

The boys slept soundly throughout the flight, their calm demeanor offering a brief distraction from the flood of worst-case scenarios that filled my mind. Even as we descended into Boston and passed through the gates of the Angelos estate, my nerves still felt uneasy.

But as soon as the doors of our armored SUV swung open at the front entryway of the house and I stepped out, a wave of emotion washed over me.

My eyes took in the grandeur and beauty of the home I had left behind against my will two years ago. It held both some of my best and worst memories.

"Are you ready to go in?" Xander's voice broke through my thoughts as he and Theo stood on either side of me, each carrying one of our sleeping boys in their arms.

I intertwined my fingers with theirs. "I'm ready."

As we approached the front door, the Angelos soldiers paused their duties to acknowledge us. As they saluted and said, "Angelos," I couldn't help but think of my father, Papa, who was always larger-than-life and known as the Angelos.

A chill ran down my spine. "I am the Angelos."

"Yes," Theo and Xander replied in unison.

As I stepped through the threshold of the house, I took a deep breath, savoring all the familiar scents of my childhood home. It instantly stirred a wave of nostalgia. My eyes settled on a wall adorned with pictures of our family at various stages of life.

Glancing at my boys on either side, I couldn't help but worry that anyone who saw them would know about the three of us.

"They already knew about us," Xander lifted my hand to his lips and kissed my knuckles softly.

Theo squeezed my fingers in reassurance. "Devani kidnapped you from a bed we all shared. It's pretty clear."

I chuckled softly, momentarily forgetting about the past. "I almost forgot about that."

"Did someone say my name?" A sultry voice called from the open doors of the library ahead of us.

Of course, she found a way past our state-of-the-art security and into the house.

"Did you know she was here?" I asked Xander, who was in charge of security measures.

"I suspected. It's nearly impossible to keep her away from you, even if we tried," he replied in a deadpan tone. "She's like you and does what she wants."

I couldn't help but smile up at him, grateful for their protectiveness and understanding.

"Go talk to your kidnapper, and we'll help their *Yai Yai* put them to bed." Theo patted Charis's back.

"I'd rather join this conversation," Xander countered, his voice thick with determination. "Whenever those two get together, trouble always follows, and it only brings problems for the rest of us."

"You aren't invited," Devani said matter-of-factly.

Xander scowled and considered pushing the issue but ultimately decided it was pointless. He shrugged and followed Theo and Mama up the grand staircase toward the bedrooms.

After a minute, Devani and I retreated to the sanctuary and comfort of the library I loved and missed so much.

"You look radiant, Nerine," she stated with a warm smile toward me. "Motherhood certainly suits you."

"Thank you," I replied gratefully. "I am overjoyed to have my babies back in my life, even if it wasn't under ideal circumstances."

"I can only imagine. And I'm sure you're thrilled to be reunited with Theo and Xander." She winked mischievously.

She wore a stunning emerald green velvet bodysuit paired with a sleek black choker embellished with real black diamonds. "Is this your usual attire, or just for our meeting? Wearing millions of dollars in jewels for a visit to my house seems excessive, even for the socialite known as the Queen of Diamonds."

"I left a mind-numbing event for you. Plus," Devani hummed, running her fingers along the necklace. "I believe these jewels are the perfect accessory to welcome back the Godmother of the Night for the Angelos Family. I have a beautiful dagger that matches the necklace. Would you like to see it?"

"You are seriously disturbed."

"I never claimed otherwise." She settled gracefully onto a couch across from me, exuding an air of feline grace. "Now, let's get down to business. You have some decisions to make, Godmother."

"Yes, like how to finally destroy my enemies once and for all."

Her laughter rang out like a bell, filling the room. "It warms my heart to see you haven't lost your spark."

"My time of hiding and running is over," I said as a vow. "First, we find Fiona, and then we will end it with everyone else."

"Determination looks good on you."

"Thank you." I held her dark gaze. "What information do you have on Fiona?"

"I can say one thing about your baby sister: she is brilliant," Devani smirked, a playful grin tugging at the corners of her lips. "And resourceful."

"You know where she is. I fucking knew it. Tell me right now, or I will kill you," I warned through gritted teeth.

Devani raised an eyebrow in a challenge. "I'd like to see you try."

I wouldn't last more than two seconds in a fight with her. Devani was five foot two on a good day, but the assassin knew every trick in the book and could toss her six foot four, one hundred eighty-pound husband on his ass.

My chances of survival were slim to none.

"Fine, I concede. Only in my imagination could I take you in a fight. Happy? Now tell me where my sister is."

A smirk tipped the corner of her lips. "Fiona is safe and sound, tucked away in one of my properties."

"She's what?" I jumped up from my seat. "Start from the beginning."

"There was no abduction. When Aetos's men came for her, she had the foresight to hide in the panic room in her closet. At least one Angelos knows how to follow instructions."

"If only she had been smart enough not to write that damn tell-all romance novel," I grumbled, folding my arms across my body. "Go on."

"She called me as soon as she found a safe location. She told me that she had just returned from a run when the security system notified her of a break-in at the back door of her townhouse. Without hesitation, she quickly retreated to the closet and hid."

I could only imagine the fear and panic that coursed

through her when she saw Aetos's men. They were notorious for their lack of civility and their imposing size.

"While in the safe room, she listened through the speaker system and overheard them discussing using her as leverage. Then they received a call mentioning something about your boys and that Fiona was no longer important. Their new objective was to take Charis and Hayes."

A shiver slid down my spine. "Oh, dear God!"

"She knew she had to get a warning to you, but they stayed in the townhouse for hours searching the place. Once they finally left and she felt safe, she grabbed whatever cash she had and snuck out through a bedroom window. Since she was too scared to use a credit card, she paid for a hotel room for a few days with the cash before contacting me."

"Why didn't she contact me?"

"She was worried they had tapped your phone and were watching you. That's the same reason she didn't reach out to your mother. The next day, when she sneaked into your mother's house, she found it ransacked and searched, which only increased her fears. She didn't know if anything had happened to you or the boys or if you were hiding together. She finally bought a burner phone."

My heart raced, and my hands shook at the thought of what could have happened.

"I can't believe this!" I exclaimed, my voice trembling with pent-up emotion. "Thank God she's alive. These fuckers will stop at nothing for revenge."

I couldn't shake the image of Xander's face when I revealed the truth about how Zoe had died. The pain and anguish etched into every line of his features haunted me, even now. And now they were targeting my sons; it was almost unbearable.

But in this life, there was no space for weakness or mercy. I understood the cruelty of my enemies all too well. They had taken my father and younger brother.

They showed no regard for targeting innocent children. To them, Zoe and Linus were not enough. The coldness and brutality of their actions no longer shocked me.

It left me feeling disgusted.

Still, it wasn't about my feelings or how much I hated the way things had to unfold. The only way to defeat them was to play by all of their dirty and despicable rules. Anything less would mean certain death in this game.

My heart skipped a beat as I thought about Fiona's safety. Was she really being guarded well enough? The idea of any harm coming to her because of this book made me want to scream.

"Are you sure she's safe?" I asked Devani, my stomach twisting in knots.

"She's fine, Nerine. You don't need to worry," Devani assured me, running a hand through her wild curls.

"All of this over a book," I muttered with a sigh and then shook my head in disbelief.

"But it was a damn good book." Devani laughed, winking at me playfully. "You have to admit that."

I couldn't bring myself to agree. "No, not at all," I argued.

"Come on, Nerine! That double penetration scene? It was delicious!" she teased, her eyes sparkling mischievously.

I felt my cheeks flush with embarrassment. "Devani, please ... never mention those words again," I pleaded.

"What about that one scene where the heroine was tied up and pleasured by her two lovers at once? Oh my god, it was pure fire!" Devani continued, ignoring my discomfort.

"Stop!" I cried, covering my ears with my hands. "Please, no more!"

"How can you be such a prude when you are living the experiences in that book?" She laughed.

"I am not a prude," I retorted defensively. "I simply prefer to keep my personal life private. And I have no idea where Fiona got these ideas from. I certainly don't discuss my sex life with my little sister."

"Well, it's not hard to imagine why Fiona wrote those scenes. Just look at the way Theo and Xander stare at you every time you enter the room," Devani pointed out. "I know they've fucked you senseless plenty since they found you in Vegas. I'm surprised you can walk straight."

"It's not like—" But I stopped myself, knowing there was no point in arguing. "I'm not discussing this anymore."

"I rest my case. Prude."

I glared at her and stood up, making my way to the bar cart in the corner of the room. Pouring generous amounts of whiskey into snifters for both of us, I returned and handed one to Devani before sitting down next to her.

After taking a hefty swallow and allowing the alcohol to settle my nerves, I said, "I'm considering a drastic move, Devani. I need your guidance. It's a dangerous risk."

"In this lifestyle, any decision you make has risks. You are the head of your organization. Your choices have consequences for everyone you lead."

"Exactly. That's what worries me."

"What are you afraid of, specifically?"

"Failure? Bringing more pain to my family? I'm trying to end these rivalries, but will they ever stop? Is that even possible? Or am I doomed to a life filled with fear? I have my sons now, Devani. Everything has changed. The game has shifted. It's not just my life and the lives of my sisters and mother that are at risk here."

"That's true," she said slowly, nodding as she took in my words. "But please, Nerine, allow me to remind you of a few things you seem to forget."

"Please do. I welcome your insight," I replied, leaning back and sipping my whiskey.

Knowing Fiona was safe, the chaos of everything else I tried to manage churned and bubbled, building like a caldera ready to explode.

The weight of my responsibilities felt burdensome, pressing down on me and reminding me that my actions had consequences.

"What is your name?" Devani asked, peering at me as if she could see deep into my soul.

She was breathtakingly beautiful with her dark golden skin and striking onyx eyes. She had the power to topple dynasties with her skill. She was formidable, unyielding, and cunning. I was grateful she was on my side, as the thought of having her as an enemy sent shivers down my spine.

"Seriously?" I scoffed. "I know who I am, Devani."

"Do you?" she asked. "Say it out loud."

I frowned. "I'm Nerine Angelos."

"No. Who are you?"

I sighed. What over-dramatic game was she playing now? Fine. I'd humor her.

"I am Nerine, the Godmother of the Night, Queen of the Angelos Syndicate. The soldiers call me the Angelos Angel."

"Stand up," she instructed, reaching for my hand and pulling me to my feet.

I let out an exasperated sigh and stood up, letting her lead me to a large mirror on the wall opposite the towering bookcases. It was a priceless antique, intricately gilded in gold and ornately carved in the eighteenth century by a renowned artist whose name I had long forgotten. I vividly recall walking in on my father one day and catching him admiring his reflection in it.

It had been one of the last days of his life, and that image had lingered with me for years afterward. I hadn't thought about it in a while, but the memory surfaced as I stood there. I studied myself closely, noticing subtle changes I hadn't noticed before.

My eyes felt different. Perhaps it was simply the effects of childbirth, but they appeared older now—more solemn and reflective. I couldn't quite pinpoint it until Devani spoke again.

"Repeat your name," she instructed, soft and gentle yet commanding.

I took a deep breath before speaking, attempting to

steady the nerves fluttering in my stomach. "Nerine, Godmother of the Night, Queen of the Angelos Syndicate."

"That's right," she said, her gaze flickering over me with pride and surprise. "You aren't the same woman who left this place two years ago, Nerine."

She pointed at my eyes, her finger tracing a line along the dark circles created from years of sleepless nights and stress.

Devani nodded approvingly. "That's right. You have grown and changed since you left this place two years ago, my dear. You are undeniably more mature and graceful now—physically, emotionally, and mentally. You have become wiser and stronger from all that you've experienced." She pointed to my eyes. "Your gaze holds a newfound confidence and determination. You have shed the selfishness of youth, the rebellious spirit of your past, and the uncertainty of your leadership."

I couldn't ignore Devani's words. I had tried my best to maintain a brave front as I stepped into Papa's role as head of the family, but doubts and fears continuously crept in. Even when I killed Andraius, it had been with a trembling hand and a fearful heart.

"You slayed that weak version of yourself while you were away, Nerine," she stated.

She was right once more. Pregnancy, giving birth, and the miracle of holding my cherished sons in my arms have transformed me profoundly and irrevocably. Moreover, leaving them with my mother and going into hiding has changed me as well.

It had given me an unbreakable strength I didn't even know I possessed.

"Fate placed you in this body, right?" Devani continued, her eyes searching mine. "Look at you. Your flesh, bones, and blood carry the genes of those who came before you. When I look at you, I see your father. I see your mother. And your grandparents too. They're all a part of you. That reality is something you will never change. Like those who came before, you couldn't choose to be anyone else."

She paused, taking a sip from her glass and letting me absorb her words.

"Tell me, Nerine," she said, leaning slightly forward. "Did your father tremble in fear? Your grandfather? Of course, they did. And did they waver? Did they doubt themselves? Sure, maybe. But did they hesitate to strike when it came to defending themselves, their loved ones, or even the family business and fortune? No, they did not. They stepped up, claimed their rightful place in a long line of Angeloses, and took charge when it was their moment. Did they make mistakes?"

I scoffed and shook my head. "Plenty."

"Exactly," Devani confirmed. "And now you have to clean up those mistakes and carry on the legacy. But that is your responsibility as an Angelos."

I gazed into the mirror, locking eyes with my reflection. The resemblance to my paternal grandfather was uncanny at that moment, and I couldn't help but feel a shiver run down my spine. I shared so many of his features—those same ones passed down to Papa.

"Duty," I repeated Devani's words with a bitter laugh.

"Nerine, what name will you give your sons? Will they take the Angelos name?"

The conversation on the plane with Theo and Xander came to mind. Xander and Theo intended to take my last name, suggesting they believed the boys would do the same. That was convenient, given that their birth certificates already listed them as Angeloses.

"Yes," I replied with a sense of pride and determination. "They already have it."

Devani turned away from her reflection in the mirror and poured herself another glass of whiskey. I sat beside her on the couch, feeling thankful for her company.

She took a healthy sip of her drink and said, "And before we know it, those precious babies will grow into men, trying to make sense of their heritage and place in this chaotic world as descendants of the Angelos name. The choices you make now will shape their future."

Her words struck me deeply. While I understood my actions would affect my children's lives, I hadn't fully comprehended their weight until now. My head swirled with thoughts and concerns.

"I don't know who to trust besides Theo, Xander, and my mother," I sighed. "And you, of course," I added with a smirk.

Devani was more than just a friend; she was a mentor and a confidante in a way I never realized I needed. Women like her are rare. She was a decade older than me, possessing the knowledge and experience to tell me when I messed up and to help me without expecting anything in return.

"And therein lies the problem," she said wearily. "I'm facing similar issues with the Solon agents. But technically, I'm not supposed to involve myself in these matters. It annoys the current director."

"What about your husband? Won't he object?"

"He can object, but I do what I want." She pursed her lips. "He knows who he married. Besides, if I let him help me occasionally, he isn't so grouchy about it."

I wasn't going to touch that with a ten-foot pole. The thought of anyone 'letting' her husband, who was a ruthless underworld boss, do anything was something I couldn't imagine. Still, it made sense that two psychos fell in love.

Instead of holding onto that train of thought, I informed her, "I'm considering something so drastic it will drown out any traitors on my side."

Curiosity sparked in Devani's eyes. "I can't wait to hear about it."

"It's merciless," I warned her, then I smirked. "You may think less of me after hearing it."

She shook her head. "You are the Angelos godmother, my dear. I have nothing but respect for you. Also, I've got a few years under my belt with the merciless thing."

"I bet."

"Before you ask, I'm here if you need help. However, it's time to have confidence in yourself, your decisions, and your power as an Angelos. You were born for this role and have spent your whole life learning things you may not even realize. Trust your instincts."

Goosebumps prickled my skin as Devani's words sliced through my doubts and insecurities.

"Thank you," I said sincerely. "Your belief in me means more than you know."

"I wouldn't have taken you under my wing if I didn't see potential in you," she reminded me.

I was the Godmother, the Angelos Queen.

And it was time to start acting like one.

Taking a deep breath, I shared my plan with her, feeling the fire of vengeance blaze within me.

"Alright, here's what I'm thinking," I started. "We're going to put an end to these feuds once and for all. It might get messy. There could be bloodshed. It may even backfire and ruin everything that generations have built. But perhaps, just perhaps, it will succeed."

Devani's eyes lit up with excitement. "Oh, now I'm intrigued."

"Once we plot out the initial plan, I want to bring in Xander and Theo."

"Of course. But first, make sure your house is in order. Your men are quite excitable and might object to several of our decisions."

"I believe you are right. Timing is crucial." I extended my hand to Devani. "Come sit at my desk, Director Patel-King. It's time to stir things up."

TWENTY-ONE

T HEO

The grand foyer of the Angelos estate was a stunning sight. The crystal chandelier above sparkled with a rainbow of colors, casting a warm glow over the Italian white marble floors that gleamed underfoot.

As we gathered at the base of the grand staircase, my heart swelled with both awe and respect for Nerine, who stood with confident grace at the center of it all.

She radiated power and authority.

Her hair, now restored to its original lustrous black, fell in an elegant cascade down her back. She donned a suit made of the finest French silk. The black pencil skirt hugged her curves closely, accentuating her shapely frame, and her tall black suede heels added inches to her already regal stature. She commanded the room like a queen on her throne.

But beneath her polished exterior, I could see the changes that motherhood had brought Nerine. She was no longer the insecure girl forced into a cruel marriage or the abused woman living in fear. Now, she stood before us as a determined and confident leader, commanding the undivided attention of her loyal soldiers, who remained at attention at her feet.

I couldn't help but feel a wave of desire for this beautiful and strong woman. My cock throbbed painfully in my pants as I imagined her in bed, naked and writhing in pleasure.

Our Angel had never looked more stunning.

Nerine's favored soldiers stood at the front of the line, their faces filled with reverence and deep respect for their leader. This respect was well-deserved. Nerine had taken excellent care of them and their families over the years under Andraius, often at a personal cost, earning their undying loyalty through trust and devotion.

"First and foremost," Nerine began, calmly addressing her soldiers. "I want to thank each of you for your unwavering loyalty to my family. Your efforts have not gone unnoticed and will be generously rewarded."

She took a deep breath, her breasts rising and falling in the perfectly tailored suit that hugged her frame. I couldn't tear my eyes away as she continued to address her men.

She gestured to a group of five men to her side.

"Georgios," she said to the soldier nearest her. "I'm assigning you the most important task of all. Your responsibility is to ensure my mother's and sons' safety. Your team must never leave them unprotected, not even for a second. Our enemies will stop at nothing to harm them."

Georgios, one of her longest-serving soldiers and the group leader, stepped forward with a confident nod. "You can count on me, Angelos. We will protect your family. Nothing will happen to them while I'm on duty."

"Thank you, Georgios," Nerine said, recognizing his dedication and loyalty.

"As for the rest of you," she addressed her other soldiers, "stand by for further orders. In the meantime, keep a sharp lookout on the estate from all sides. We could be attacked at any moment."

With one final commanding glance at her soldiers, Nerine dismissed them.

I felt proud and inspired by this powerful woman who had claimed her rightful position as the Godmother of the Angelos family. Xander and I stood back willingly, knowing we would always stand beside her and support her every move.

With a confident stride and a serious expression, Xander beckoned me to a secluded corner near the foyer. "She's back where she belongs," he said in a hushed tone.

"I'd be lying if I said her confidence didn't make my cock rock hard," I admitted. "I want to fuck her so badly right now."

"Same here," Xander murmured in agreement. "There's just something about her that's so damn sexy."

"The session with Devani in the library helped her more

than I initially realized," I remarked. "She has stopped constantly worrying and questioning everything and has accepted herself and her role. Especially today. She's wearing her godmother's cloak like a weapon."

"Her whole demeanor is as calm as a winter lake," Xander observed, a hint of caution in his voice. "It makes me nervous."

"I wonder what Devani said to create this change," I replied. "Have you managed to get any information from our angel?"

"No luck." He shook his head. "And you?"

"Not yet," I sighed. "We need to tread carefully, or we won't get a single answer out of her. Remember, she's stubborn on a good day."

"There is also a chance she'll eat us alive." Xander chuckled wryly. "We've tasted her sharp tongue plenty of times before."

"Best to avoid it then," I agreed, gripping my hair in frustration.

"Do you have any idea what her plan is?" I asked Xander, nodding toward Nerine, who was engaged in a deep conversation with Georgios.

"All she told me was that she needed to get her household in order before she could bring us in," he replied with a frown. "I don't like it."

I thought for a few moments, trying to work out the possibilities of what Nerine planned.

Then it hit me.

"I have a feeling she plans to call a gathering of representatives from all the New England families, including the Aetos family," I speculated.

"It won't be easy. Aetoses rarely attend and only if they see value in it," Xander added, his gaze never leaving Nerine.

"If that's her plan, we better prepare for trouble," I warned. "Remember the last meeting?"

"How could I forget?" Xander scoffed. "It turned into a bloodbath, and our angel even ended up stabbing someone."

"Exactly," I nodded grimly. "We have to protect Nerine at all costs. The danger could come from any direction."

"And she'll fight us every step of the way," Xander added.

"She can insist on whatever she wants," I said firmly. "I'm not letting her out of my sight."

"Me neither," Xander vowed fiercely.

"It's like some twisted game of chess," I muttered in frustration. "We're constantly strategizing against each other, even though we're supposed to be on the same side."

"Yeah, she drives me crazy sometimes, too," Xander admitted with a small smile.

"I suppose that's just part of being in love with an angel," I replied with a gentle sigh.

Nerine's piercing cobalt gaze found us, urging us to follow her down the hallway and into the library. Xander and I trailed closely behind like eager puppies, unable to resist her.

Once inside the library, Nerine turned to face us with her arms crossed and one stiletto-clad foot pointed to the side. She exuded confidence and sex appeal, making it almost impossible for me to keep my hands off her. My arousal was evident as I felt my cock twitch.

"I know that look on your faces," she stated, a smirk playing at the corners of her lips. "Standing in the corner together, whispering. What are the two of you planning?"

She scanned our faces with a critical eye before continuing.

"Crossing your arms like that makes you look like an army sergeant. Is that what you're aiming for? Are you planning to discipline us?"

My question brought a faint blush to her cheeks. However, before she could respond, Xander interrupted.

"We're waiting for your orders, Angel."

His words lingered in the air because I had nothing to contribute. Technically, what he said was true; we hadn't developed a solid plan yet.

Nerine's lovely face scrunched up as she appeared lost in thought. At last, she directed her attention to Xander.

"Did you search this room for any monitoring devices?"

Xander's jaw twitched in irritation, a sign I recognized all too well. He took his responsibilities seriously and had undoubtedly checked every room in the house. Nerine questioning his diligence would surely irritate him.

But then she winked, and the tension dissipated as we shared a gentle laugh.

She knew as well as I did how meticulous Xander could be, not only in his job but also in other aspects.

"This stays between us," she began, her tone serious. "But I know where Fiona is now. She's safe."

"Why can't we tell our soldiers?" Xander asked. "Or your mother?"

"I'm worried about Mama's reaction," Nerine sighed. "She's extremely worried right now and won't be able to keep this to herself. She'll spill the news to all the wrong people that we've found Fiona. I can't take that risk. As for our soldiers, I'm not sure who we can trust with this information. So, for now, we trust no one."

"That complicates things," I said, glancing over at Xander to gauge his reaction, which was unreadable.

"You're telling me," Nerine muttered as she paced the room. Frustrated, she ran a hand through her long, dark hair. "Fucking Fiona and her need to dive headfirst into things. Even if it wasn't intentional, that book messed us up, and now we're stuck in the middle of this damn mess."

"True," I agreed, aware that Nerine was nowhere near finished with the rant bursting out of her.

She walked over to the window, still muttering under her breath. "I mean, what was she thinking? She didn't think. That's the problem! She never thinks things through. She's always so stubborn and convinced she's right about everything! It's infuriating! I hoped she'd grow out of it before she could cause real damage. Well, that was a big mistake."

Her voice grew louder as she started to pace.

I shared a smirk with Xander.

I restrained the impulse to tell Nerine that, in many ways, she had just described herself. Stubbornness appeared to run deep in the Angelos family, and perhaps it was some inherited trait. In fact, Nerine was likely the most stubborn of them all.

This wasn't good. At least one, if not both, boys were bound to take after their mother in this.

"Tell us where she is," Xander interjected, trying to get her back on track. "Do we need to mount a rescue mission?"

His urgent tone sliced through the tense atmosphere like a knife. "Please, tell us where she is. Is she in danger? Do we need to rally help for a rescue mission?"

Nerine shook her head, frustration etched into every line of her face.

"There's no rush. She doesn't need rescuing. She's been safe this whole time." She released a heavy sigh. "Fiona was inside her penthouse when the Aetos's men broke in. She managed to hide and overheard their conversation and plans to abduct Hayes and Charis."

"Who do I have to kill then?" My anger burned bright at the thought of anything happening to those babies.

"No one. Not yet, anyway," Nerine replied, the furrow between her brows deepening. "Fiona staged her kidnapping to protect the boys. She was too scared to seek help but finally reached out to Devani."

"Are you saying she orchestrated all of this?" I asked, unsure if I had grasped the situation correctly.

"In a way, yes," Nerine said with a wry shake of her head. "Can you believe that?"

I snorted in response. Considering it was Fiona, it wasn't too far-fetched an idea.

"But that doesn't make sense," Xander interjected, his

confusion evident in his tone. "Staging her kidnapping doesn't address the issues that drove her into hiding in the first place."

"And who exactly was planning to take the boys? Aetos, Santos, or one of their allies?" I demanded, my blood boiling with rage. "That's the first thing we need to figure out."

"You're right," Nerine said grimly, her eyes glinting with determination. "I'm tired of all of this. I have a plan to end it once and for all.

"What's your plan?" Xander asked cautiously, studying her closely.

"I'm going to fight fire with fire," Nerine whispered darkly, sending chills down my spine. "Our enemies have shown no mercy, using our families and children as leverage. They killed my brother and Zoe, all for some twisted vendetta that can only be satisfied with the blood of innocent children. What kind of monsters do that?"

"Those that deserve to burn in hell," I growled, sensing where she was headed and hating every word.

"We have to show them that we are not weak. If sacrificing the lives of their beloved and innocent family members is the only way to get through to them, then that's what we'll do," Nerine declared, lifting her chin defiantly.

The darkness in her eyes was chilling, filling me with dread for what she was about to propose.

"Wait ... are you suggesting we kill the youngest children of our enemies?" Xander's disbelief was palpable in his words.

"I am," Nerine confirmed, a menacing edge creeping into her voice. "But not just one child. All of them."

Twenty-Two

Nerine

I waited, allowing my words to sink in, knowing an explosion was imminent, considering the gravity of the situation.

"Nerine. Are you freaking kidding me?" Xander exclaimed, his voice rising in alarm and disbelief, his eyes wide with shock. "You can't be serious."

"You won't do that. Tell me I heard it wrong." Theo stared at me as if he was seeing someone he never met before. "All of who?"

I lifted my chin, "All of their children."

They both shook their heads, their skepticism rolling off them in waves.

"No, I refuse to believe you would do something like this." Theo gripped the back of his neck.

Xander walked toward me but suddenly halted, staring with eyes filled with horror and confusion.

I hated the way they looked at me. Hopefully, once I explained my reasons, they would accept them. My plan was cold, calculating, and cruel. There was no denying that. But this was the only way to make a powerful statement and push our enemies into submission.

"We need to hear every single detail of your plan, Angel," Xander growled, struggling to maintain his composure but failing. "You might as well have detonated a bomb."

"Why do you think I brought you in here?" I gestured to the library surrounding us.

"No, you're not doing it!" Xander roared, unable to contain his anger any longer.

I narrowed my gaze but maintained my calm. "It's already in motion."

"What the fuck do you mean it is in motion?" Xander asked, anger burning in every word.

There was no trace of the patience he typically showed toward me. That part of Xander was completely absent.

I anticipated this reaction from Theo, not from Xander. My relationship with Theo was explosive and volatile, while with Xander, it was gentle and calm. However, it seems that the roles have reversed.

"Exactly what I said, Xander." I held his furious, dark stare.

Theo approached me. "Let me guess, Devani is involved

in this. Taking children is right up her alley. And if one dies, that's just collateral damage."

"That's right," I confirmed, staying composed despite their explosive reactions and my irritation that they could think I had become a ruthless child killer.

Dumbasses.

I wasn't a heartless killer and would never stoop to such lows. However, that didn't mean I wouldn't use children as leverage if necessary. It was all part of the game.

Locking eyes with them defiantly, I said, "With Devani's help and a few personal connections, I've gathered a reliable team from the Drakos and Mykos conglomerates. They are quietly accumulating assets from the families we intend to target."

"Assets?" Xander repeated in disbelief, his eyes widening even further. "You mean their children?"

"Yes," I replied with a nonchalant shrug. "But discreetly, of course. Most of these families rarely pay attention to their children anyway. They're typically sent off to some boarding school or left in the care of nannies. This way, they won't suspect our true intentions until it's too late."

"Nerine, how could you implement such an extreme plan without consulting us first?" Theo asked, becoming increasingly frustrated. "This is incredibly dangerous."

Xander's expression turned from shock to anger.

"This is not a good plan at all, Angel," he fumed. "You should have thought this through more carefully before taking action."

"Oh? Are we arguing about who's in charge again?" I

shot back, my patience wearing thin as their criticism persisted.

"That's not what we meant!" Theo protested, his dark eyes flashing with frustration and anger.

"I'm not questioning your authority!" Xander added quickly.

"No?" I challenged, raising an eyebrow sarcastically. "Just my judgment then?"

Xander released an exasperated growl and turned away as Theo approached to confront me.

"We all share the same goal here, Angel. We want to keep our boys safe. But this is an incredibly risky plan you're suggesting," he said, his voice filled with concern.

"It's more than a proposal," I reminded them firmly. "It's already in motion."

"Goddammit!" Xander exclaimed, throwing his hands up in exasperation. "What the hell is wrong with you?"

I was over this anger. I wasn't their subordinate. I was the fucking Angelos.

I stayed quiet, trying to calm my temper, especially as the tension in the room felt thick and suffocating around us.

Once I gathered my sanity enough not to throw a knife at one of them, I said, "I would never harm innocent children. You know this."

"What game are you playing, Nerine? Don't you trust us?" Xander asked, his words filled with disappointment. "Is that the issue? Is that why you've withheld so much from us after all this time?"

My blood boiled at his accusations.

Theo chimed in, his voice filled with frustration. "Is this how you want things to be now?"

"Now you're not even listening," I said, my voice rising in anger.

"Learning about it after the fact is insulting," Theo agreed. "Why don't you trust us?"

"Of course, I trust you!" I insisted, keeping my voice steady and calm despite my raging emotions. "Why do you think I'm telling you this now?"

"You should have told us sooner!" Theo shouted.

His face was flushed red, his eyes small and unyielding. His fists clenched at his sides as he paced back and forth in front of me.

His unreasonable behavior only intensified my anger. How dare he question me like this?

"You question my authority?" I shouted, getting right in his face. "Have you forgotten who I am, Theo?"

We stood facing each other, our noses inches apart, our breaths warm against each other's skin. Theo's dark eyes blazed with fierce anger, and for a moment, I felt a familiar fire ignite deep in my belly.

"As if that's even a possibility," Theo sneered. "You never let us forget for a second, do you?"

Anger pulsed between us, the tension thick and palpable. Xander stood by, undoubtedly ready to step in if things escalated. At least, he chose to revert to his usual role of peacemaker between Theo and me.

"Tell me," I asked, lowering my voice to a dangerous whisper. "Would you question my father's judgment the same way you're questioning mine? Would you expect him to consult his subordinates before making a decision?"

Theo's eyes widened with frustration. "It's not the same thing."

"It's the same thing," I pressed, waiting expectantly with a raised brow. "Tell me how it isn't."

He didn't respond.

"Since Theo has no answer, maybe you can respond for him, Xander." I pressed on, waiting expectantly with a raised eyebrow.

There was no response from Xander either.

At that moment, we all knew I was right. Whether they appreciated the reminder or not, I was still speaking the truth.

"You wanted me in this role. Now I'm doing my job," I explained, my voice rising. "I'm protecting my people. To do that, I must display my power and claim it as my own. The other families need to see this and understand that I am in charge. When I left, everything I gained disappeared! This time, it will only be worse."

"We're not questioning that!" Xander insisted.

"No, you just want me to run everything by you first, and why?" I shot my words out like sharp daggers, fueled by the anger and frustration boiling inside me. "Because you don't trust me to make smart decisions? Do you think I don't see the seriousness of my role? I know exactly who I am. Even in my darkest moments, I've never forgotten when I wished to be anyone but myself. For years, I prayed to wake up in someone else's body. But not anymore!"

My voice rose to a roar as I stood before them, my chest heaving with emotion. "Now, I stand proud before you, the Godmother of the Night, Queen of the Angelos family. It would be wise for both of you to remember that."

"As we mentioned earlier, we could never forget either," Theo's gentle words acted as a soothing balm on my simmering anger, immediately easing the tension in the room. "You mean everything to us."

I took a deep breath and exhaled slowly, feeling the fire within me fade. Theo and Xander may not always see eye to eye with me or understand my decisions, but their trust in me was all that mattered. We were a team bound by blood and purpose. Together, we could face anything that came our way.

I loved these men with every fiber of my being.

We were meant to present a united front, working together as a team. Perhaps my men were correct that I should have consulted them, but I was trying to make things right at that moment. Time was of the essence.

"Theo," I turned to him, my eyes softening as I spoke. "I am so grateful for your unwavering loyalty and service to my family while I was away. I know it wasn't easy. And while I value your advice, there are times when I must follow my instincts. When I am certain about a path, you both need to trust that it is the right decision for our family."

"I thought we were equals," Theo interjected, his hurt lingering in his tone.

Heat radiated off his body, and despite our current disagreement, I couldn't help but admire his powerful form.

"I am the one ultimately in charge," I stated firmly. It was time for them to accept that.

My tone might have been harsh, but I needed to get through to them once and for all. I stood tall with my arms crossed over my chest.

That's when Xander stepped closer, encroaching on my personal space from the other side. His dark eyes locked onto mine as he challenged me.

"I am the boss," I insisted, forcing myself not to reveal any signs of fear.

We all knew they were physically stronger than I was and could overpower me if they wanted to. But deep down, I was certain that wouldn't happen because we were a team.

But leave it to them to always take things personally.

I couldn't help but think it was a man thing. They always seemed to need to assert their dominance, especially in front of a strong woman. It was frustrating.

Xander's eyes roamed over my body. When they met mine again, a hint of desire mixed in with his remaining upset. My body responded immediately, my core pulsing with need as I fought to keep my composure.

"Look at you, Angel," he crooned. "Taking charge and standing firm in your 'take no prisoners' attitude, ready to bulldoze through the world without looking back."

He meant for his words to provoke me, but I refused to give him the satisfaction.

"You can mock me all you want, Xander, but that doesn't change the truth."

"We would never mock you," Theo said, his energy matching Xander's now. "We're only stating facts."

They were ganging up on me, communicating silently with each other, but I refused to let them intimidate me.

I lifted my chin. "Is that so?"

"You've changed, haven't you, Nerine?" Theo asked, his sharp gaze darting down to my exposed cleavage and then back up. He cocked his head to the side, analyzing me with a hunger that made my skin tingle. "Not just your full breasts you keep displaying. Or that curvy ass you keep sashaying around us seductively. But motherhood. It changed you in deeper ways, didn't it?"

He pushed a strand of hair away from my face, his fingers brushing my cheek and sending a shiver down my spine. I tried to resist their allure, but it felt almost impossible. My body fought against me every second of the way.

"You're stronger. More determined. More serious now," Xander added, stepping forward with an air of authority.

"Perhaps," I admitted, taking a deep breath to steady myself. "But that doesn't —"

"You want to seem more assertive. Is that right?" Theo interrupted me with a crooked smile as he closed the distance between us.

"Like I said, I'm in charge now."

"Of the Angelos estate? Of the Angelos fortune? Of the fate of the Angelos name?" Theo said, shrugging nonchalantly. "Sure."

"We're not questioning that, are we, Theo?" Xander interjected without even glancing at him.

Theo shook his head slowly, and together, they approached me with a sexy, sultry confidence.

I swallowed hard at the sight of the raw, savage hunger gleaming in their eyes.

Taking a step back, I found myself cornered against my mother's heavy wooden desk. It was her favorite piece—a seventeenth-century antique with intricately carved legs and corners, passed down through our family for generations. With my back pressed against it, I felt them closing in on me.

"No, we're not questioning that at all," Theo replied, his voice low and seductive, his intense gaze burning into mine. "But I believe it's important to clarify who is in charge when it comes to our relationship, Angel."

He reached up, cupping my chin and forcing me to meet his heated gaze.

"Surely, you haven't forgotten that, Nerine?" Theo growled.

The bastards.

Rage and lust battled within me. Theo and Xander knew precisely how to provoke my feelings buttons. How to make my insides melt. But I wasn't ready to give up that easily. I'd battle them every step of the way, if necessary.

"Our relationship is not relevant right now."

My words were a dare that hung between us, taunting them. The truth was that even in our most vulnerable, primal moments, no matter how much dominance they chose to display, we all knew I was still in charge. With just one word, I could shut the whole thing down.

But that didn't mean we didn't enjoy playing the game from time to time.

"Now that we know Fiona is safe and we're not in a rush to find her, maybe we should show you who's in charge here. Unless you need some convincing first?" Xander spoke with a hint of menace in his tone.

His words hung heavily in the air between us.

"This isn't a game," I insisted. "I mean what I said. I'm the—"

Xander scoffed, his eyes flashing with wicked intent. "You don't quit, do you?"

"About my family? No. Never."

He reached out and grabbed my wrist, his fingers encircling it tightly.

"Careful," he warned, his voice dropping to a low, rough tone.

"Or what?" I snapped, trying to pull my hand away, but his grip was unyielding.

I knew where he intended to take this. It always ended up being the same place—all three of us stripped bare, taking our frustrations out on each other.

But right now, I wanted them to take me seriously. I was tired of having to prove myself to everyone, especially them.

"This isn't happening!" I shouted.

Rage pulsed through my veins, desperate to escape the trap they had set for me. Drawing on the training I had received from Devani, I twisted my arm in the opposite direction, fighting against his grip until I forced him to release me.

I pushed them away with all my strength and jumped back against the door.

But before I could escape, Theo's hand shot out and grabbed my bicep, spinning me around to face him once more. My heart pounded as his lips crashed against mine, fierce and relentless. Suddenly, Xander's body pressed against my back, his mouth exploring the nape of my neck, sending shivers down my spine.

I cried out in protest, struggling to push them away once more. But their touch ignited a fire within me that I couldn't resist, even though my mind screamed for me to. Xander's fingers found my nipple, expertly pinching it and causing another cry to escape from my lips.

Driven by anger and desire, I broke free from their hold and turned to confront them.

"No!" I exclaimed, resolute in my decision to defend myself. "If you can't acknowledge my strength, I won't offer you my body!"

"Angel," Xander growled possessively. "We've known about your power since we were kids."

"But here, when we're alone," Theo added, "you belong to us. Don't forget that."

Despite their words, fear still churned inside me.

But as I lifted my chin defiantly, I felt a spark of desire ignite again.

"I'm the boss," I declared boldly, though the strength in my voice wavered.

Theo said softly, "You are our leader."

"The one in charge," Xander whispered with reverence.

They reduced the distance between us until I found myself pressed against the desk once more. My heart raced as I stood before them, looking up into their eyes, searching for any sign of acceptance, understanding, or respect.

Was this it? Had they finally accepted my power and comprehended who I was? Or were they using their typical hypnotic magic to undermine my resolve?

Xander's hand pushed my blazer aside, sliding it down my arms before carelessly tossing it onto the floor behind the desk. As he did this, my once-strong determination crumbled beneath his touch.

Theo's hands were now at the hem of my camisole, slowly peeling it off my body and flinging it behind him. Xander took hold of my hips and turned me around as he unzipped my skirt, and then four eager hands slid it down over my thighs.

Turning back to face them, I stepped out of my skirt and stood before them in nothing but my black lace bra and panties. The French lace stockings, held up by a matching garter belt and stiletto heels, completed the seductive ensemble.

Their hungry eyes scanned every inch of me, sparking a fire within them that radiated warmth against my bare skin.

Theo leaned in close on my right side, his warm breath brushing against my ear as he whispered words that sent shivers down my spine.

"Yes, we know who you are, my love," Theo's voice was low and seductive as he spoke to me. "But here, behind closed doors with us? Don't deceive yourself."

I gasped and turned my head to face him, but he captured my mouth in a searing kiss before Xander's fingers grazed my chin. He pulled me away from Theo's embrace, his intense gaze holding me captive.

"You know he's right," his words dripped with a dangerous edge. "Once the public's eyes are no longer on us, the power dynamic shifts. You may rule your soldiers, but you'll never truly control us. Don't even think about pretending otherwise."

He threaded his fingers through my hair and tugged my head back. Instantly, a surge of desire shot through me.

Theo's hand slid between my legs, his palm pressing firmly against the thin lace covering my soaked center. I shuddered at the heat radiating from his touch.

"Already wet for us, aren't you?" He chuckled darkly. "See? You are ours. This sweet pussy? It knows that it belongs to us."

Xander's other hand cupped my left breast, squeezing and teasing my nipple through the fabric of my bra. "And this body? It's ours," he sneered.

My breath caught in my throat as their words echoed in my mind. I wanted to resist them. I tried to maintain control and tell them that their manipulative tactics wouldn't work on me, but deep down, I knew they were right.

They knew exactly how to push my buttons.

They knew how to make me submit to their desires.

And most importantly, they were right about what went on behind closed doors. Although I might have ultimately been in control, and they would never take me without my consent, they had a way of coaxing my deepest and most uncontrollable desires out of me. They did this effortlessly, time and time again, by tapping into the intense love and passion that burned between us like a blazing wildfire, impossible to extinguish.

"Your soul, Nerine," Theo's voice was a low, seductive hiss in my ear.

Xander's lips brushed against my other ear. "Ours."

My body responded, fire igniting deep inside, my pussy quivering and flooding with desire.

I matched their intense passion with an insatiable hunger, lifting my chin defiantly. I surrendered to the primal urges within me, yearning for their touch and their dominance over me.

"Claim me then," I demanded. "Take me."

Theo's eyes darkened with desire, and Xander released a low, dangerous growl.

They descended upon me like wolves pouncing on their prey, pushing me back onto the top of the desk. Their hands gripped my thighs, spreading them open and exposing me completely to them. With my legs splayed before them, they gazed down at me with heated intensity in their stormy eyes.

"Say it," Theo demanded, his hand landing on my pussy once again.

"Yes, Angel," Xander urged, his hand sliding up my thigh. "Let us hear you say it."

I hesitated for a moment before responding. "What does it matter what I say?"

"It matters because we said so," Theo replied firmly.

"Have you forgotten who you belong to?" Xander asked, his fingers tightening around my throat. "Do as we tell you, Angel."

"Make me," I challenged, locking eyes with Xander. "Prove I'm yours. As I said, claim me if I really belong to you."

"Why are you so fucking difficult?" Xander growled before claiming my lips in a fierce kiss.

His tongue intertwined with mine, and his fingertips pressed possessively into my neck. He pulled away briefly, only to be replaced by Theo, who kissed me just as passionately.

When Theo stepped away, he left me breathless and craving more. Xander reached for the sides of my panties.

I lifted my hips to help him slide them off, but he had other plans. With a swift tug, the lace fabric ripped away from my body, leaving me exposed between my stockings-clad thighs.

"You're the sexiest, most stubborn woman in the world," Xander growled, his eyes raking over my naked form.

Theo unclasped my bra skillfully and pushed the straps from my shoulders. My breasts spilled out into his palms. He squeezed and pinched the tips. The pleasure-filled pain was so delicious I couldn't help but arch into his touch.

I gazed at my two beautiful lovers, the veil of anger lifting. The relentless resistance and stubbornness that typically coursed through my veins now felt harmless and weak.

Bare, vulnerable, and naked in front of them, my soul exposed as much as my body.

I met their gaze and slowly opened my legs wider, welcoming them into me eagerly.

I wanted them to know I needed them as much as they needed me.

The truth between us was undeniable now. We all belonged to each other equally. But as soon as the fabric separating our flesh fell away, my body belonged to them completely.

Xander shed his clothes quickly, and in seconds, his magnificent cock bobbed, throbbing and ready between us. My pussy clenched at the sight, the memory of the pleasure that beautiful cock could give me, leaving me quivering with anticipation.

"I need you now, Angel," he growled, grabbing my hips and shoving his cock in deep and hard and fast. I cried out as he slid inside of me easily, my arousal leaving me soaking and quivering at his sudden piercing.

He stared down at me, his gaze shadowed with fierce passion.

"You're mine, Nerine," he demanded. "Mine and Theo's. Don't you ever forget that. Do you want us to claim you, Vixen? You want to be fucked so hard you'll never forget for a second that your body, your pussy, your entire being belongs to us?"

I laid back on the desk, submitting shamelessly and spreading my thighs as wide as possible as he slammed into me, over and over, the strength of his thrusts increasing with each and every slide.

"You're mine, Angel!" He growled, fucking me so hard

he was pushing me across the top of the desk until I was writhing beneath him, gasping and panting for breath, pleasure rolling through my head and down my chest and into my belly until crescendoing deep in my pussy, until I was crying out uncontrollably.

He hammered into my pussy, never stopping for a second through my orgasm, my pussy spasming feverishly around his hardness.

"Take my cock, Angel," he said, pressing in deeper. "Take it all."

I wasn't sure I could, my pussy was gripping him so tightly, but he pressed in further, his shaft inching even deeper into me, driving my need higher and higher.

"More, please more," I begged him for his cock like I was starving for it.

My orgasm rushed up on me, taking my breath away. It was like a switch went off in my body, and I craved even more and needed his cock deeper and harder.

My head fell back, and I closed my eyes, losing myself in the feeling of being so thoroughly and deeply fucked, relishing in the intense pounding Xander was raging upon my pussy.

"Open up, Angel," Theo's voice broke through the trance.

My eyes fluttered open to find his beautiful, throbbing shaft in my face, Theo's fingers wrapped around the base, his rugged face staring down at me as he brought it toward my lips.

With a slow, sensual smile, I licked my lips, then

opened my mouth to let him slide his thick, hard length inside. Velvety and smooth, he pulsed hotly against my tongue. The sound of his moans ricocheted through me like a shock of electric desire as he pushed deeper into my mouth.

Xander continued to roughly pierce my pussy, his cock pistoning in and out of me mercilessly.

"Fuck, that's sexy to watch," Xander growled, his eyes glued on Theo sliding in and out of my mouth. My pussy gripped his cock tighter at the sound of his sexy words, and his hard shaft swelled in response. I lost myself in the pleasure of being fucked by Xander and Theo, unable to think of anything else but the intense pounding and ecstasy they provided.

Xander's hips moved in a primal rhythm, his cock thrusting into me with unrelenting force. I moaned and writhed beneath him, my body consumed by the raw pleasure he was giving me. With each powerful stroke, my pussy tightened around him, desperate to cling to this feeling forever.

Theo's fingers tangled in my hair, guiding me as he pounded my mouth with abandon. He gripped the back of Xander's head, pulling him in his direction. Their mouths collided in a primal kiss, which drove my need higher and higher.

I sucked harder, and Theo let out a guttural cry of pleasure against Xander's lips that sent shivers down my spine.

My gaze then drifted over to Xander, his hips rolling in a sensual motion as he took me to new heights of ecstasy. His fingers dug into my skin, marking me as his as I surrendered completely to their touch.

I lay back and let them have their way with me, giving in to the vulnerability and submission that came with being their lover. Their primal passion consumed me, exploding through all my senses and taking me on a journey of pure physical bliss.

They were my beautiful men,

My gorgeous lovers,

The fathers of my children.

And as they used my body for their savage pleasure, I couldn't help but feel overwhelmed with love and desire for them.

They broke apart as the ride to climax neared. The intensity of their thrust grew relentless. They came mere seconds apart. I took everything Theo had to give as Xander poured himself inside me.

Xander barely circled my clit, and my pussy clamped down on his still hard cock. Waves of intense sensations cascaded through me, leaving me quaking and weak in their embrace. My moans mingled with theirs as we rode out the ecstasy together, our bodies intertwined and pulsing with passion.

After we caught our breaths, they carried me to the couch, knowing that my legs were too weak to support me. We lay there, skin glistening with sweat and hearts full of love, basking in the aftermath of our shared pleasure.

But it wasn't long before their hands roamed over my body again, rekindling the desire that had barely ebbed. And as we lay there tangled up together, I knew deep down that this was where I belonged— with these incredible men who loved me fiercely.

"I love you both," I whispered, my heart overflowing with emotion.

Theo kissed my neck and whispered, "We love you too, Angel."

Xander tightened his embrace and nodded in agreement. "We do love you. More than words can express."

They were right. Our connection ran so deep that even I couldn't deny it. We were destined to be together.

"And no more secrets," Xander added sternly. "We're a team now."

I nodded in agreement, willing to promise them anything at that moment. Our bond was unbreakable, and we were stronger together.

"And now that that's settled," Xander growled playfully. "It's about time you two got married."

His words lingered in the air, heavy with truth. Theo gazed into my eyes with a gentle smile, and I realized without a doubt that he didn't need to ask. He already knew I belonged to him and Xander in every sense.

In marriage.

In life.

And even in death.

Twenty-Three

X ANDER

Nerine's stilettos clicked sharply against the polished black marble floors beneath our feet, the sound echoing down the long corridor as we made our way to the conference room. Theo and I walked on either side of her, our movements in perfect sync, projecting a formidable and united front.

Since our intense argument and later reconciliation, we have discovered a sense of harmony and unity among our group. As long as Nerine understood that when our clothes came off, she belonged to both of us, everything ran smoothly.

We strode confidently down the hallway, exuding an air of authority and power.

One family.

One force.

Behind us, our loyal soldiers followed suit, their weapons ready. Even Nerine was armed, her slender frame most likely concealing hidden daggers all over her body.

Walking into the conference room filled with enemies was a risky move. The tension in the air was palpable, and my nerves were wound tight like a coiled snake.

Godfathers of the Night from all New England families awaited our arrival, including rival factions of the Angelos Syndicate. The fact that even the Aetos Syndicates were present spoke volumes about how seriously they took Nerine's message.

Our enemies believed that Nerine had control over their children, using them as leverage or threatening to harm them if she didn't get what she wanted. However, our allies' offspring were safely hidden away in their families' strongholds. Keeping those loyal to us informed about our plans helped prevent issues from arising at inconvenient times.

We played a dangerous game in a world full of powerful individuals.

Nonetheless, Nerine's intentions were not harmful. While she had technically taken these children, they were safe and well cared for in a private, luxurious facility with skilled caregivers. They likely received better care than they had at home or in boarding school, where they faced neglect or abuse from families that regarded them as mere pawns.

Fortunately, Nerine never experienced this in her youth. Peter Angelos wanted his children close and loved them deeply. The only time he softened was with his wife and kids. However, even then, unbeknownst to him, his death caused his daughter to sacrifice herself for her sisters.

The image of my little sister, Zoe, flashed through my mind. She had always been so innocent and carefree, and I had failed to protect her from the dangerous lifestyle we were all part of. The thought of her dying at such a young age, caused by the ruthless Aetos family, filled me with uncontrollable rage.

"What's wrong, Xander?" Nerine asked.

Theo chimed in, his dark eyes searching mine. "You're fuming. What's on your mind?"

The two of them could read my thoughts like an open book.

"I was just thinking about those Aetos bastards. And Zoe," I replied through clenched teeth.

"Ah, yes, the sins of our past coming back to haunt us," Theo muttered, nodding in understanding.

Nerine touched my arm gently, halting our progress down the hallway.

"Can you control yourself and refrain from ripping off a few heads? Or do you need a few moments to compose yourself before we face them?"

I took a deep breath, trying to calm the rage bubbling inside me. "I'll do my best but can't make any promises."

"Theo spoke up with a smirk. "Trust me, the thought of beheading these fuckers gets my blood pumping too."

"Save your hard cocks for after the meeting, boys,"

Nerine teased with a wink before leading us the rest of the way to the conference room. "I might need them later."

"You know they're always hard for you," Theo reminded her with a playful grin.

I shook my head at their banter and growled, "We could all end up dead sixty seconds from now, and you two are talking about sex."

"Some things can't be helped," Theo shrugged casually.

"Enough," Nerine interjected decisively. "It's time to take down these assholes."

We wiped away the jokes and replaced them with determined expressions as we followed Nerine into the room filled with our enemies.

All eyes turned to us, and our soldiers lined up behind us as we faced the room.

The atmosphere was tense, resembling a storm forming on the horizon. It seemed nearly impossible for everyone to leave this room unscathed.

As Simon Drakos, one of our few allies, stepped forward to greet us, I felt a wave of relief. Nico Mykos and Anthony Galani flanked him, both on our side. However, a formidable wall of enemies loomed behind them, watching our every move.

"Welcome, Nerine," Simon greeted her with a polite bow.

"Thank you, Simon," Nerine replied with grace and composure. "Hello, Nico. How are the young ones?"

She displayed no nervousness or anxiety with her question, radiating only an aura of calmness and peace.

The corners of Nico's lips curved. "Tucked away and safe."

I clenched my teeth. The annoyance still lingered from Nerine involving the Mykos brothers in collecting all of the children. I understood they had resources in places no one could link back to us, but Nerine left us out of the loop completely before taking action.

Nerine's next question snapped me out of my brooding, "And the ones belonging to you and your brothers?"

"On vacation with their *Theia* Nyx."

Now, that explained why Nyx Drakos, Simon's wife, hadn't made an appearance at the house after our arrival back in Boston. She was as close to Nerine as Devani and was the one who introduced Nerine to Devani in the first place.

Nico glanced at Simon, "I'm sure *Theios* Simon is disappointed to miss the holiday with his wife."

"Not in the least," Simon muttered. "I'd rather see who the Godmother disciples today."

I held in my grunt. My gut told me we wouldn't leave this room without some bloodshed.

Anthony Galani, a tall, tanned man in his late twenties, approached us. He had dark blue eyes and black hair styled to appear both disheveled and tidy.

"Let me start, Ms. Angelos, by stating clearly that I've resolved the issue with my father," Anthony announced, bowing his head respectfully. The corners of his lips curled into a small smile before he continued. "My loyalty will always lie with the Angelos family."

I raised an eyebrow in surprise and admiration.

Managing his father's attempted coup must have been no easy task. His father was notorious for his ruthless and cunning ways. However, Anthony controlled the purse strings, and even the best-laid plans can fall apart without funding. Realizing he had cut off his father's access to funds was a relief.

However, he succeeded. I was grateful for that.

"Thank you, Anthony," she said with a sincere smile. "That's one less worry for me. Your loyalty means a lot."

"What is your feeling about your peers in this room?"

Nerine's directness wasn't something I expected. But then again, Anthony was young like her, and having to prove his worth was a battle he continually faced.

"Excluding Aetos and Stratos. The consensus is to watch the outcome of your interactions with them. They will follow based on the outcome of that battle."

"They have no fear for their children or what I might do to them?"

Anthony smiled. "They sat at this table with your father and saw a lot of his style in you, which led them to believe you shared his views on the value of children."

"As long as they don't turn against me, they have nothing to worry about."

"I will pass on the message," he nodded and stepped back in line with Simon and Nico, nodding slightly.

Nerine's gaze swept across the room, patiently waiting for someone to speak up. It was crucial to allow the two self-important assholes who caused this mess to reveal their agendas.

As the room stayed silent, Nerine walked to the head of the table and took her seat with poise and authority, prepared to address the group.

"I appreciate you all taking the time to be here today," she began, her voice steady and without inflection.

Whenever she exhibited this level of control, I couldn't help but feel a surge of desire. Today was no different. Yet beneath my want, I stayed vigilant for the tension that charged the air around us. Nothing would deter me from safeguarding my queen.

"Yeah, it's bullshit that you forced us here," Gusto let out a bitter laugh. "What's the fucking point of all this?"

Nerine's eyes blazed as she raised a perfectly shaped brow at his blatant disrespect. My fists clenched at my sides, the urge to destroy these insolent men surging within me.

"You're upset, gentlemen," Nerine remarked coolly. "That's unfortunate but understandable. I am upset as well."

"That's a mild word for what we feel," Gusto spat back. "I don't know who you think you are, taking the children and summoning us here like a queen."

Nerine's calm smile did little to hide her irritation at his words. "Because that is exactly who I am. Why do you always feel the need to be so contrary? I don't answer to you, and I never will. Do you really believe that just because I am a woman, I am in any way lesser than you?"

"That's absurd!" Gusto interrupted, his face turning red with indignation.

But Nerine ignored his outburst and continued calmly. "Do you really believe my gender diminishes my abilities as a leader? Let me assure you, Gusto, I am just as powerful as you think you are just because the Y chromosome gave you that little mushroom between your legs."

Her sharp words cut through the air like knives, and Gusto fumed in his seat.

"Are you sure it's not your sordid relationship with these two brutes standing beside you that gives you any semblance of power, Nerine?" Tobias spoke up with a mocking smirk on his face. "You're right. It's not what's between your thighs that makes you powerful. It's the people you align yourself with, wouldn't you agree?"

We expected this type of dealing from Stratos. His ego couldn't accept rejection, so taunting was a way to save face.

Idiot.

Nerine viewed her relationship with Theo and me as an asset, not a weakness. Nothing any of these bastards said could change this.

His eyes glinted with malice as he continued. "And from what I've heard, you've certainly aligned yourself with them more than once." The disgust in his voice was palpable. "So tell me, what does that make you? I can't imagine these two let their little whore have much control behind the scenes."

Around the table, some gasped while others laughed at Tobias's words. I noted how each person reacted and planned their punishment accordingly. Theo stood stoic at Nerine's side, but I could sense the anger and frustration boiling within him.

Nerine lifted her chin, undaunted by Tobias's insults. I had never been prouder of her.

But the final straw came when Tobias focused on our children.

"And now you have two young boys of your own," he mocked. "Congratulations, by the way. We all wondered where you'd been for the last two years. It turns out you were busy giving birth to the consequences of your promiscuity. Are they even their fathers? How can you be sure when you open your legs for both of them?"

"Enough!" My voice echoed sharply, laced with fury. I stepped forward, poised to tear Tobias apart. Theo matched my movements, eager to join in.

But Nerine held up a hand, halting us both.

"Tobias," she said coolly, her tone laced with disdain. "You were an ugly soul. And just like your friend Gusto here, you think that flaccid noodle in your pants gives you the right to spout nonsense without consequences."

She leaned forward and then lowered her voice to a mocking whisper. "And by the way, I don't know if you've heard the rumors, but there's some doubt about your ability to produce viable sperm. That's why you used alternative methods for conception. It seems the mother of your children has started questioning whether the sample used was yours. You know, DNA tests are pretty simple these days. You don't even have to provide anything but spit. Just like you're spitting out those despicable words at me."

His eyes widened as he processed her words, a mix of disbelief and anger boiling inside him.

"How dare you imply such a thing?"

"You have some nerve with your outrage," Nerine continued, her voice laced with disdain. "Get over yourself. I'm sure those poor kids are praying they don't inherit any of your genes."

Tobias felt the sting of her words like a physical blow. He clenched his fists in frustration, knowing that Nerine was right. He and Gusto were no match for her in this verbal sparring match.

"This is completely fucked up!" Tobias exclaimed, slamming his fist down on the table. "We demand to know where our children are!"

Instead of providing an answer, Nerine smirked and shook her head slowly. "I'd be more concerned about discovering who their real parents are," she taunted.

Tobias's face turned beet red with anger at her insinuation.

"How about you tell me where my sister is first, Tobias?" Nerine asked. "Then maybe I'll update you on the legitimate and illegitimate offspring of everyone in this room."

But before he could respond, Gusto interjected. "Do you really think we'll just hand over whatever you want, Nerine?" he growled. "Do you think you're the only one who can stoop this low? Don't forget that Hayes and Charis aren't as safe and untouchable as you might believe."

Rage surged within me. The very mention of my sons' names by these heartless monsters unleashed waves of anger. I understood that it would require strength to refrain from lashing out.

I pictured them bleeding out on the floor, their lives slipping away as I watched with satisfaction. In reality, however,

I had to settle for imagining their destruction while keeping a watchful eye on Nerine.

"Do you dare to threaten my boys, Gusto?" Nerine asked. "I must admit, I greatly underestimated your intelligence."

"Enough!" Simon's voice resonated in the room as he stood at the table.

The tension in the air shifted, and I shared a warning glance with Theo. "Gusto, this is only making things worse!" Simon exclaimed. "You're not just harming yourself and your family, but also future generations to come. Have some foresight, and stop focusing solely on yourself! Don't forget we're all in the same boat. If one goes down, we all go down together."

His words struck each of us like a brutal reality check. He was right. We were all guilty of turning against one another at times, but ultimately, we needed each other to survive.

Nerine leaned back, a cold smile playing at the corners of her lips. "Simon, your words might be lost on Gusto," she said, locking eyes across the table. "His interests have always consumed him. But did you think I wouldn't know? That I wouldn't find out?"

"Find out what?" he spat, his voice dripping with disdain. "You know nothing!"

"I know you killed my brother," Nerine replied calmly. "And I know it was a pathetic attempt at revenge for your brother's death."

Despite her accusations, Gusto lifted his chin defiantly, challenging her to take action.

But instead of reacting with violence, Nerine simply took a calming breath and stood up. She strolled around the table.

"Round and round we go, huh?" she mused with a sardonic smile.

"Apparently," Gusto grumbled in reply.

"How about we call it even now?" Nerine suggested. "An eye for an eye. A brother for a brother. We can end this here and now."

Nerine strode purposefully, her heels clicking against the hardwood floor until she stood directly across from Gusto and Tobias. She paused to take a deep breath, her piercing gaze sweeping across the table before settling on Gusto again.

"But if that's not satisfactory to you, there is always another option," she said coolly.

Gusto raised an eyebrow in response.

"Is that so?" he asked, his voice tinged with skepticism.

"Absolutely. I don't like it very much, but I won't hesitate to carry out my plan if needed. Make no mistake, despite my recent venture into motherhood, I am still a ruthless businesswoman."

The Godfathers around the table sat still, hanging on every word that fell from Nerine's beautiful yet unforgiving lips.

Tobias could no longer contain himself. "Well, spill it," he demanded. "We don't have all day."

A calm, serene smile spread across Nerine's face as she turned to look at him. It was evident that Tobias was walking a thin line.

I expected Nerine to pull a dagger from her suit pocket at

any moment and strike him down for his disrespect. No one spoke to her like that without facing the consequences. Instead, she kept talking.

"This is your other option: for every child you take from the Angelos family, I will take one from you. Then we'll call it even."

Her words lingered in the air until Tobias's voice pierced the silence. "You can't do that!"

"I can do anything I want," she stated boldly. Gusto set the standard for this negotiation: a child for a child. I was willing to accept that our past losses were enough to settle the debts between our families."

She turned her attention to Gusto, her gaze hardened. "Don't you have a daughter?"

Gusto's face drained of all color as he realized the gravity of her words.

"She's about the same age that Xander's little sister Zoe was when you killed her. Isn't that right? I mean, if she's actually yours," Nerine continued, her tone casual and detached. "I've heard rumors about your kids that are similar to those about Tobias's children. But you know what I mean."

The thought of innocent children being murdered to atone for their families' sins was unsettling, but I knew it was all just empty threats from Nerine. She would never do such a thing. There was no doubt about that.

Yet the men around the table were trembling with fear, believing every terrifying word.

Once it became clear that Gusto and Tobias would not

respond, Nerine returned to her position at the head of the table.

"Very well," she declared confidently. "If no one else has anything to add, I'll take your silence as agreement to my terms. Allow me to outline those terms clearly and concisely to avoid any misunderstandings. Please listen carefully."

She took a deep breath while I watched the others, expecting someone to make a move at any moment.

"No one will speak of my family's debt again. Is that clear?" Nerine declared firmly. "The feud between our families is over. Boston belongs to the Angelos family, and there are no ifs, ands, or buts about it. You will leave my city immediately. You can contact me individually whenever business arises here. However, let me be perfectly clear—the Aetos family is never welcome in this city again. None of you will ever threaten the Angelos family or our allies again. You will never bring harm to any of our family members."

She paused, allowing her words to sink in. Gusto appeared crestfallen and defeated, his bravado and ego deflated like a balloon.

"Thank you for your cooperation," Nerine said with a nod. "Your children are safe and will be returned to you shortly."

She paused for a moment before concluding, her voice filled with finality. "I'm taking your silence as approval of this agreement."

Nerine turned on her heel and led the way to the door with a determined stride. Theo and I followed closely behind her, aware of the tension in the air.

"You forgot to ask for our approval on your relationship, you whore," Tobias spat, his voice dripping with venom.

Nerine halted, her back stiffening at the insult. Tobias stood up from his seat with a sneer, his eyes darting accusingly toward us.

The air hummed with electricity, charged with hostility and danger. Clearly, the jerk had a death wish. I watched Nerine closely, bracing for her reaction. A glint of metal flickered in the reflection of the overhead lights.

"I don't need anyone's approval, Tobias," she spat through gritted teeth. "For anything at all."

In one swift motion that seemed almost too fast for the eye to follow, Nerine unsheathed her dagger and hurled it across the room with lethal precision. The tip of the blade struck directly between Tobias's beady eyes, drawing blood that trickled down his face like a scarlet ribbon.

He crumpled to the ground at his brother's feet, a look of shock frozen on his face as reality dawned on him. Nerine gave Nixos a pointed look.

"Congratulations, Nixos. You are now the head of the Stratos family. Will you be an ally or an enemy? The choice is yours." Her voice carried a hint of warning and a promise of better things depending on his decision.

Nixos stared with wide eyes, too afraid to move. In fact, every man in the room remained motionless.

Nerine swept out of the room with a haughty smile, closely followed by Theo and me. Our power solidified as we strode down the hallway, accompanied by a loyal army of soldiers, leaving our enemies stunned and silent.

Twenty-Four

N ERINE

As I gazed into Fiona's piercing turquoise eyes, the flames of the fireplace danced behind her in my office. The warmth from the fire contrasted with the tension in the room as I spoke to my sister. She sat beside me, her features reminiscent of my own at a similar age. It served as a disconcerting reminder of our bloodline and the weight it carried.

"You might think you live in a bubble, but that's not true," I said, hoping to share some wisdom with my sister. "The blood that runs through your veins carries a rich history you can't ignore. Believe me, I've tried to escape it myself. But now, I understand the value of embracing and leveraging our heritage to our advantage."

Fiona shifted uncomfortably in her seat, her voice brimming with determination. "But I believed I was doing the right thing by writing the book. Once I found out they were coming after the boys too, I thought..." She trailed off.

Despite my recent conversations with Theo and Xander about family unity, it was my turn to convey this message to my sister. "Communication is essential for our family," I gently reminded her, feeling a pang of guilt for my hypocrisy. "We are a team, and no one should act alone."

"Do as I say, not as I do," I said with a rueful tone, which made her smirk and relax the tension in her shoulders.

"I know," Fiona reluctantly conceded, her impulsiveness overshadowed by regret. "I won't act thoughtlessly again. I didn't think about how my actions would affect our family. That was a mistake."

"I'm always here for you," I reassured her, offering a comforting hand on her shoulder. "You can come to me no matter what, and we'll figure things out together. We must always stand united against our enemies."

"I understand," Fiona admitted, her earlier determination replaced by humility. "I've learned from this."

"Good," I said warmly, kissing her forehead. "You'll keep growing and learning like we all have."

Man, I sounded like an old lady.

What the heck?

Fiona's face lit up with excitement. "I have some fantastic news," she exclaimed.

Her infectious smile spread to my face. "Tell me! I could really use some good news."

"I got accepted to Boston University!"

"What!" I couldn't hold back my excitement. "That's amazing!"

"Yeah, I didn't want to tell anyone until I was accepted, but I plan to start once my semester at Arizona State is over."

"Fiona, this is wonderful news!" I hugged her tightly. "And you'll be so close to family now! I was worried about your loneliness after Mama and the boys moved back here. This is perfect!"

"Thanks, Nerine," she said with a grateful smile before leaning in for a kiss. "With all the craziness in our lives over the last few years, I'll feel much safer being closer to home. And to you."

I narrowed my eyes playfully. "You're just coming back to sneak in and take my job?"

"That too," Fiona beamed. "But there are also two little boys who are a big incentive."

"They're all yours," I said, shaking my head with a smile. "But be careful; they're pure chaos in human form. Charis managed to get to the other side of the house last night. Hayes even found one of the secret passageways. Who knew he was strong enough to push open a false wall?"

Fiona laughed with me. "I can't wait for the twins to arrive. We'll have to have them babysit and see how long it takes before they run out of the house screaming."

My heart swelled with love and happiness for my sister as I watched her carefree and silly after everything we had been through together.

Fiona's voice bubbled with excitement. "Do you think

the boys are awake? I want to read them a story. I bought them a new book."

"I think Theo and Xander have already put them to bed," I replied, pausing for a moment. "You know what? They might be asleep on the floor in the boys' room. Hayes and Charis aren't used to the routine, and they can be difficult to settle down and get to bed."

Fiona laughed, tilting her head to the side in amusement. "You look happy, Nerine. The shadows in your eyes have vanished."

"I've never been happier," I reassured her. "Having my family together at last, after all this time? I can't even express how relieved I am."

"I know it was hard for you to be away from everyone," Fiona said sympathetically. "I'm so glad to see your little family together now. You truly deserve this."

"Thank you." My eyes filled with tears of gratitude.

"I can't wait until we start planning the wedding."

I held in my moan. "I'd rather a justice of the peace officiate it and have it over and done with, but Xander and Theo overruled me."

"Of course they did." The outrage on Fiona's face was almost comical. "You have to celebrate everything you've overcome."

"You sound like Mama," I grumbled.

"You had to know she wouldn't take your side on this. You're her eldest child. She wants that big wedding, even if you aren't taking the traditional path."

"I suppose you're right. At least it's going to be sooner

rather than later."

"Meaning?"

"Late June."

"That's barely a month from now." She cocked her head to the side. "Are you insane?"

"It was either that or the justice of the peace."

She hugged me tightly, whispering, "I love you, sis."

"I love you too," I whispered back.

As we released each other, we said goodnight and went our separate ways.

I walked down the hallway to my suite of rooms, which felt less private now with the boys so close to the bedroom I shared with Theo and Xander. At least there was a small sitting room separating us from the babies, considering their fathers' sexual appetites and my inability to keep quiet.

Regardless of how drastically our lives had changed, I couldn't help but feel a surge of happiness.

But as I walked down the hall, instead of toys scattered on the floor, I found random pieces of men's clothing. They were all damp. I glanced up at one of our guards, who pursed his lips as if trying to stifle a laugh, then shrugged in response to my questioning look.

What would I discover upon entering the room? Taking a deep breath, I turned the knob and stepped inside, bursting into laughter at the chaotic scene that unfolded before me.

Theo and Xander lay in their underwear, sprawled on the floor beside the boys' cribs. On top of them were two diaper-clad boys who still seemed to have soap on their bodies. The room was a complete mess, with bath toys and towels scattered everywhere.

I couldn't help but pull out my phone to snap a few pictures. This is what life is really about.

My family.

My loves.

My children.

For the first time in ages, I felt truly happy.

Xander's eyes flew open, and he frowned. "Are you filming us?"

"No, just taking some pictures," I laughed.

"It's the same thing. Get rid of them. I don't want any evidence of this." He stood up and placed Charis in his crib.

Before I could say anything else, Theo stirred and opened his eyes. "What's going on?"

I giggled, trying to hold back my laughter. "I have a question for both of you."

"Don't even say it," Theo groaned sleepily.

"I'm just curious," I insisted, wearing a mischievous smile.

"You'll pay for it," Xander warned as he walked toward our bedroom.

As I followed him, I stoked the flames. "Who had more trouble at bath time? You or the boys?"

"That's not funny," Theo huffed, setting Hayes down next to Charis in his crib.

But I couldn't help but laugh at the sight of two grown men exhausted by two tiny babies, needing a nap themselves.

"You're going to pay for that," Theo said with half-seriousness. "And you need to keep your voice down, or you'll wake the boys."

My heart raced at the warning. "Um, I have an early morning tomorrow."

Xander shook his head, a sly grin spreading across his lips as he approached me. "You know the rules. You must face the consequences of your actions."

Suddenly, I realized I had backed myself against a wall instead of moving toward the door that led to the adjoining living room. I tried to find a way around them, but Xander blocked my view.

"How about a rain check?"

Theo stepped closer, a mischievous glint in his gray eyes. "We don't accept IOUs."

"So, what do you accept?" I asked nervously, feeling a blend of anticipation and fear.

"You'll find out soon enough," Xander said mysteriously. "Now, make your way into our bedroom and take off your clothes."

EPILOGUE – CHAPTER

XANDER

"Where the hell are you?"

Theo's message flashed on my phone, and I couldn't help but laugh.

I craved a moment of solitude before the ceremony.

Nerine had confined us to a distant wing of the estate, ensuring we wouldn't cross paths before the wedding.

Even though I wouldn't have my name listed on the marriage certificate, and I'd be the one marrying Theo and Nerine, it felt like I was getting married to both of them myself.

I wasn't nervous. I wasn't anxious.

I felt completely at ease with our plans for today. They seemed long overdue.

Theo and I should have acted much sooner to marry our

angel, but the chaos with our enemies delayed us. Now that we'd overcome the worst, it was time to move forward.

I was more than ready. As I adjusted my tie, I noticed the tension I had held for years was finally dissipating. Today, I felt genuine unrestrained happiness in my heart.

The dark, empty space I had drowned in during Nerine's absence was finally filled by her light and healed by her love. I reflected on the turmoil I had faced—the sleepless nights consumed by anger and alcohol that I had wasted, overwhelmed by worry and distress, haunted by countless unanswered questions that tormented me endlessly.

I didn't know whether Nerine was alive or dead. Then she returned, alive and well, with our boys. It felt as though all my prayers had been answered.

Yet, I hadn't prayed—not once. Not in my darkest hour. Instead, I had raged and cursed at God, even threatening to harm those I thought God might care about.

But in the end, all I did was hurt myself. And yet, here I was, slipping into my tuxedo jacket, the loves of my life waiting for me at the altar. I combed my hair again, adjusted my tie in the mirror, and stared myself in the eye.

A movement in the reflection drew my attention, and I turned just in time to witness the door behind me swing open. This additional bedroom led to a small private terrace through that door, which provided access to the rear of the estate grounds.

I felt at ease.

Happy.

Smiling.

And when I turned, I expected to see Theo—or possibly my future mother-in-law.

But never, in a million years, did I expect to find Gusto Aetos looking back at me.

Suddenly, all the tension returned. Alarm and anger washed over me like an unexpected wave, and I stepped back, preparing my body for whatever this fucker planned.

"Gusto!"

"Xander," he nodded. In his hand, he held a revolver aimed straight at me. He wore the same clothes I had seen a caterer wearing earlier.

"What the fuck are you doing here?"

"It's obvious. I'm here for your wedding, of course."

"You weren't invited."

My mind raced as I evaluated my surroundings. Distanced from my bedroom and firearms, I found myself utterly defenseless here. I might as well have been standing there with my dick in my hand.

"I wasn't? Forgive my rudeness," he joked.

I took a deep breath, my eyes flicking to the door behind him.

"Don't even think about it."

"What's the end game here?" I asked.

"You're an asshole, Xander, but you're smart. That's a stupid fucking question, don't you think?"

"Fair enough," I said. "I thought we were past this, Gusto."

"Nerine thought we were past this. I never agreed."

"Your silence was agreement," I reminded him.

"Fuck that," he said. "I'm here for revenge."

"Yeah? A life for a life?" I asked.

"Exactly."

"You realize what's going to happen if you kill me, right? Nerine already warned you. If you mess with the Angelos again, you're signing your little daughter's death warrant. Nerine will show you no mercy."

"That's a risk I'm willing to take."

"You're an idiot," I scoffed, shaking my head. "How the fuck did you rise to the head of your family with that IQ?"

His face twisted in anger, his breath quickening. I took a step forward, and he jutted the gun toward me.

"Don't move!"

I stopped, raising my hands.

"Can I talk you out of this?" I asked.

"I've made up my mind," he replied, lifting his chin defiantly.

I noticed his fingers tightly clutching the gun, with one finger on the trigger.

His hand trembled, and a drop of sweat rolled down his temple into his sideburn.

For someone who planned to kill me, he was certainly moving slowly. He appeared to be more anxious than I was. Then it struck me.

Had he ever even gotten his hands dirty?

He achieved prominence in his family only because his predecessors had passed away. Born into wealth and comfort, he likely never cleaned a dish himself.

A slow smile spread across my face.

"Gusto," I said, chuckling. "Why are you so nervous?"

He took a step toward me but stopped again, waving the gun around.

"I'm not."

"Have you ever killed anyone?" I asked, tilting my head to the side. "You haven't, have you?"

"I'm about to kill you."

I nodded, my eyes scanning up and down his body, assessing him.

"You've found yourself at the head of a mafia syndicate. But you've never done your dirty work yourself, have you? Why are you here now?"

"I told you. Revenge."

"But you don't want anyone to know. What's your plan? Sneak out without being seen? Do you really think nobody will notice you?"

"I took precautions," he said, eyes darting to the camera outside the door.

"Is that so? What did you do?"

"I recruited a Harvard student to assist me in breaching your security system. He programmed it to loop so that no one would notice my entry," he said, a sense of pride evident in his voice.

"I understand. So, you plan to kill me, and you took it upon yourself to do the job to avoid any snitches, correct? It must be difficult for you to have so little faith in your own people."

"You don't know what the fuck you're talking about."

"Don't I?" I asked, lifting a brow. "If you were a real

godfather, I wouldn't have seen you coming, and you'd be on your way back home after having left me on the floor to bleed out. But you're not, are you? No, you use the only strength and power at your disposal to get things done—money. What a fucking coward you are, Gusto."

My words hung true and heavy in the air. His eyes dilated with anger, and I knew I had called him out correctly. I tried to avoid smirking, but his incompetence was amusing.

My phone buzzed from its spot on the table, and I figured it was probably Theo again. I hadn't replied to his first text, so he was likely getting antsy.

It was almost time to start the ceremony.

I thought about Nerine. She probably looked like an angel already in her wedding dress. I couldn't wait to see her walk down the aisle. I had dreamed of this day for years.

And I wasn't about to let this prick take that opportunity away from me.

Not a coward like him.

Another bead of sweat slid down his face, his hand still trembling.

I weighed my options. I needed to move this along. Which meant I needed to kill this asshole so I could go marry the loves of my life and begin the next chapter of our story.

There was no fucking way I was going to let this be the end.

"People are looking for me," I said, pointing my chin toward the phone.

"Let them look."

"You're going to make me late for my wedding, Gusto."

He laughed, shaking his head. "You're not going to make it."

"Right. You're going to kill me," I shouted, calling his bluff. "Well, go ahead and do it, then!"

He raised the gun higher, his hands shaking with fear.

"Shoot me, you bastard!" I yelled, my voice carrying through the air.

His eyes widened, and his finger wiggled against the trigger.

"Come on! Do it, you prick," I urged even louder this time.

"You're the prick," he shouted. "This is payback for my brother's death.

He took a step forward, placing the barrel of the gun against my chest. He was so close that I could smell his breath.

He was so upset that he trembled like a child, his face pale and glistening with sweat. I recognized that this kind of fear was a dangerous mix. Terror like this—unchecked, wild, and unrefined—was precisely the kind of situation that could lead to someone ending up dead.

But I also knew I wasn't going to become a corpse today. Gusto summoned his courage, a wild and uncontrollable storm raging in his eyes as he wrestled with his emotions.

EPILOGUE –
CHAPTER TWO

THEO

"What the fuck, Xander?" I muttered to myself as I looked down at my phone, waiting for his reply.

He mentioned needing a few moments alone to gather his thoughts and said he would return shortly. The ceremony was about to begin, and he should have already been in position. We definitely couldn't start without him.

The door to my room swung open, and Nerine's mother poked her head in.

"I have a surprise for you," she said as the boys clung to her legs. When they saw me, they reached out their arms and insisted that I pick them up.

"Papa!" they exclaimed together. As quintessential twins, they synchronized their actions and words perfectly. Even at under two years old, they created more chaos than the older children.

"I love these surprises." I bent down to pick them both up, then leaned over to kiss their grandmother's cheek. "How's Nerine?"

"She's beautiful," she replied.

"I have no doubt about that." I smiled. I couldn't wait to see, kiss, and make that stunning woman my wife.

"Where's Xander?" she asked, scanning the area.

"He needed some time to himself. He'll return shortly."

"I understand," she said, nodding. "Theo, I wanted to speak with you and Xander privately. Things will get hectic once the ceremony wraps up, and we won't have the chance to talk."

"Is everything alright?" I inquired, feeling worried.

"Yes," she nodded, tears welling in her eyes. "I wanted to express my gratitude to you and Xander for making my daughter so happy and being such great fathers to the boys. You've brought me happiness too. I sleep much better at night knowing Nerine is with you both."

"Nerine is perfectly capable of caring for herself," I reminded her.

"I know. But a little extra protection never hurts."

"Nerine is the love of my life," I explained. "I don't need thanks, but I appreciate the sentiment."

"Welcome to the Angelos family." She beamed at me.

"I feel like I've belonged to your family forever. This makes it official."

"Yes, I agree," she replied. Taking a deep breath, she reached for the boys. They eagerly went into her embrace, and she set them down, holding their hands.

"I'll see you out there," she said.

"Yes, if Xander ever shows up," I said. "I'm not sure where he's gone off to."

"He'll show up."

"True," I nodded. "He always does."

"He's a good man, just like you."

I kissed her on the cheek once more before she walked off with the boys and returned to the mirror to adjust my tie. I took a moment to assess my appearance, hoping I looked good enough for Nerine.

"As good as it's going to get," I muttered.

The three of us had come such a long way to arrive at this day, and now that it was finally here, I was excited, but honestly, I wanted to get this day out of the way so we could be a happily married throuple.

Perhaps the concept of justice of the peace wasn't such a bad idea after all.

I should have listened to Nerine. I shook my head. I was never going to share that thought with her. I loved that woman more than any other in the universe, but she didn't need to hold that over me.

I picked up my phone from the dresser and messaged Xander once more. If we arrived late for the wedding, Nerine would undoubtedly drive her dagger straight into our hearts. I drew back the curtain and glanced outside. From my vantage point, I could see the wedding party assembled below. Although we kept the guest list small, the caterers and production crew were occupied with preparations, so at least a hundred people were gathered outside.

We'd only invited family and allies. I watched for a moment as they all mixed and mingled with each other, eager smiles on their faces and drinks in their hands. At least the guests were well taken care of. I looked at the clock on my phone and saw we only had twenty minutes until we were supposed to be in our places.

Needing to ease my nerves, I walked over to the bar cart in the corner, poured myself a snifter of bourbon, and downed it quickly. The warm amber liquid gave me just the shot of courage I needed.

I wasn't afraid of marrying Nerine and Xander, not by a long shot.

But I was afraid of screwing something up and stumbling down the aisle.

Saying the wrong vows or something.

I chuckled at my thoughts, aware that none of this mattered, yet I was determined to give Nerine the perfect ceremony and wedding day she deserved. Nevertheless, a nagging feeling lingered at the back of my mind—a peculiar sensation creeping up my spine—that made me ponder how Xander was doing.

If only he'd fucking reply…

"Fuck this," I muttered and decided to find him myself.

Xander wasn't the kind of person to arrive late without a reason. I hoped everything was okay, and he'd lost track of time.

I stepped outside through the door leading to the garden and was instantly surrounded by guests eager to wish me well. I tried to evade them, but then I encountered Nyx

Drakos, who stood at the edge of the crowd talking to Devani.

"Well, well, well," Devani said. "Don't you clean up nicely?"

She ran her fingers along the lapel of my tuxedo, smiling up at me.

"Thanks, Devani," I replied. "Have you seen Xander?"

"No." She shrugged. "Is everything okay?"

"Oh, yes, of course," I assured her.

"Great. Nerine is truly fortunate to have both of you by her side." She placed her hand on my arm, giving it a gentle squeeze.

Being touched by a woman other than Nerine, regardless of the context, felt entirely alien to me.

"Thanks again," I said. "I have to keep moving. The show is about to start!"

"Good luck, Theo," Nyx replied. "I'm so happy for you. You're lucky to have each other."

"I'm the lucky one," I said, then turned away and walked back toward the house to continue searching for Xander, leaving the crowd behind as the music from the nearby speakers boomed.

The Angelos estate was stunning today. The sunlight dancing through the trees brought pure joy to my heart. It was a beautiful day to make our union official. I smiled as I wondered how Nerine was feeling at that moment. Was she filled with nerves? Was she laughing with her sisters and mother? Was she having second thoughts?

No, there were no second thoughts with Nerine. She made a decision and jumped in headfirst.

As I walked through the garden at the back of the house, I looked back at the crowd of people. They appeared joyful and relaxed. Despite the day's festivities, there was also an underlying tranquility.

It felt like even our guests knew this was the right choice. I took a deep breath and paused, looking up at the large cypress tree where Nerine, Xander, and I shared our first kiss. We had rushed there to escape her father's constant watch and his guards, breathless, our hearts racing. We had no idea our lives would lead us here at that moment. We were young and naive, lacking a clear vision for the future. All we understood was the need to embrace the emotions pulsing through us and to stay close together.

Today, on our wedding day, that tree stood tall and sturdy. Much like our unwavering resolve to embrace the bond that united the three of us, the tree remained steadfast.

I closed my eyes, savoring the moment as a wave of thoughts flooded my mind, wanting to imprint this day in my memory forever.

I remembered the sensation of Nerine's lips on mine for the first time, feeling a profound surge of joy and love echo within me as I revisited that memory. She has always been my guiding light, while Xander represented the shadows. I truly need both of them in my life.

"Thank you," I whispered a prayer to the universe for my good fortune.

The tree danced in the breeze, as beautiful as ever.

"I'll never take this for granted," I vowed.

Warmed by love and smiling gently, I resumed my search but immediately froze at the sound of Xander's muffled shouts.

Epilogue – Chapter Three

XANDER

"I'm waiting," I taunted Gusto.

Rage and fear twisted his features, but his ego wouldn't allow him to back down. "I'll do it. Don't think I won't."

As I was about to reply, I spotted a shadow in the bedroom's open doorway. I instantly recognized it was Theo before even seeing him.

In a blur of movement, Theo raced up behind Gusto and glided his blade across Gusto's neck.

Gusto's eyes grew wide as blood streamed from his wound. He let the gun slip from his hand while clutching his neck. Then, as effortlessly as he had entered uninvited, he collapsed onto the floor that accursed Aetos blood, responsible for so much suffering, now spilling onto the polished parquet.

It was a beautiful fucking sight watching Gusto struggle

for his life at our feet. He deserved every second of the pain coursing through him.

"Thank you for that," I said to Theo as he stared at me in disbelief.

"What the hell is this?" he asked. "You didn't answer, so I came to find you. That's when I heard you yelling."

"Yeah, that was my plan." I shrugged. "Either that or dying at Gusto's hand on our wedding day."

"Like you'd ever let that happen," he chuckled. "But thank the universe, it didn't. Now we have to explain why Gusto is lying on the floor in our extra bedroom."

"Not really."

"No?"

"Gusto fucked himself. He found someone who could hack into our security system, turning off our cameras and sneaking in as a caterer to gain access. I'll handle the security issue later. Additionally, he came here secretly without informing any of his allies or men. We can use his precautions to our advantage. All we need to do is get rid of the body. Gusto will become another missing asshole in the world. And, of course, we know fucking nothing because we were here at a wedding, surrounded by more than enough witnesses."

"Do we tell Nerine?" Theo asked.

"I want to shield her from this. However, we agreed that there would be no more secrets."

He sighed and nodded. "True. But we should wait to tell her."

I said, smiling at him, savoring the moment. "Let's not spoil this day."

"It was hard enough to get her to agree to the wedding," he replied, running his hand through his hair, a loose strand falling over his eye.

He had saved my life for what felt like the hundredth time. Yet, he appeared completely unfazed by it, not a drop of blood on his hands.

"You look damn good in a tux," I said, taking him in.

He smirked. "You're just saying that because I saved your life again."

"Maybe." I laughed.

We looked down at Gusto together, watching as he gasped his last breath before his body shuddered and stilled.

"What are we going to do with this guy?"

"Let's leave him. We'll deal with this later," I stated, taking his hand and drawing him near for a kiss.

After a few moments, I pulled away, smiling at him.

"We're late. Let's go marry our queen," Theo said.

Epilogue – Chapter Four

NERINE

"What on earth is going on, Fiona?" I paced around my bedroom while my twin sisters darted alongside me, trying to keep my train from getting caught on the bedposts.

"Will you sit still?" Ariana complained.

Christina huffed as she held up the embroidered lace. "Running around while you worry isn't as easy as you think."

Glancing at the clock, I saw it was exactly ten minutes before I was supposed to start walking down the aisle. I peeked out the window again, wishing Xander and Theo had somehow shown up. Unfortunately, I only saw a crowd, now more nervous than ever, sitting in their seats.

Waiting.

Awkwardly.

"Stop looking out there!" Fiona demanded, yanking the

curtain from my hand and shoving me away. "You're not supposed to see them before the wedding!"

"Well, believe me, I'm not. They still aren't out there! Where the heck are they?"

Panic and confusion wrestled within me. I trusted both of them with my life. We'd been through so much together.

My God, we had the boys!

Surely, they wouldn't betray me.

"Well, isn't it obvious? They've run off with a couple of strippers!" Ariana said, flashing me a teasing smile.

"This is no time for joking, Ari!" I stopped to glare at her.

She shrugged her shoulders. "I was only trying to lighten the mood, and it got you to stand still for a second."

"Seriously, Nerine..." Fiona rolled her eyes, making me want to shake her. "Can you hear how ridiculous that sounds? Whatever's happening, I'm sure there's a reasonable explanation. Those two would go through hell for you."

"I'm going to set them on fire myself!" I insisted, resuming my pacing.

The door to my room flew open behind me, and I turned with anticipation, hoping to see them there with a reasonable explanation.

But it wasn't a sheepish Xander in the doorway.

Nor was it my infuriating Theo.

Instead, it was Mama with Hayes and Charis in her arms. Anxiety was etched all over her face, leaving a heavy lump in the pit of my stomach.

"Did you find them?"

She shook her head slowly. "It doesn't make sense. I took the boys to see Theo and spoke with him."

"And then?"

"I asked him where Xander was, and he said he would return shortly. But now..." She paused, setting the boys on the ground, who immediately ran toward Fiona.

"What is it, Mom?" I asked intently.

"Nerine, I'm sorry. They're both gone."

My blood ran cold. I sat on the bed, not caring anymore that I might be wrinkling the luxurious silk.

"Everyone is looking for them," she assured me.

I looked at Fiona with alarm. The smile she gave the boys as they came toward her disappeared.

"Devani," she said, picking up Hayes and Charis, setting them on the sofa beside her, and pulling out her phone from her clutch. "She will handle this."

"Call her now," I urged, unable to mask the panic in my voice. "See if she can have her team search for them."

She nodded and got up from her seat, and right away, Mama took her spot to keep the babies in check. At least the boys being a handful was typical for the day.

We needed to find their fathers.

They wouldn't disappear together unless something were seriously wrong. Given how they pushed for the wedding, there wasn't a chance in hell either of them would get cold feet.

I headed for the door, but Fiona stepped in front of me, her phone tucked against her neck, her arms folded, and a glare on her face. "No."

"Get out of my way, Fiona. I have to look for them!"

"As Mama just said, everyone is searching for them. Devani's on the line. She's gathering her people to join our soldiers in finding them. And she told me to tell you, don't leave the room, or she will kick your ass."

I clenched my jaw. "I hate it when the two of you gang up on me."

Fiona smirked and continued her conversation with Devani, completely ignoring me.

"She's right," Mama replied. "You need to stay here. If something is wrong, we can't give them another target."

Ariana huffed, "Mama. That's not helping the situation. Don't put those thoughts in her head."

"Don't worry so much, Nerine. They're probably just having a drink or two and lost track of time." Christina adjusted my train, draping it over a nearby chair.

"If they are just fucking around to mess with my head, I'm going to kill them."

"Maybe you should rethink that glass of rosé," Christina suggested.

My head spun, and I tapped my toe against the floor. "Fine, get me a glass."

"Coming right up." Ariana ran to the bar cart.

"It's probably nothing, right?" I said, looking over at her hopefully as she poured me a glass.

The last thing I wanted to do today was think about the violence and possibilities of our world. For just one day, I needed to put aside my duties as the Godmother of the Angelos family.

For twenty-four hours at least, couldn't I just be a fucking bride?

"Absolutely," Ariana assured me, handing me the wine and gesturing for me to drink.

I followed her instructions, attempting to rein in my racing thoughts.

Please let whatever was going on be something stupid.

And if it was something stupid, I planned to either make their lives a living hell or murder them with my bare hands.

"You can't kill them on your wedding day," Fiona said, shaking her head at me.

I scowled at her. "You're a mind reader now, are you?"

"I'm your sister, and I know how you think." She shrugged. "The moment they piss you off, you want to reach for your blades."

"Am I that predictable?" I laughed, downing half the glass.

I needed the warmth of the buzz to take the edge off just a little. If this wedding ever happened, I needed to ensure I wasn't drunkenly stumbling down the aisle.

"You have another option," Christina hummed.

"I'm worried what you will say, but okay, I'll bite."

She gave me a beaming smile and said, "Just fuck them almost to death."

"Oh, for the love of all that is holy," Mama exclaimed. "How have I raised you to say such things?"

"Honestly, Mama. We're aware of everything about you and Papa, so there's no need to act surprised," Ariana remarked in her straightforward manner, which only infuriated Mama further.

"Stop picking on her, you two. Our knife-wielding mother doesn't want anyone to know she's a bloodthirsty badass who sinned before marriage." Fiona shot me a grin as she walked over to the window.

"Feel free to enjoy yourself at my expense. This is what occurs when the Lord blesses me with daughters—not just one, but four." Mama sighed dramatically, making me laugh.

God, I loved these women. Their antics always helped ease a stressful situation. A moment later, a cheer rang out from the crowd outside the window, and a wave of relief washed over me.

"Looks like your princes have arrived," Fiona said, glancing into the gardens.

"My kings," I replied.

She nodded in agreement. "I stand corrected."

I rose to face her, excitement coursing through my veins.

Fiona's phone buzzed, and she signaled to Mama, who came over to me.

"It's time, my sweet girl."

She reached up and swept a lock of hair over my shoulders, smoothing the curl. Tears filled her eyes, and mine widened in surprise at her sudden outpouring of emotion. "I hope you know how beautiful you are, Nerine Angelos."

"Thank you, Mama," I replied, pulling her close, my heart overflowing. "I love you."

"I love you too," she said as I pulled away. "Now, go get your happily ever after."

Mama extended her elbow, allowing me to slip my hand through it. We stepped out into the hallway together. Just outside the door, Ariana, Christina, and Fiona formed a line, grinning widely while clutching bouquets of red lilies. In front of them, Hayes and Charis looked adorable, holding baskets filled with red rose petals. They fidgeted restlessly, and Fiona did her best to manage them.

I smiled, my heart soaring with pride for them. I was so happy they were here with us and would have the memory of their parents getting married. Mama handed me my bouquet from the bedroom, a beautiful spray of red and white lilies that matched the ones my sisters carried. "Thank you," I said. We took our place in line behind the girls and headed outside. As we approached the door, I heard the music change, and the rumbling of the crowd subsided.

My heart raced with anticipation.

The moment I'd dreamed of all my life had finally arrived.

I closed my eyes, trying to drink in the feeling, wanting to remember it forever.

When the doors opened, and the boys walked out first, the initial oohs and aahs erupted from the crowd, and I felt tears welling up.

I hastily blinked them away, not wanting to be a sobbing mess by the time it was my turn to walk down the aisle. I tried to peer around my sisters' bobbing heads as they waited in front of me, hoping to sneak a glance at my loves.

With each moment that passed, my breath grew shallower. My anxiety shifted to eagerness and impatience as Mama gently pressed her palm against the back of my hand.

"Are you alright, darling?"

I was too overwhelmed to respond. Breathing felt nearly impossible.

So, I simply nodded.

As my sisters stepped aside, disappearing down the aisle, the crowd parted like a sea, revealing Theo and Xander.

I gasped as I saw the two of them anxiously peering down the aisle, seemingly just as desperate to look at me as I was for a glimpse of them. My entire soul lit up at the sight of them.

They looked striking in their matching tuxedos, exuding a captivating charm. My heart swelled with profound love.

"Here we go," Mama whispered close to me, and together, we walked toward them, stepping into my new life, my new role, my destined future.

As we approached, the beaming crowd seemed to fade away, leaving only the two of them in my focus. Seeing them stand side by side, waiting for me, was better than I had ever dreamed.

Xander moved ahead, speaking loudly yet gently.

"Mrs. Angelos, are you here to present the bride?"

"I am," Mama said quietly. She turned toward me, wrapped her arms around me, and kissed me on the cheek.

"I love you so much, Mama," I replied.

She caressed my cheek and smiled brightly at me. Then, she took my hand and placed it in Xander's.

Xander's dark eyes gazed into mine, warm and tender.

Silently, he guided me up the two small steps to my other waiting love, Theo.

Xander offered my hand to Theo with a subtle bow.

"You two are late," I whispered.

"Sorry about that, Angel," Theo replied with a wink. "It won't happen again."

I laughed at his joke, aware that we'd never marry again. My gaze swept over them, absorbing every detail, desire coursing through my body.

My eyes caught a splash of color on Xander's collar, and I focused on it intently. Initially, the vivid red reminded me of lipstick, and Devani's joke about the stripper resonated in my mind.

But then I looked closer. *Blood.* My eyes widened at the sight, and I looked at Xander with a questioning look.

He nodded slowly, sharing a knowing smile with me.

"Shh, we can talk later," Xander whispered.

Curiosity bounced around my mind. Perhaps they had been detained for a valid reason, after all. A gradual sense of relief began to flow through me. No matter what had happened, they were both here now.

Theo squeezed my hands, and I turned my focus to him. We all knew I'd have a million questions later, but for now, this—our future waited, wide open and full of possibilities.

"Dearly beloved," Xander started. "We are gathered here today..."

EPILOGUE – CHAPTER FIVE

NERINE

We decided to leave for our honeymoon in the morning rather than right after the ceremony. We arranged for everyone else, Mama, my sisters, the boys, and most of the soldiers overseeing the estate, to stay at a hotel, keeping only a few on-site for the evening.

After a night filled with exquisite dining, drinks, and dancing, our guests gradually departed, loading into hired cars that took them to various luxurious hotels.

Eventually, Theo, Xander, and I found ourselves alone for the first time that evening. We were tired and a bit tipsy, the excitement of the day surrounding us like the setting sun in the distance. Standing together, we gazed over our property, our arms wrapped tightly around one another.

The warmth of their bodies and their love enveloped me, making me feel cozy and joyful in their embrace.

"That went quite well, almost flawlessly," I remarked as we looked at the pink and blue streaks in the sky above us.

"Almost," Theo replied, glancing back at Xander with a wink.

I withdrew from their embrace and turned to face them.

"I suspected you both were up to something. What was it?" I inquired. "Are you finally going to explain why you were late?"

They crossed their arms and shook their heads before saying in unison, "Nope."

Frustration bubbled inside me, nearly suffocating my happiness and intensifying my irritation.

"You promised there would be no more secrets between us. I believed that vow applied to both of us."

"Relax, Angel," Theo said, wearing an annoying smirk.

"Don't you dare tell me to—"

Xander silenced me with an intense and passionate kiss. His tongue slipped between my lips immediately. I pulled away, my annoyance rising, even though his mouth felt incredible.

"Don't ask me to relax. We can't begin our marriage with hidden truths!"

"We aren't being dishonest," Xander reassured me. "And there won't be any secrets. Something did happen earlier that caused our delay."

"I knew it!" I exclaimed, gesturing to the bloodstain on his shirt.

"We both recognize your investigative skills, Angel," Theo replied. "We will share everything, just not tonight."

"That's why we asked you to relax," Xander added.

"Is everything okay?"

"Yes, absolutely," Theo confirmed.

"We have everything under control. We sincerely apologize for the delay regarding our wedding. Please forgive us."

I smiled at them, my annoyance dissipating, and my heart warmed by their expressions.

"I forgive you," I replied, my tone gentle and full of emotion.

They each took one of my hands and kissed the back of it, their warm lips grazing my skin at the same time, sending shivers through me.

"You are the most stunning bride I've ever seen," Theo whispered.

"Yes," Xander added, his voice low and laced with desire that reflected the shadows in his eyes. "And the most alluring."

Heat flooded my cheeks.

"We're married now," I breathed, a sense of wonder swelling in my chest as the truth dawned on me.

"And we're alone," Theo replied.

"Alone," I echoed, nervously biting my lip.

They looked at me with the same intensity as in my dreams, filled with a raw, savage hunger. But tonight, with the moon glimmering and the city lights sprawled below us, reflecting in their eyes, there was an added depth to their gaze.

A sense of belonging.

A sense of pride.

A sense of possession.

Both leaned in, kissing my cheek before their lips brushed against my ear.

"You belong to us," they growled in unison.

My pussy spasmed at their words. My heart lifted with a mix of love, lust, and all that lay in between.

I let out a soft moan at their words, my head tilting back slightly as my eyes closed. Together, they lowered themselves to lift me from the ground. Theo cradled my head while Xander secured my feet, my dress trailing down to the ground below.

I laughed as they carried me toward the house like a sack of heavy potatoes.

"Is this necessary?" I exclaimed.

"Carrying our bride across the threshold? Absolutely, it is," Xander replied.

Theo reached the front door and kicked it open, both of them effortlessly lifting me inside. They continued down the hallway to our bedroom and finally set me on my feet in front of them by the bed.

I beamed up at them, overwhelmed with love.

"Our queen," Theo murmured, pressing a gentle kiss against my neck.

"Our angel," Xander added, kissing the opposite side.

"Oh," I sighed, savoring the sensation of their lips. My back arched toward them, my breasts pressing against their chests.

"This evening," Theo breathed close to my ear, "we're going to have you scream for us."

He pressed his warm lips against my collarbone, igniting my skin.

"Exactly, darling, we will ensure you know who you belong to."

Xander's breath was warm against my ear, his words cutting through my mind like a blade.

My knees threatened to buckle under the weight of my desire for them.

However, I realized that if I rested on the bed for a moment, they would leap at me and consume me, leaving no opportunity to wear the exquisite lingerie I had ordered from France for our wedding night. With a slow smile, I took a step away from them.

"I need to get out of this dress first," I said.

They exchanged a glance and shrugged.

"Take your time, Angel," Xander reassured. "We have all night."

"Exactly," Theo chimed in. "We need to handle something anyway."

I regarded them with suspicion but chose not to inquire. They had promised to share everything eventually, and I trusted them. The last thing I wanted to engage with tonight was any business-related matters, and I had an uneasy feeling that I was involved here.

"We'll be right back in fifteen minutes," they stated before vanishing and leaving me alone in the room.

With a sigh, I turned toward my closet and began undressing. It took a bit of work, but eventually, I'd peeled off the dress and stood naked and alone in my closet, staring at myself in the mirror.

I looked at the scar on my belly that Andraius had left; it was nearly faded now. Soon, it would be gone altogether. The only remaining scars would be those buried deep within me. However, I felt sure that with the unwavering love of my men, even those would eventually disappear over time too.

Despite all the trauma I faced, everything eventually turned out well.

For me.

For Theo and Xander.

For our boys.

I couldn't feel more thankful.

With a joyful grin, I slipped the black negligee over my bare skin. I had chosen black, rejecting the conventional white bridal nightgown. Our union wasn't traditional, and our lovemaking wouldn't be either.

Soft and silky, it was crafted from the finest black pongee silk and red Chantilly lace. I felt feminine and alluring in it, and I eagerly anticipated seeing the look in their eyes.

I returned to the bedroom and lit candles around the room, enhancing the dim lighting as the sun set outside the window.

I wanted to see them tonight.

I wanted to memorize every expression on their faces.

I knew we'd spend countless nights in the future, making love until the break of dawn together, hours spent passionately embracing and exploring the depths of our bodies' pleasure. And I did not doubt that those countless nights would fade to a blur eventually, just as the ones that had come before.

But tonight? Tonight was special.

I lay on the bed, waiting for my lovers to arrive.

And it was only seconds later that they did, appearing totally nude, their eyes full of hunger and love, their cocks standing at attention already.

They stopped just inside the door, their hot gazes raking over my body, adorned in lace and silk, spread out before them, waiting for them to take me and claim me as their wife, once and for all.

"My god, you look like an angel," Xander growled as they approached me.

"Maybe the Angel of Darkness," Theo hissed. "You've never looked sexier."

They joined me on the bed, wrapping their arms around me and pulling me close. Theo kissed me, slow and longingly, the love flowing between us strong and pulsing.

He pulled away, staring down at me gently. "We're married."

I managed to whisper. "We made it."

"Finally," Xander added.

We intertwined our bodies, the three of us tangled, unsure where one ended and the other began.

This was how it had always been. The three of us united, exactly where we were meant to be.

And it would always be that way.

"I love you both," I murmured.

"And we love you, our queen. Always and forever."

Books By Sienna

Rules of Engagement

Rule Breaker

Rule Master

Rule Changer

Politics of Love

Celebrity

Senator

Commander

Gods of Vegas

Master of Sin

Master of Games

Master of Revenge

Master of Secrets

Master of Control

Master of Fortune (Nyx and Simon)

Sweetest Sin

Intrigued By Love

Street Kings

Dangerous King

Vicious Prince

Deceptive Knight (Lilly and Rey)

Ruthless Heir (Devani and Sam)

Violent Delights

Claim

Defy

Own

Sin and Lies

Sin and Betrayal

Sin and Deception

Sister of Wrath

Legacy (April 25, 2025)

Influence (June 6, 2025)

Power (June 27, 2025)

Sinful Gods

Forbidden Empire (Sept 3, 2025)

Dark Alliance (2026)

Broken Crown (2026)

Collections

Reckless Romeo

Take Me To Bed (2019)

Meet Me Under The Mistletoe (2021)

Nightingale (A charity anthology in support of Ukraine) - (2022)

Darkly Ever After (An Organized Crime Anthology) (2022)

RARE Melbourne Anthology (2023)

About the Author

USA Today bestselling author Sienna Snow loves to craft dark and extremely sexy stories centered on anti-heroes and the strong, unapologetic women who bring them to their knees. Her books immerse you in a world of indulgence, suspense, and undeniable steam.

Her heroines are vibrant and self-assured, often discovering love and romance under unconventional circumstances. Sienna offers her readers enticing glimpses of steamy romance filled with empowerment and indulgent satisfaction.

Sienna loves a life filled with travel and adventure. She plans to explore even the farthest corners of the world and revel in experiencing the diverse cultures along the way. When she isn't writing or traveling, Sienna is focused on her "happily ever after" with her husband and children.

Sign up for her newsletter for notifications of releases, book sales, events, and so much more.

http://www.siennasnow.com/newsletter

contact@siennasnow.com